RUNDIMAHAIR

Rundimahair

LARRY FORKNER

HIGHEST STAR PRODUCTIONS

Published internationally by:
Highest Star Productions
www.higheststar.com

Cover designed by Amy Hansen

ISBN: 978-0-578-84905-8

Highest Star
Productions

This book is dedicated to my great friend and partner, Amy Hansen, who also happens to be my beloved daughter. I would likely have never succeeded as a novel writer, music composer or playwright without her great talents, creative abilities, and encouragement. Many thanks for all you do, sweet Amy!

Prologue

May you have hindsight to know where you've been,
The foresight to know where you are going,
And the insight to know when you have gone too far.

~ Old Irish Saying ~

The storm seemed to be growing in intensity with each passing minute. The skies that were partly sunny, when Sean Quinn left Portland several hours ago, were now filled with thick, dark, brooding clouds. Bruised, purple clouds finally let loose a mighty downpour, and gale-force bursts of wind lashed torrents of rain against Sean's windshield as it rushed down Highway 101 on the northern Oregon Coast. It was all he could do to keep his Cadillac SRX on the highway.

"I understand why they're upset, Jennie. They want to keep things just the way they are, and I want to change them. We can't all be happy, so we'll have to settle for me being happy. Just get the crew going, and if we have to, we'll call in the police to deal with the nut cases. Standing in front of our bulldozers is a crime—trespassing if nothing else," Sean Quinn said with a touch of exasperation creeping into his voice.

"You got it, boss man," his office manager replied in her usual cheerful, confident manner. "I actually agree with you on this one, Sean. They're not willing to give at all on their unrealistic

1

demands. I'll start the…" Jennie's voice was cut off as the cell phone signal disappeared. As if to accentuate her dislike of modern technology, Mother Nature let loose a deafening boom of thunder, which seemed to explode inches above the roof of his SUV.

"Jennie, can you hear me? Are you still there?" Sean shouted over the rumbling thunder. "What else can go wrong?" Sean growled, tossing his useless cell phone onto the passenger seat of the Cadillac.

Sean took a deep breath and relaxed a little. His good friend and office manager, Jennie Mason, would handle this issue in her usual efficient, compassionate manner. When it came to business practices, they didn't always agree on the best course of action, but on this project, they were on the same page.

At twenty-four, Sean was already a very successful businessman. He was tall and well-built, with thick sandy hair and large hazel eyes. He was a handsome man by anyone's estimation, and most women seemed to find him irresistible.

Despite his relative youth, Sean was already a very successful property developer, who specialized in projects along the picturesque Oregon Coast. He was driven to succeed no matter what the cost. Those who assumed he was too young to be a serious player in the real estate game, had often found out the hard way they were sadly mistaken.

He'd departed from his office building, in downtown Portland, early this morning to check out a large parcel of land near Lincoln City. It was part of a real estate auction taking place in a couple of days. Since it was only an overnight trip, he hadn't packed for stormy weather. Anyone that spent as much time on the coast as he did, should have known better. This time of year, the weather could change dramatically in a matter of minutes.

Another sudden gust of wind forced his attention back to the problem at hand. If he wasn't careful, his brand-new Cadillac would end up in a ditch or at the bottom of a ravine. Sean concentrated on getting through this storm and put the rest of his problems on the back-burner for the moment.

Lightning began streaking across the sky, showing off Mother Nature's savage beauty, as the storm's intensity increased. It seemed he was the only person foolish enough to be out in this weather, since he hadn't spotted another vehicle for quite some time.

A sudden, massive and jagged streak of lightning flashed across the sky, striking an enormous old fir tree alongside the highway. A deafening crack followed as a large section of the tree split and fell across the road. It was less than 30 feet away, leaving him only seconds to react. Sean instinctively veered hard right to avoid crashing headlong into the massive tree blocking the road. Almost immediately, he realized this was a terrible mistake. He was only a few feet away from the edge of the road, and beyond that was empty space falling into a very deep ravine.

Sean swung the steering wheel hard in the opposite direction, deciding his chances of survival were much better by striking the fallen tree, as opposed to falling into the deep, rugged ravine. When he tried to swing the Cadillac back onto the road, the front bumper struck the tree, causing the rear wheels to spin out of control. The impact slammed Sean's head into the driver's side window frame, and he was mercifully unconscious, while his vehicle veered sharply toward the ravine's deadly darkness far below.

Chapter One

The sound of gentle rain tapped out a pleasant rhythm on the Cadillac's roof. This was the first thought that crossed Sean's mind when he regained consciousness. The searing pain from a world-class headache quickly vied for his attention and dominated his thoughts. A trickle of blood was running down the left side of his face, which seemed to be coming from his scalp.

It was now very dark outside, meaning he must have been out for several hours. The stiffness in his body seemed to confirm that conclusion. The wind had all but stopped, and the rain was reduced to a steady drizzle. The good news was that the SRX was still running and didn't seem to be too badly damaged. For some reason that troubled his dazed mind, but he was unsure why.

He lifted his head off the passenger side windshield and was immediately assailed by blinding pain. It began in his left temple and quickly traveled through his neck and left shoulder. He dropped his head onto the headrest and hoped the pain would diminish. After several minutes, the pounding headache began to recede into a dull throb, but the neck pain was still ferocious.

Keeping his head very still, Sean tried to reason through what he'd just experienced. His mind still felt sluggish, but he was beginning to recall most of the accident. He'd struck the fallen tree—losing control—and the SRX crashed through the flimsy guard rail and fell into the...

"Where's the ravine?" he said aloud, sitting up to look through the front windshield.

Pain erupted from his injured neck and head, but he did his best to ignore it. To his great relief, the Cadillac was sitting in the middle of a narrow, paved road, instead of at the bottom of a deep ravine. Sean had been so sure that the car was headed into the ravine when he'd lost consciousness.

He turned gingerly to look behind him. About a hundred yards back was Highway 101, which he'd been traveling on. The fallen tree was still lying in the middle of the highway, so he hadn't imagined the accident. But instead of falling into the deadly ravine, he'd veered onto this narrow lane. Then he'd apparently brought the Cadillac to a stop and put it in park before he passed out. The confusing part was Sean couldn't recall doing any of that. He didn't even remember seeing the narrow lane his car was sitting on.

It was too much for his pain muddled mind to reason through. He would deal with the confusion once he'd gotten medical treatment and some much-needed rest. The fact that he was alive and safe was all that mattered now.

Sean reached for his cell phone that was still on the passenger seat beside him. Frustration burned within him when he saw it still had no signal. He sighed deeply and started to turn the Cadillac around to get back on Highway 101. He wondered how far he could travel in his present condition, but he really had no choice. Just as he began turning the wheel, he noticed that it wasn't complete blackness ahead of him. A few lights were burning about a half-mile down the road. He had no idea what small town lay ahead, but right now it was any port in a storm.

He drove down the narrow lane, heading toward the unknown town at a slow and steady pace. The pain in his head and neck was nearly unbearable, but he was alive and that was more than what seemed likely a few hours ago.

As he neared the town, Sean noticed a large, semi-circular, cut of myrtle wood along the side of the road. The multi-colored grain made for a beautiful piece of wood. Someone had carved a few words, in the wood, in elegant, old-world script, *Welcome to Rundimahair, A Bit of Heaven on Earth.*

Sean knew this area of the Oregon Coast fairly well, but he'd never heard of this little town. Life was full of surprises, and he'd already had more than his share today.

The few lights that he'd seen in the distance multiplied dramatically as he reached the edge of town. He couldn't be sure of the population, but judging by what he could see, Sean guessed there were about five or six thousand residents. This was a fair-sized town, by coastal standards, and he was still amazed he'd been unaware of its existence.

The ride suddenly became bumpy and a little uneven when he drove down Main Street. In his headlights, the cause was plain to see; the road had turned from pavement to cobblestone. That was something Sean hadn't seen very often. It was appealing but not very practical—unless the town was trying to attract tourists to the area with an old-world look. That was likely, since most of the homes and businesses had something of an old world European look.

The small town seemed very out of place with a surreal aura that made Sean feel a little uneasy. It was probably just the aftermath of the accident, which left him feeling groggy and uncomfortable. He reasoned that everything would look better after a good night's rest. If he still felt disoriented in the morning, he'd seek medical attention. Right now, all he wanted to do was go to bed.

Sean tried to focus on the surrounding buildings, hoping to find a motel or bed-and-breakfast where he could stop. It seemed the more he tried to concentrate, the more confused he became. His vision was becoming blurry, and he began to feel like he would pass out again. He tried to pull over but lost consciousness just as he turned the wheel. Sean was out cold and the Cadillac was heading straight for the oldest building in town.

⸎

A deep, resonant voice was intruding on Sean's peaceful slumber. At first he ignored it, but the voice seemed to become more insistent the longer Sean resisted. Finally, the disembodied voice almost shouted Sean's name and he reluctantly began to respond. It was a struggle to clear the fog from his mind and open his eyes. Most of the fog lingered, but his eyes slowly squinted open.

"Well, well, there is somebody to home after all," the voice said.

There was a pleasant, lilting quality to the voice that made Sean think it was a foreign accent. The type of accent eluded him; he was too busy trying to fight the bright glare of sunlight that assaulted his eyes. He finally gave up and closed them again.

"A bit too much of the sunshine, is it? I think we can take care of that for you, young fella."

Sean felt the glare decrease as he heard the shades being drawn. He cautiously opened his eyes again and the room slowly

8

came into focus. He was expecting to see some type of hospital room but was surprised to see he was lying in a large, beautifully furnished bedroom. The furniture appeared to be antique and beautifully preserved or restored. Sean loved antique furniture and had many expensive and unique pieces in his Victorian home, sitting high in the hills above Portland.

Despite his confusion about where he was and how he got here, Sean's attention was drawn to the oystered cherry armoire. The stunning piece of well-aged furniture sat grandly against the wall, near the window, where the older gentleman was drawing the shades. It was a Louis XV bonnet-topped armoire with the doors highlighted by chevron parquetry and was restored to mint condition. That was just one of several unique antiques in the room. The armoire's value alone would be near $20,000.00.

"So you had a little accident, judging by the lump on your head," his host said.

"At least one accident," Sean replied. When I passed out again, here in town, I seem to recall an old building directly in front of me. I don't know if I ran in to it or not."

"Fortunately not," the older fellow replied with a smile. You were headed right for my furniture shop, but you weren't going very fast. Young Billy Crandall was able to pull the driver's side door open and put on the brakes for you."

"Remind me to thank him once I'm on my feet again," Sean said.

"That I will."

"So how did I end up here?" Sean asked.

"Ah yes, forgive my shameful manners, young man. Here you are in a strange bed and I've not even introduced myself. I'm

Eamon Cahir and you're resting in the guest bedroom of my own home, so you are."

Eamon stepped forward and offered his hand to Sean. His handshake was firm, and Sean was surprised to realize that Eamon's hand was even larger than his. Eamon was a tall, lean man, a couple of inches over Sean's six-two. Sean had a bit more muscle on him at 190, but Eamon had the look of a man with wiry strength. He realized Eamon wasn't as old as he'd first assumed, even though his light brown hair had a fair touch of gray at the temples. His well-trimmed beard was showing a bit more gray, but Sean decided he was probably no more than his fifties instead of the sixties he'd initially assumed.

"We sent a crew out to clear the tree off the road. We don't want any other traveler to come upon that hunk of trouble in the middle of a dark and stormy night," Eamon said.

"Good idea. I'm fortunate that I spotted your town after the accident. I don't think I'd have made it to the next town in the condition I was in. It's funny, but I'm already starting to feel better now."

"I've always been a great believer in the restorative powers of a good night's sleep," Eamon said. "I'm sure you'll be right as rain in no time, Sean."

A strange chill went through Sean at the mention of his name. Had he told Eamon what his name was? He was pretty sure he hadn't, although he couldn't be sure what happened the night before. Maybe someone had gone through his wallet when they'd found him to find who they were dealing with.

"I see you know my name. Did I introduce myself last night, Eamon?"

"I'm afraid you were in no condition to be making introductions last night. No, it was my nosey daughter who checked your driver's license. She wanted to be sure you weren't some nefarious character who might murder us all in our beds. Not that you had the strength to do any such thing when we found you."

"That's fine, Eamon. I'd have probably done the same if I were in her shoes. I appreciate the hospitality you've shown me."

"And what else could we do for a wounded traveler, stranded in our humble community? We hope you'll stay for a few days until you're well enough to continue your journey."

"I was afraid I'd be laid up for a week or two but the way I'm feeling now, I think I'll be out of your hair sooner rather than later."

"In the meantime, I'm guessing you're well overdue to put on the feedbag," Eamon said.

"If I've ever been hungrier, I can't recall when," Sean said.

"That's all well and good since my own sweet daughter will have breakfast on the table by the time you're up and dressed. The guest bath is right through the door nearest to your bed and your luggage is in the closet just there," Eamon said, pointing to another door across the room. "If you need any help, be sure to give me a holler."

Sean managed to shower and get dressed in near record time. His head still ached when he was on his feet, and the dizziness seemed to flare up if he tried to move too fast. Otherwise, he was amazed by how quickly his health seemed to be returning. Of course, the delectable aromas wafting from the kitchen were a great motivator to hurry him along.

Following the aroma of bacon frying, Sean pushed through the café doors that led to a large country kitchen. The kitchen looked like a vintage painting from a farm house built hundreds of years ago. Everything from the wood-burning oven to the large butcher-block table seemed to belong to a time long past.

The only exceptions were a large stainless-steel side-by-side refrigerator/freezer unit, resting in one corner of the room, and a large capacity dishwasher next to the sink. The stainless-steel finishes were buffed to a brilliant shine, just like everything else in the kitchen. The old oak floors and the knotty-pine cabinetry were spotless and finished with a high-luster varnish.

There were two black cast-iron skillets sitting on the stove with bacon crisping nicely in one and over-easy eggs frying in the other. Since no one else was in the kitchen at that moment, and Sean was practically drooling over the wonderful smell of bacon cooking, he reached for one of the bacon strips.

"And didn't I tell Da we might have a scallywag among us? Stealing the bacon, the moment a poor girl's back is turned."

Sean was startled by the voice from behind him and quickly pulled his hand back from the frying pan. He turned to see who'd entered the kitchen behind him and saw a lovely young woman walking toward him.

"Sorry," he stammered. "It smelled so wonderful I couldn't resist."

She walked past him, frowning tolerantly, as she took up her position in front of the stove. She deftly grabbed a strip of bacon out of the pan with her tongs and set it on a napkin.

"If you're that bad off, then you'd best have a strip before you faint away right before my eyes," she said, letting a smile touch the corners of her mouth.

"Thanks," he said, taking the bacon she offered to him. "I can't remember the last time I was this hungry."

"I suppose trying to run your car over a fallen tree gives a man a healthy appetite," She said, turning back to the stove.

"So it seems," he agreed, munching on his bacon strip.

He watched her for a moment, while she pulled the eggs out of the pan and onto a serving plate. By the look of her, Sean guessed she was in her mid-twenties. She had thick, shoulder-length, auburn hair and vivid, sparkling green eyes. Her complexion was peaches and cream, and her long, curvaceous figure was outstanding — curves in all the right places. This woman was a classic Irish beauty, except for her unusual height. She had to be nearly six-feet tall.

"Seen enough or would you like me to strike a couple of other poses as long as you're ogling me," she asked calmly.

Sean felt a blush burn up his neck and flush his cheeks as he quickly looked away. He seemed to be getting off to a very bad start with this woman.

"I didn't mean to stare, ma'am. I just…I guess I'm just not myself this morning," he stammered.

"Ma'am, is it? I don't look a day older than you, and my name is Ashling, Ashling Cahir. And I know you're Sean Quinn, a fine Irish name, or so says your driver's license," she said, stepping toward him and offering her hand.

"Yes, I'm Sean Quinn and it's a pleasure to meet you, Ashling. So you are Irish. I thought you might be after listening to your lovely accent."

She smiled as they shook hands. "Oh yes, we're Irish through and through, although our accent has faded a bit since we've been gone from the homeland for so many years."

"So you were born in Ireland. When did you immigrate to the United States?"

"It seems like two lifetimes ago," she replied wistfully.

For a moment Sean saw what appeared to be sadness or longing in her eyes. It was there and then gone so quickly he couldn't be sure he'd seen it at all.

"Do you still miss Ireland so much?"

"I do indeed. Don't get me wrong. I've grown to love our little piece of heaven on earth here on the Oregon Coast. In many ways it reminds me of home."

Sean wanted to ask more questions, but the café doors opened behind him and Eamon strolled into the kitchen.

"I see you've been given a taste of my dear daughter's cooking," Eamon said, as he stood next to Sean and rested a hand on his shoulder. "Believe me; you have no idea how fortunate you are. Ashling has been known to inflict serious bodily harm on those caught sneaking a wee taste from her kitchen."

"Go on with you, Da. You'll be having our injured guest believing I'm a dangerous woman to be around," Ashling said.

"That you are but well worth the risk, since you're also an extraordinarily lovely lass and the finest cook that ever graced a kitchen."

"Enough of the blarney," she said, smiling and kissing her father's cheek. You two go sit at the table and I'll bring your breakfast to you."

When they were seated around the table, Sean went to work on the bacon, eggs and golden hash browns like a man who'd missed his last few meals. He couldn't believe how hungry he was and how delicious the simple, well-prepared food was.

"Are you sure the man wasn't lost alongside the road for days before he tried to run into your furniture store, Da? He's eating like he hasn't seen food for a week or more," Ashling said.

"And what's wrong with a young man with a hearty appetite, Ashling?" her father said. "I'm sure he's a hard-working fella and needs to keep his strength up."

"He'd better be hard working with an appetite like that or he'll soon be as big as our house," Ashling said.

Sean felt his cheeks redden for the second time that morning and wondered how long it had been since he'd blushed like a school boy. He decided that it must have something to do with the strange surroundings and his accident, since he didn't normally embarrass easily.

"Sorry if my manners are lacking. I just can't remember being this hungry before, and you're fine cooking has raised my appetite to new heights," Sean said.

"Well said, Sean. You're obviously a man of fine words and an easy tongue. I admire that in a young fellow, but I've found it sometimes difficult to believe everything a fast-talking man has to say," Ashling said.

"What a thing to say to a perfect stranger that you've just met, Eamon said incredulously. For all you know, he could be a man of the cloth, spreading the word of God around the countryside."

"It's all right, Eamon, Sean said. "I've known a few fast talkers in my time, and I don't have any use for them either. Of course, the one person I know who could tell a pack of lies faster than any other happens to be a woman. One of the richest people on the entire west coast and she got that way by lying and conniving her way to the top. So, you see, Ashling, it's not only men who are born with a silver tongue."

"I couldn't agree more," Mr. Quinn. Like you, I've known many men and women with the devil's own gift for blarney," Ashling said. I suppose it's made me over cautious when it comes to strangers. My apologies if I've offended your delicate sensibilities."

Sean put his knife and fork down and looked directly at Ashling for a moment before he replied. Her eyes were as open and innocent as a young child, but there was a hint of a mischievous smile at the corner of her lovely mouth.

"My sensibilities may not be as delicate as you seem to think," Sean said. "It'll take more than a passing comment from a young woman to upset me."

"Ashling darling, would you be kind enough to bring us a loaf of that fine bread you bake along with a dab of butter and jam?" Eamon said.

Ashling smiled at her father and nodded her head slowly. She hurried off to the cupboard without another word. While she was gone, Eamon turned back to Sean.

"Don't mind Ashling, Sean. She can be a bit temperamental around someone she doesn't know well, but she's truly a darling girl once you get to know her," Eamon said.

"Believe me, I understand completely. She seems like a fine young woman, and I'll do my best to put her mind at ease while I'm here," Sean said quietly.

"And how long will that be, Mr. Quinn?" Ashling asked, as she returned to the table. "How long do you intend to be with us, I mean?"

Sean was amazed that she had overheard what he said from across the kitchen. He thought she must have supersonic hearing.

"I'm not sure how long I'll be. This is a part of the countryside I've never seen before, and I would like to look around a bit, once I'm fully recovered from the accident. I surely wouldn't think of imposing on you and your father's gracious hospitality while

I'm here. I'll gather my things and find a hotel or bed-and-breakfast to stay in. Surely you have one or the other in town," Sean said.

"Indeed we do," Eamon replied. "We'll not be sending you off to one of them, however. I insist that you stay with us while you're mending and doing whatever sightseeing you might wish before you head for home. Isn't that right, Ashling?"

"Of course, father dear. We won't let it be said that a Cahir didn't show an injured stranger all the kindness he deserves."

She was smiling at Sean as she talked, but he thought he still felt an undercurrent of mistrust in her words. He wondered if it was a particular incident or life in general that caused her to be mistrustful of a stranger. Her father certainly didn't seem to share her concerns.

"It's settled then," Eamon said. "You'll stay with us while you're on the mend, and Ashling will be your tour guide. She'll show you all there is to see in and around our beloved little town of Rundimahair."

Sean was sure that Ashling was about to object when a look passed from father to daughter, and she smiled and nodded instead. Whatever her true feelings, she wasn't going to argue with her father in front of him.

"I'll do the best I can, Father. Not that there is all that much to see," she said.

"What may seem familiar and ordinary to someone who's lived here all of her life may strike an outsider as extraordinary and full of possibilities," Sean said.

"Oh, I didn't mean to say Rundimahair was ordinary," Mr. Quinn—quite the opposite in fact. You could travel far and wide and not find so pleasing a place to live out your days," Ashling said.

"Well, despite my youth, I have traveled far and wide and seen much of what the world has to offer. I look forward to adding Rundimahair to my list," Sean said.

"Now don't be getting your hopes up too high, Sean," Eamon said. "Sure, it's a grand place and all, but I doubt anything too interesting or exciting will take place while you're visiting our little town."

"Still, I look forward to learning all I can while I'm here, and I'm grateful to have such a lovely and intelligent tour guide to teach me everything she knows," Sean said.

"Oh yes, a silver-tongued devil indeed," Ashling muttered.

Chapter Two

There are only three kinds of Irishmen who don't understand Irish women—
old men, young men, and men of middle age.

~ Old Irish Saying ~

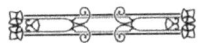

Ashling agreed to begin her duties as tour guide that afternoon once she'd finished going over the books for the furniture shop with Eamon. Father and daughter adjourned to the library of the home, carrying on a hushed conversation as they went. Sean was fairly certain that he was the topic of discussion.

After eating a large breakfast, Sean decided he would get a little exercise. He thought it better to wait until Ashling was available to show him around the interior of their home. It looked to be a lovely day, so he decided he'd begin with a tour of the grounds of the Cahir home.

After he'd walked out to the front gate, Sean turned to look at the stately old home from a distance. It was a charming two-story, with tall, white stucco walls. Four evenly spaced dormers protruded from the steeply pitched roofline, where warm, brown-toned tile covered the roof. The multi-colored stone chimney that climbed the north end of the home looked to be hundreds of years old. A wide, brick-lined walkway led to an impressive double-door entry that appeared to be made of ancient solid oak. The entire home appeared to be very old but meticulously maintained.

Sean found a gray stone path at the edge of the front yard that led around the side of the home and into a spacious backyard. At a glance, he estimated the grounds to be well over two acres in size and as well maintained as the beautiful home. The large expanses of grass were a lush green, and the many large trees and shrubs were perfectly trimmed and shaped.

The path led him to the middle of the back yard and into a breathtaking flower garden that was surrounded by a perfectly shaped hedge of privet shrubbery that was easily ten feet in height. The hedge was a deep green with sweetly scented small white flowers blooming throughout. In the center of the flower garden, the stone pathway split and followed around both sides of a large, circular fountain. The walls of the fountain were about two-feet-high and appeared to be constructed of the same stone material as the main house. In the center of the circle was a fountain pushing a spray of water eight feet into the air, before it fell back into the pool at the base of the fountain.

Sean was amazed by the intricate detail of the structure and the entire garden. He was surrounded by roses of all shapes, colors and sizes. It was obvious that someone spent a great deal of time caring for the flower garden and everything else he'd seen on the grounds of the Cahir home.

The Cahirs didn't behave like a typical wealthy family, but Sean knew enough about housing and real estate to realize that it would take a fair chunk of change to maintain the large, beautiful home and grounds.

After touring the exterior of the home, he was very anxious to wander through the rest of the interior. There were probably many interesting surprises awaiting him there, as well, judging by what he'd already seen.

Fatigue began to overtake him as he circled the fountain to get a closer look at the many roses in the garden. He assumed that the accident had taken more out of him than he realized, since he was normally fit and full of energy. Reluctantly, he turned back to the house, thinking a quick rest might do him some good.

As he walked, Sean looked around him and smiled at the warm, sunny day and gazed up into the clear blue skies. He was amazed at the mild, pleasant day since it was the middle of February. Weather on the Oregon coast was usually cold, wet and often foggy this time of year.

Another thought struck him, and he turned to look back at the flower garden. It was without doubt one of the most beautiful settings he'd ever seen, and that was part of what bothered him. How had they managed to have a rose garden in full bloom in the middle of February? He made a mental note to talk to Ashling about it when they began their tour.

By the time he made it back to the house, he was feeling very tired and decided he'd go directly to his bedroom for a short power nap. He struggled up the stairs, wondering why he was feeling so weak and sleepy when it was only mid-morning.

Sean dropped onto the bed, turning onto his right side and wrapping the quilt over him. Just a short nap would do him a world of good, and then he'd seek out Ashling and see if she was ready to begin her duties as tour guide. He realized that he was looking forward to spending time with her, which shouldn't be too much of a surprise. She was a very attractive and interesting woman that any man would enjoy spending time with. His thoughts continued to dwell on Ashling, and he was soon fast asleep.

When he finally opened his eyes again his room was dark and the house quiet. A quick glance at the bedside clock told him he'd slept through the remainder of the day and well into the night. It was now a few minutes before two in the morning.

He was amazed by the passage of time and realized his body must have needed the rest. He made another mental note to not over do it for the next few days and give his mind and body a chance to recover.

His thoughts were suddenly interrupted by a strange clanking noise outside his bedroom window. His first instinct was to ignore it, but the clanking was soon joined by the sound of metal scraping on rock and his curiosity got the better of him.

Sean rolled out of bed and stumbled to the window, still feeling a bit lightheaded. He pulled aside the drapes, hoping to identify the source of the strange noises. At first he didn't see anything, but when the scraping sounds began again it was apparent they were coming from behind the large willow tree in Eamon's back yard.

He lifted the sash on the window about an inch. The metal on stone sounds rang louder in the quiet night air, followed closely by what seemed to be urgent whispered voices. Sean couldn't make out what they were saying, but they seemed to be trying to quiet the source of the noise.

Before he could decide what to do, Sean was surprised by a sudden golden glow that emanated from behind the tree. It was a soft golden light that seemed to pulse with a gentle energy. To add to his confusion, two very short men rushed out from behind the tree, dancing a jig as they hummed a quiet tune.

Sean was having difficulty wrapping his mind around what he was seeing. After a moment's consideration, he decided to alert Eamon to what was going on in his back yard. He was about to stand when he heard a soft sound directly behind him.

"Who is. . ." is all he could say before he felt a sharp twinge at the base of his neck. Within seconds a feeling of pure weightlessness overwhelmed him, and his mind was filled with absolute peace and joy. It was a sensation that he'd never experienced in his entire life. Sean tried to move, but all the strength had drained out of him. He collapsed onto the floor and descended into unconsciousness before having a chance to identify his attacker.

Early morning sunlight filtered into the room through the window facing the back yard. Birds were chirping merrily in the large willow tree, inviting anyone within earshot to get out of bed and enjoy the bright, clear morning.

Sean groaned and reluctantly opened his eyes. He sighed and struggled to sit up on the edge of the bed. His head ached dully, and his body felt stiff and tight. When he tried to stand, dizziness washed over him as he collapsed back onto the edge of the bed.

He scratched an itch on his right shoulder and felt the familiar, soft fabric of his favorite pajamas. Something vaguely troubling touched his mind when he looked down at his pajamas and bare feet. When he searched for the cause of his disquiet, he realized he couldn't recall much of anything about last night.

After several moments of struggling to clear his thoughts, Sean began to recall some of what he'd done the day before. The breakfast with Eamon and Ashling was clear in his memory, and he was beginning to recall the stroll around the grounds of the home. He'd gone upstairs to rest for a short time and the next thing he could recall was waking up this morning feeling the worse for wear. It seemed impossible that a one-hour nap had turned into sleeping away most of yesterday and all night too. He knew he'd been tired when he went upstairs, but this was ridiculous.

He took a deep breath and steeled himself for another attempt to stand. His legs were still a bit wobbly, but he managed to stay on his feet. The dizziness began to diminish, as he made his way into the bathroom and turned on the cold water. A couple of splashes of very cold water on his face, nearly took his breath away but helped clear the cobwebs out of his mind.

"What a mess," he mumbled as he stared at his reflection in the large bathroom mirror. "You look like twenty miles of bad road."

He grabbed his toiletry bag and dug through it until he found his toothbrush and toothpaste. He gave his teeth a vigorous brushing and felt better after rinsing his mouth with cold water.

"There's no hope for that without a hot shower and shampoo," he said, while trying to smooth down his bed hair with one hand.

Sean smiled at his unkempt reflection, but then his smile turned into a frown. He rubbed his hands over his pajamas again and recalled the unease he'd felt when he first looked at them this morning.

"When did I get into my pajamas?" he mumbled.

When he'd come upstairs for a power nap, he was sure he'd flopped on the bed with all his clothes on except his shoes. It came to him, with a start, that someone must have helped him into pajamas before bed last night. Sean had no recollection of that taking place, but the evidence of it was right before his eyes.

"Let's hope it was Eamon," he grumbled, shaking his head.

After a shower and shave, Sean felt much better, although the dizziness and weakness were still there as background irritants.

While dressing, he continued to wonder how he'd lost almost an entire day to sleep. Even taking the accident into account, it just wasn't like him to sleep like he was in a coma.

He glanced out the window to see if he could spot Ashling or Eamon outside. When his gaze fell on the willow tree, a strange feeling rumbled through him. He closed his eyes and tried to recall a bit of memory that was there, just out of reach. After several moments, he gave up in frustration. He recalled that his mother had once told him to leave it alone if he couldn't recall something. She promised that it would come to him sometime soon when he was busy thinking of something else. He'd found that she was usually right and tried to relax and not worry about whatever was troubling him.

Sean glanced at his watch as he descended the stairs and was surprised to see that it was already after ten. He was afraid he'd missed breakfast, and he was absolutely starving. When he stepped into the kitchen, hoping to find something he could whip up for a late breakfast, he was amazed to see a plate full of waffles sitting on the table. Someone had prepared a gourmet quality breakfast of waffles with sausage and bacon on the side. Three flavors of syrup were also on the table, along with butter and orange juice.

"It's feels like it just came out of the waffle iron," Sean said, surprised to feel the warmth coming off the plate.

It was almost as if someone knew the exact moment, he'd be coming downstairs and set the breakfast table at just the right moment. That was a little strange, but certainly not the strangest thing that had happened to him over the past two days. Strange or not, he was going to enjoy breakfast.

Sean sat down and dug into his waffles, after drowning them in butter and syrup. He'd worry about his cholesterol another day.

He went through the waffles in record time and was enjoying a juicy sausage when he heard the saloon doors to the kitchen swing open.

"And who told you to help yourself to my breakfast, Mr. Quinn? After I slaved away at the stove to get everything just the way I like it. Sure and true, I've never seen the like of this," Ashling said from behind him.

Sean stopped his fork full of sausage halfway to his mouth. He felt a surge of heat rush up his neck and into his cheeks and knew he was blushing deep red again.

"I…It never crossed my mind that…I'm so sorry to have just assumed all of this was for me," he finally stammered as he stood and faced her.

To his surprise, Ashling was covering a smile with her hand, and a wonderful merriment filled her sparkling green eyes. Sean understood immediately that she was having fun at his expense and smiled as he shook his head.

"You must enjoy seeing a grown man blush, Ashling. In my entire life, I don't think I've gone beet-red as much as I have since meeting you."

She couldn't hold back a giggle, and the sound of her laughter charmed Sean and he chuckled too.

I'm so sorry to be teasing you all the time, but you must confess you're an appealingly easy target," Ashling said.

"Others who know me wouldn't agree, but I admit I've been easy fodder for your quick wit."

I appreciate you being good-natured about it, Sean," she said, as she put her hand on his shoulder and guided him back to the table. "Now sit down and finish your breakfast. I really did make it just for you. Of course, I had no choice since the rest of us ate hours ago."

Sean laughed as he sat down. While he finished off the sausage that was still on his fork, he realized how pleasing it was to feel her warm hand on his shoulder. "Well, I have been sick, you know. But I must say that I've never slept away almost an entire day and night before."

"Well, if you continue to sleep like the dead, you'll be back among the living in no time."

"I do feel pretty well this morning. Are you up to showing me around town, or do you have a load of work ahead of you?"

"As it happens, I have my rounds to cover this morning. If you don't mind mixing my errands in with a bit of sightseeing, then we can soon be on our way."

"Sounds like a very exciting day."

"I doubt you'll find going on rounds all that exciting, but at least you'll see the sights and meet some town folk."

Sean had a sudden impression he was being set up as Ashling's target again, but it was probably just his imagination.

Chapter Three

You can't kiss an Irish girl unexpectedly.
You can only kiss her sooner than she thought you would.

~ Old Irish Saying ~

By the time Sean had finished breakfast and rinsed his dishes in the sink, Ashling had gathered her things together. Sean grabbed his light jacket since there was a chill to the air despite the bright sunshine.

He had dressed casually in jeans and a pullover sweater. Sean was surprised to see that Ashling had changed into a pretty, flowered dress with a black belt that cinched the dress tightly around her trim waist. She wore a cream-colored, brushed cotton cardigan sweater over the dress. Add in her thick auburn hair and sparkling green eyes, and she looked every inch the classic Irish beauty.

"What's in there?" he asked, pointing at an old, brown, leather bag she was carrying. "It looks like an old leather doctor's bag from the days when they still made house calls. Don't tell me you're the doctor in Rundimahair."

"Oh no, we have a fine doctor here who runs a state-of-the art medical clinic. It's as fine as any you'd see on the west coast. I'll take you by there if we have time."

"So, what's in the bag if you're not a doctor?"

"They're just odds and ends that I carry with me whenever I make my rounds. I'm what you might call a naturopath—a person who uses herbs and natural potions for healing."

"I'll have to introduce you to my office manager. She's a great believer in all things natural. She's always trying to get me to take some foul-tasting concoction or another."

"I take it you're not a true believer in Mother Nature's healing arts then."

"I'm open minded about it for the most part. I must admit that the vitamins Jennie gives me seem to work wonders. But if I'm really sick, I think I'll stick with an experienced doctor. One who preferably graduated from medical school in the top of his class."

"I'll keep that in mind if you happen to have a relapse while we're wandering around town."

While they were enjoying talking together, they'd walked into the center of town. Sean was impressed by the layout of the small town. The center was a town square that was mostly green grass, trees and playground equipment. In the center of the square was a large gazebo that looked like it was used as the centerpiece for concerts or town gatherings. It all looked like something right out of a movie set.

The streets were narrow by today's standards, but they were well laid out in a grid around the town square. It was a much better design than Sean had seen in many old coastal towns.

Most of the buildings were two-story attached with a thick stucco finish, painted in a variety of bright colors. The roof overhangs were all finely detailed, decorative wood painted in more subdued colors that blended well with the building's primary color. The look and style of the commercial buildings and most of the homes seemed old European, although it was obvious they had been updated and renovated over the years. Sean was impressed by how well maintained the town was. Everyone seemed to take great pride in keeping their property in near-perfect condition.

"What do you think of our little town so far?"

"It's a wonderful place, Ashling. Most coastal towns I visit are not so beautifully cared for. In fact, some of them are quite run down."

"We're a close-knit group, and we're all anxious to keep Rundimahair a place we can all take pride in."

"The pride of ownership really shines through. It looks to be older than any town I've come across on the west coast. The age and the old European style are quite unique. With all the Irish accents I'm hearing, I assume the town was founded by Irish immigrants. Do you know when it was first settled?"

"The origins of the town are something of a mystery. No one seems to know exactly when it was settled or by whom. I don't think it's as old as it appears, but we all love the original style and have worked hard to maintain it. That's why we still have cobblestone streets, even though asphalt would provide a much smoother ride."

He wasn't sure what it was about her response that bothered him. On the surface, it seemed to answer his question, but it didn't really satisfy his growing curiosity about Rundimahair. Every time he asked a question about the town's history, she gave what seemed to be a well-rehearsed response without ever answering his question in depth.

"Here's my first stop," Ashling said, turning into the yard of a small but well-kept home. "You're welcome to look around town on your own or accompany me on my visit with Mrs. O'Leary."

"A fine Irish name," Sean said. Would I be in the way if I came in with you? I'm curious to see the inside of some of these old homes."

"Not in the least; I'm just checking in to see how she's doing. She's been a wee bit under the weather the past month or so, but I think she's well on the mend by now. To tell the truth, she'll love the company. Mrs. O'Leary is quite a talker, and she'll enjoy having someone new to share her stories with."

"Lead the way. I'm always up for a good story."

A diminutive woman answered the door almost immediately after Ashling's gentle knock on the heavy, mahogany door. She must have been waiting by the window, watching for them.

She looked to be in her late seventies or possibly early eighties. Despite her advanced age, Mrs. O'Leary had fiery red hair with only a touch of gray in it. She wasn't much over five-feet tall and was slightly stooped. If Sean had to guess, he'd say she was barely a hundred pounds—if that. He wondered if her withered appearance was due to the illness Ashling had mentioned.

Her home was decorated very simply but beautifully. Sean began to wonder if everyone in town was a professional decorator. The colorful oval rugs that lay over the immaculate mahogany floor were obviously old, but still very attractive. The furniture looked like it came over with the original pilgrims. The solid oak frames could have used a touch of refinishing, but the plush cushions looked to have been recovered recently.

Sean noticed that the plumbing and electrical looked like it had been added long after the home was built. The lighting and the kitchen sink appeared to be right out of the 1920s.

Mrs. O'Leary had a small fire going in the large stone fireplace. The fireplace, with the old oak mantle and the gray stone hearth, provided a warm, comforting centerpiece for the home.

"And how are we this fine day, Mrs. O'Leary?" Ashling asked, as she set her leather bag on the couch and gave the old woman a gentle hug.

"Oh, as good as a worn-out old woman can be. And is all well with you, my darlin' girl?" Mrs. O'Leary asked, returning the embrace with surprising strength.

"Couldn't be better if I tried," Ashling replied, smiling.

"And you look as good as you feel, dearie. It's a never endin' mystery how a beauty like you hasn't been snatched up long ago."

"Now, now, none of your matchmaking today, Mrs. O'Leary," Ashling said. "I've come to visit you, not discuss my pathetic love life."

"And truer words were never spoken than when I say, there isn't a man within a hundred miles of here that deserves a sweet lass like you. But I see you've brought a fine-looking outsider with you. Could he be the apple of your eye, then?"

Sean and Ashling both had to laugh at that audacious comment. Mrs. O'Leary smiled, pleased to have gotten a rise out of both of her visitors.

"He is the man who nearly ran his vehicle into my Da's furniture shop. He's staying with us for a few days while he recuperates from his accident. I'm just showing him about our little town and introducing him to some of our most illustrious citizens. Of course we started with you," Ashling said.

Sean held out his hand and smiled at Mrs. O'Leary. "I'm Sean Quinn; it's a pleasure to meet you."

"Oh and a fine Irish name to boot," Mrs. O'Leary replied, shaking his hand vigorously. "How long do you expect to be with us, Sean?"

"It will probably be just a few days. As soon as I fully recover from the accident, then I'll be on my way," he replied, as he pulled his hand back from her two-handed grip.

"Isn't it a stroke of the good Lord's luck that you had your accident in Rundimahair, then? There isn't a finer healer in this great wide world than our dear, Ashling. She'll fix whatever ails you and have you fit as a fiddle in no time, she will."

"Speaking of healing," Ashling said, interrupting Mrs. O'Leary's long-winded praise. I've brought you another month's supply of your tonic. I'm fairly certain that you won't be needing anymore when this bottle is gone."

"And you're that sure that I'm going to be as well as I can be after this month's dosing? If that's so, then I suppose I should be grateful that I'm still on my feet and walking about, even if each step I take pains me something awful."

"We should all be as fit as you are, Mrs. O'Leary," Ashling said, laughing. Your color is better than it's been in months."

"Oh and speaking of color, did you bring my other bottle of . . . medicine?"

"Are you sure you need it? Your hair is as fiery red as I ever remember seeing it."

"There you go telling secrets in front of your fine young beau," Mrs. O'Leary said. "Is it a sin of vanity if I want my hair to stay the same color it was when the good Lord sent me into this world of trouble and strife?"

Sean laughed and said, "It would be a tremendous loss to the world if your fiery mane was toned down in the slightest, Mrs.

O'Leary. Whatever has to be done to maintain the natural beauty you were born with is an essential duty."

"Oh my, my. Strong, handsome and a silver- tongued rascal along with it. You're a lucky girl to have found a man such as this," Mrs. O'Leary said to Ashling.

"I'll grant you the silver-tongued devil part of that. However, as I explained, Sean's not my beau, Mrs. O'Leary."

"So you say, dear. So you say."

"Be off with you. If you don't stop, I'll give your hair potion to Mrs. Flannery," Ashling said.

"And why would you be doing such a terrible thing to a dear old lady like her, Ashling? It's not dignified for a woman as senior as her to be trying to turn back the clock. Besides, her gray hair suits her personality to a tee."

"She's at least twenty years younger than you," Ashling replied, smiling.

"Be careful, dear. This is how vicious rumors get started. I was no more than a glint in my dear father's eye on Annabelle Flannery's wedding day."

"So you say. So you say," Ashling said. "Now, if I can get you to be still for a few minutes, I'll check to be sure you're as well as you seem to be."

"I'll be as still as stone, I will," Mrs. O'Leary said.

For the next few minutes, Ashling examined Mrs. O'Leary. It was nothing like anything Sean had ever seen before. She held a clear crystal about the size of a golf ball up against Mrs. O'Leary's chest, while she touched her forehead for about thirty seconds. Ashling's long, slender fingers repeated the process, moving to her patient's eyes, chin, temple and the base of her throat.

"All is well and you're sure to outlive us all," Ashling said when she'd completed her strange exam. "Finish the potion I gave you, and I'll be back to check on you next month."

"And will you be bringing Sean with you again?" Mrs. O'Leary asked hopefully.

"I'm sure Mr. Quinn will be long gone back to the real world and making money hand over fist by next month."

Something in her tone bothered Sean. It almost sounded like Ashling was condemning him for being a successful businessman. After pondering her words for a few moments, Sean decided he was being too sensitive. She probably didn't mean anything negative at all. Most likely it was just a passing comment.

Over the next hour they visited four other families, and each home was a delight to walk through. Sean felt like he was on a tour of homes from the original 13 colonies. They all seemed to be classically historic, in the age of the homes and the design.

The last home they visited was a two-story with one large dormer dominating the front roofline. The limestone walkway, leading to the front porch, was lined by brightly colored lilies, daffodils and daisies. Sean wondered again how they could have flowers blooming in February.

A wildly excited group of young children opened the door and ran out to greet Sean and Ashling before they were halfway to the front porch. There were five children that looked to range in age from two up to eleven or twelve. They were all neatly dressed and very well groomed. They each wore a bright smile as they rushed toward Ashling.

"Ashling," the older girl called out just as she embraced her in a warm hug. "What took you so long to get here?"

"Nothing but the usual, Jennie dear. Perhaps I should come to your house first next month."

"But then we wouldn't have anything to look forward to all morning," one of the boys said.

"That's a true quandary, Devin," Ashling said. "Perhaps you're right; I should stay with my usual schedule."

Ashling swooped up the youngest child, a fair-haired beauty with a pleasing patch of freckles across her button nose. Sean was instantly taken with all the well-mannered, pleasant children. He was already looking forward to meeting the parents.

"Top of the morning to you," a young woman called out from the doorway as she stepped onto the porch. "I see the children are making the usual nuisance of themselves."

"The darlings couldn't be a bother if they tried, Kaitlyn. "I see Kayla is the picture of health again," Ashling said, nodding toward the toddler she was holding.

"Yes, and it's all thanks to you and your magic healing arts, Ashling. She's been as slow as a late dinner to get her energy back, but since your last visit her recovery was nothing short of remarkable," Kaitlyn said.

Sean smiled listening to the colorful speech and phrases the young woman, Kaitlyn, used. He was beginning to feel like he was on the coast of Ireland instead of Oregon. She wasn't as beautiful as Ashling, but she was still a lovely and perky. All in all, she seemed to be a very pleasant person.

"And you've brought us company," Kaitlyn said as they settled in on the overstuffed couch and chairs in the large, open living room.

"That I have. Kaitlyn, children, this is Sean Quinn. He's here visiting Da and I for a few days, so I'm showing him the sights," Ashling said.

"Ashling has a boyfriend, Ashling has a boyfriend," two of the boys began singing. The other children giggled with delight and joined in the chant.

"That will do, children. Can't you see you're embarrassing our guests?" Kaitlyn said.

"Not at all, Kaitlyn. It will take a wee bit more than that to get me blushing. I suspect Mr. Quinn hasn't blushed for many a year, himself. Am I right, Sean?" Ashling asked.

Sean enjoyed the beautiful, wide smile that Ashling turned his way. She had caused him to blush only that morning at breakfast and was now enjoying teasing him about it.

"I believe a man that's not afraid to blush is a man in touch with his true inner feelings. Isn't that bound to make him a better husband and father when those joyful days arrive?" he responded.

"Oh how I wish my Patrick could talk that way, Ashling. You've got a keeper there you do," Kaitlyn said.

"I assure you he's not mine to keep. Sean is the gentlemen that nearly ran into my Da's store after having the accident on the highway. Have you not heard the gossip about that?" Ashling said.

"Aye, we've heard it all right. Well, he looks none the worse for wear, then does he?" Shandra, the eldest daughter said."

"He's doing well, all things considered," Ashling said. Speaking of doing well, let's set up shop and see how the lot of you are faring."

"They're all good as gold except for Kayla," Kaitlyn said. "And she's doing so much better that I can hardly work up the energy to worry about her."

"Good to hear. I wish all my visits went so well. It's a sign of what a fine mother you are, Kaitlyn," Ashling said sincerely.

"More likely a sign they inherited their father's iron constitution, but thanks for the kind words just the same," Kaitlyn said.

Ashling smiled and turned her attention to the little girl, Kayla. "Can you sit very still on your mother's lap, dearie?" she asked.

"Mommy said I can have a cookie if I'm good," Kayla said.

"Well then you must get a lot of cookies since you're such a fine young lass whenever I visit," Ashling said, as she opened her old leather bag.

Ashling brought out a beautiful crystal for the examination of Kayla. It was sky-blue with flakes of white scattered through it. The crystal was about a half-inch thick and four inches tall and shaped similar to an arrowhead. She held it up against Kayla's chest, directly over the heart.

For a few moments, nothing happened while Ashling held the crystal over Kayla's heart and stared intently into the little girl's eyes. Slowly, the crystal began to change color. Where there were only traces of white in the stone at first, now it was nearly half white.

Sean couldn't help feeling a bit uneasy watching the strange crystal turning from mostly blue to nearly all white. He looked up at Ashling and saw that she was whispering something into Kayla's ear, and the young girl almost seemed to be lost in a trance.

He didn't know a lot about Naturopathic medicine, but he certainly hadn't heard of anything like what he was witnessing now. A lot of questions were piling up that he would like to ask Ashling when they were alone again.

The crystal appeared to be glowing now, almost like it was turning white hot. A high-pitched wail seemed to be emanating from the glowing stone, which was now bright white, without a trace of blue.

Sean jumped when a ferocious growling and barking started up from behind the door about five feet to his right. That seemed to break the spell that the crystal had cast over the room, and the children began laughing at Sean's sudden fright.

"You're not afraid of a little doggy are you, mister," one of the boys asked. Sean thought his name was Devin.

Sean jumped again when the ferocious barking was joined by the sound of something very large slamming into the door. He was sure that was no little doggy trying to tear that door apart.

"It's the crystal's song that sets him off," Ashling said, smiling. "The pitch is so high that it doesn't really grate on human ears, but animals are another matter."

She pulled the crystal away from Kayla's heart and the sound quickly died away. The glow faded as well, and within moments it was back to the original sky-blue color.

The barking and growling stopped but was immediately replaced by a whimpering sound that made it clear the family dog wanted to join the party. Sean wasn't so sure he wanted to see the animal up close and personal.

The youngest boy, Duncan, hurried to the door and started to open it. Sean braced himself and tried to prepare for whatever might come through the door. It would probably be a man-hating Doberman if Sean's luck with animals held. He didn't mind most animals, but they had never really taken a shine to him over the years.

"Duncan! What did I tell you about Gorten while we have company?" Kaitlyn asked.

"To not let him out of his room," the oldest girl, Jennie, said before Duncan could answer.

"Oh yeah," Duncan said, grinning. "Sorry, Mother."

Duncan started to close the partially open door, but before he could get it closed, a large, furry, gray head shoved its way into the opening. The head was soon followed by the largest body Sean had ever seen on a dog. The curly-haired dog, with a long bushy tail, was bounding toward him with his eyes bright with excitement and his long, red tongue lolling out of his open mouth. This dog was easily four-feet high and six-feet long and had to weigh close to two-hundred pounds.

"Gorten Abernathy!" Kaitlyn shouted. "Stop this instant or you'll be spending the night in the back yard, so you will!"

If the massive dog heard Kaitlyn, he didn't seem to be listening, since his headlong rush at Sean continued unabated. Sean decided he had a better chance for survival on his feet than he did sitting down. At least he'd have a few inches of height on him, even if the dog outweighed him.

Sean's standing up must have appeared as an open invitation for play to Gorten. He rushed forward and jumped up, placing both gigantic paws on Sean's chest. It was no contest, as Sean toppled over backwards onto the couch as the children scattered to get out of the way.

Once Gorten had Sean pinned on the couch, he began licking his face enthusiastically with his large, wet tongue. Maybe other dogs didn't take to Sean, but Gorten had found a new best friend.

Sean thought he saw motion out of the corner of his eye and turned his head to see Ashling touch her hand to Gorten's side. The dog jumped like he'd received an electrical shock and let out a yelp of pain. He quickly heaved his bulk off Sean and sat still in front of Ashling, his mouth open and tail twitching across the floor.

"Spare me the theatrics, Gorten," Kaitlyn said. "I swan, for such a big bruiser; you're really quite the baby. Ashling barely touched you, and she saved you a few lashes from my hickory stick besides. What were you thinking, mauling our guest like you're some untrained alley rat? I'm ashamed of you, I am, and so are the children."

Sean sat up and tried to wipe off some of the slobber Gorten had left on his face and shirt collar. When he looked over at Gorten, the big lug was hanging his head and looking thoroughly miserable. Sean almost felt sorry for the dog-almost.

"I'm so sorry you were the victim of one of Gorten's tongue baths, Sean," Kaitlyn said. He gets a wee bit excited whenever we have company."

"Especially if it's someone he's never met before," Ashling added. "You really should be grateful that Gorten took it easy on you, Sean. Some of his victims were rushed off to the hospital, so they were," she added with merriment twinkling in her eyes.

"Well, I did come to see the sights and Gorten is quite a sight, I must say. What type of dog is he?"

"He's an Irish Wolf Hound," Jennie said. "They're known for getting very big. Gorten has lived longer than most dogs, and he just seems to keep right on growing. He's gotten so big that we had to give him his own bedroom."

"Big might be an understatement," Sean said, as he stood again. "I've seen horses that weren't as big as Gorten."

"Just go on into the kitchen-right through there," Kaitlyn said, pointing toward the back of the house. "You can wash up in there."

Sean walked warily by Gorten but gave him a soft pat on the head when he realized the dog was going to stay put. There was a lot of muffled giggling from the living room, as Sean tried to walk back to the kitchen with a little dignity still intact.

Chapter Four

May the enemies of Ireland never eat bread nor drink wine,
but be afflicted with itching without the benefit of scratching

~ Old Irish Saying ~

"I was impressed with the way you handled yourself with the Abernathy's," Sean said, as they walked toward what looked like a small river at the far edge of town.

"They're quite a hand full, but they are really the most wonderful of children. I look forward to my visit each month."

"They obviously adore you, and your rapport with all your patients is impressive. But I was talking about how you handled yourself with Gorten. You barely touched him, and he jumped to attention like an army private when the general walks by. Tell the truth; you stuck him with a safety pin, didn't you?"

"A pox on you for saying such a thing! I would never do that to Gorten, or any other animal," Ashling said indignantly. "I happen to love animals very much and find them better company than a lot of people I meet."

Sean wasn't sure if that last comment was aimed at him, but he could see he'd said the wrong thing. He'd only been teasing, but he couldn't understand why the dog would have jumped and yelped like that otherwise.

"I didn't mean to offend you, Ashling. I was just very surprised at the way Gorten reacted to your touch. It did seem like he was hurt by the way he yelped."

"I probably just scared him. He really is a big baby."

"Big being the operative word," Sean said.

"Come this way," Ashling said suddenly. "I want you to see one of my favorite parts of Rundimahair."

Sean felt like she was hurrying to change the subject. He had other questions about some of the strange things he'd seen today, but he realized now was not the right time to pursue them.

They crossed the street at the far edge of town and came to the river. It was about forty-feet wide and looked to be fairly deep as well. The slow-moving water was a soft green color in the reflected sunlight shining across the surface.

Along the edge of the street was a lush green parkway about twenty-feet wide and running the length of the town. Where the parkway met the river, there was a very old stone wall about four-feet high and a foot thick.

As Sean looked up and down the parkway, he could see that there were openings where the stone wall curved in toward the river. There were wide inlaid rock stairs in each opening, which led down to the river's edge.

All along the parkway were cherry, apple and peach trees planted about six or seven yards apart. The cherry trees were already in bloom, and their violet and white blossoms were lovely.

"This is absolutely breathtaking," Sean said, as he stood in the parkway and looked up and down the river. I don't know if I've ever seen a waterfront as tranquil and beautiful."

"If you look a bit farther down, you can see the harbor where the fishing and pleasure boats are moored. That is a fine sight to see, if you love rivers and boats as much as I do," Ashling said.

"So this river runs to the ocean?"

"Indeed it does. Many of our town folk make a fair living with their fishing boats," Ashling said.

"Not for the first time, I am absolutely blown away by the beauty and unique charm of your town, Ashling. It must be full of tourists all summer long."

"Not so much as you might think. The truth is, we don't really seek out the tourist trade here. We like our little town just the way it is and wouldn't want it turned into a tourist trap that some coastal towns are."

"I agree that many of the towns along the Oregon coast have become over commercialized and it has ruined the charm that made them worth visiting in the first place. Still, I can't believe you've been able to keep Rundimahair such a well-kept secret over the years."

"Just the luck of the Irish, I suppose."

Sean was going to say more on the subject, but he could sense that same guarded unease from Ashling, which he'd felt earlier. It was in his nature to get answers to his questions, sooner rather than later, but he didn't want to offend his tour guide again.

"Shall we head back to the house for a bit of lunch? Ashling asked.

"Sounds good to me. I'm starving and as much as I hate to admit it a little worn out."

"Perfectly natural for someone recovering from an accident and injuries like yours."

The next few days passed by too quickly from Sean's point of view. He had enjoyed every moment of his time in Rundimahair, and in particular the wonderful people who lived here. He hadn't seen much of Ashling, since she seemed to make a point of being up and gone long before he would drag himself out of bed.

He'd been very surprised by the way he slept deeply each night and usually didn't wake up until nine or ten each morning. This was very atypical for him, since he'd always been a light sleeper and an early riser. Eamon assured him it was just his body's way of healing and recovering his strength after his accident.

Sean had used his free time to wander around the town, taking in the sights and sounds of small-town life. He'd driven out of town on several occasions to look over the beautiful countryside and farmlands that surrounded Rundimahair.

The unusual layout of this community continued to fascinate Sean. Once he passed through town and into the more rural area, there were only gravel or dirt roads to travel by.

Stranger still, there were no signs of telephone or electrical poles carrying wires to the farmhouses. Now that he thought about it, there were no overhead power lines in town either. He could believe that they had underground power in town, although most rural towns still used overhead power lines.

There was no way they had underground power running to the farmsteads, which were spread out and separated by miles of open farm and range land. It wouldn't be economically feasible to have underground power ranging so far and wide.

Despite the lack of visible power lines, the few homesteads he'd visited had electrical power. They had electric lights and plugin receptacles, even if they looked a bit old fashioned.

Sean was anxious to ask about this apparent mystery, but he couldn't bring himself to question the families who'd welcomed him into their homes. Each family he'd met was kind and full of hospitality for a complete stranger.

The other strange pattern that continued was that each family or individual he met had Irish accents. Some of their accents were so strong he struggled to understand most of what they said. Others only had a trace accent.

Even in a small community like Rundimahair, it seemed extremely unlikely that every single person was of Irish ancestry. Even if that were possible, how had they maintained the pleasant, strong accents over the generations. It was true that some had less accent than others, but they all had Irish accents.

These, and many other questions, were piling up in Sean's mind. There were so many strange and seemingly unexplainable incongruences surrounding the odd but beautiful Rundimahair.

Sean's train of thought was interrupted when he drove over a hill and saw a man and woman trying to rescue a cow from a muddy quagmire at the bottom of the hill. The dirt road was dry for as far as he could see in both directions. Somehow the valley at the bottom of two hills was a muddy quagmire.

Sean drove down the hill within about fifty feet of the muddy mess in the base of the valley. When the man sitting on an old horse-drawn wagon turned to look at Sean's Cadillac, Sean could see he was quite old. Ancient was the word that came to mind. This was a scene right out of an old black and white western.

The woman he'd seen sitting in the back of the old buckboard now appeared to be more of a girl- perhaps seventeen or eighteen. She had dark auburn hair and fair skin. Like many of the females he'd seen during his visit so far, this girl was unusually beautiful.

"Hello," Sean called out as he walked down the hill. "Can I be of any help?"

The old man didn't appear to be unfriendly, but it was safe to say his expression was guarded. The teenage girl's attitude was completely opposite, as she jumped out of the rugged old wagon and smiled brightly.

"It would be a kind and generous fellow who would offer us a helping hand. As you can clearly see, we sure and truly require assistance," she said, as she walked toward him.

The old fellow climbed down off the wagon seat with slow, methodical movements. He stared at Sean approaching but didn't say a word. Sean wondered if he kept a rifle under the wagon seat, like he'd seen in so many old movies.

The pretty young girl ran up to meet Sean before he was halfway down the hill. Instead of offering a hand to shake, she embraced him warmly and said, "My name is Ailbe and you must be the ever so handsome stranger in town. Your name is Sean, is it not?" she asked when she let him go.

Sean couldn't help but smile at the girl's outgoing, confident nature. Yes, my name is Sean. It's a pleasure to meet you, Ailbe."

"Well Sean, the pleasure is all ours. As you can plainly see, one of our cows got through the fence and into a spot of trouble. Our irrigation ditch sprang a leak, so it did. most of the water ran into this hollow and made a muddy mess of things."

"He looks to be pretty well bogged down all right," Sean agreed, as they approached the bottom of the hill. "Sean Quinn's the name, he added, offering his hand to the old fellow.

The old man looked Sean over carefully before finally shaking his hand. "I go by Aengus," he said in a slow Irish accented drawl. "We don't get many strangers 'round here. We heard about you sure enough, but didn't expect to make your acquaintance. We don't get into town all that much."

Aengus still held Sean's hand in a surprisingly firm shake. He might be older than the hills, but he still had a fair grip. Sean finally pulled his hand free and said, "Are you going to pull him out with that wagon?"

"Tried that with very little success," Aengus said calmly. He didn't appear frustrated or angry, despite the messy situation he was in.

"That's because you wouldn't let me lend a hand, dear Daideo, Ailbe said with a smile.

Sean saw a sharp glance pass from Aengus to the girl. "That will be enough of that talk, dearest."

Ailbe turned and rolled her eyes at Sean. He smiled and said, "It sounded like you called him Dadyo. Is he your Dad?"

She laughed heartily before saying, "does he look young enough to be my Da? No, I called him Daideo, which is an affectionate term for grandfather in these parts."

"In the Irish language you mean?" Sean asked.

"What else would I mean, Sean?"

Sean started to offer a sarcastic response, but he thought better of it when he saw the tense look on Aengus' face.

Instead he said, "Irish does seem to be the official language around here."

"My Daideo's wagon only has two horsepower, as you can surely see," Ailbe said, pointing to the two horses pulling the wagon. "I'd venture a guess that your shiny new car has a wee bit more horses under the hood–would I be right?"

Sean couldn't resist her charming smile and chuckled, as he said, "Indeed it does, Ailbe. If you two could untie the rope from the wagon, I'll back the Cadillac down the hill. We'll tie the rope onto the trailer hitch and see if we can coax that big fellow out of the quagmire."

"A good and fine idea if I've ever heard one, Sean. "Will you be willing to let me ride along with you while we pull Gertie out of the muck?"

Sean was wise enough to look at Aengus for approval before he responded. The old gentleman gave him a tiny smile and nodded his approval.

"Come along then, Sean said to Ailbe.

"That I will!" she shouted, as she ran up the hill with surprising speed.

"That girl has the energy of a dozen good men, Sean. You'd best hurry along if you don't want her trying to start your fine car for you."

Sean turned and hurried up the hill behind Ailbe. When he got to the Cadillac, he wasn't too surprised to see her sitting behind the wheel. He was glad he'd put the keys in his pocket before leaving the vehicle earlier.

"It's the finest car I've ever laid eyes on, Sean," she said enthusiastically. "I'd bet my last dollar she'll fly down the road fast enough to take a girl's breath away." Ailbe turned and stared at Sean while giving him a 'come hither' smile. "I'd wager you know a thing or two about taking a girl's breath away. Am I right, Sean?"

While he might only be six or seven years older than Ailbe, he wasn't about to get into a flirting match with her. "No wonder your grandfather's hair is gray. I'd guess your Da's hair is the same from raising a wild young girl like you." He smiled to soften his words, but he wanted her to know he wasn't going to play her games.

"Scoot over to the passenger's seat and we'll go rescue Gertie before she disappears from sight."

She gave him a pretty pout, but to her credit, she quickly smiled and moved lithely into the passenger's seat. Sean reckoned she would be a heartbreaker in a few years, if she wasn't already.

While he drove slowly down the dusty hill, Ailbe turned on the radio. Sean had been listening to a Carrie Underwood CD and her song: Temporary Home, filled the car with her powerful but often tender voice.

"I love her music so much," Ailbe said enthusiastically. "I didn't know older guys liked her too."

Sean laughed and said, "I'm only twenty-four. It's not like I grew up in the sixties."

"I'll be eighteen in six months," she said, giving Sean a hopeful smile.

He glanced at her and said, "Ailbe, you're going to make some lucky young man a very happy guy. In the meantime, try to stay out of trouble."

She stared at him for a moment before breaking into a smile and saying, "I've got so many kinfolks watching over me that I couldn't get into trouble if I wanted to."

"Something tells me it's going to take all of them to keep you in line," he said, as they circled around and backed up to the mud hole.

Her cheerful laugh followed him as he climbed out of the car. By the time he got to the back of the car, Aengus nearly had the knot tied around the trailer hitch. "Slow and easy it goes, young fella," he said with his easy drawl.

When he put the SUV in gear and began moving slowly up the hill, he felt the resistance when the rope became taut. He continued to apply a little more gas until he felt movement behind them.

"Give it the gas!" he heard Aengus shout.

Sean pushed on the gas and after a brief hesitation, he felt the massive cow come free. He continued slowly up the rise until Gertie was walking on dry ground.

Gertie greeted him with an annoyed moo when he shut down the engine and walked to the back of the car. She looked very annoyed, but at least she was safe.

"Well and finely done, Sean," Aengus said, before giving him a firm pat on the back.

"Glad I could help," he said. "I'll be heading back to town to meet Ashling and Eamon for lunch. Good luck with wandering, Gertie," he added, as he opened the driver's side door and climbed inside.

Albie tapped on the glass and motioned for him to open the window. When Sean hit the button to lower the window, Albie leaned in close and said, with a mischievous grin, "I see how it is, Sean."

"And what is that supposed to mean?" he asked, smiling.

"Ashling is a rare beauty, if you like older women," she said with a twinkle in her eye.

"She's no more than my own age–not that it matters," he said.

"Are you sure about that?" Ailbe asked grinning, as she added, "Is it her green eyes that make you go weak in the knees?"

"The only thing that might have me a little weak in the knees is the ill effects from my accident," Sean said, returning her smile.

"Still and all, if it's green eyes you have a hankering for, then all you have to do is say so," Ailbe said, leaning in until their faces were only inches apart.

Sean couldn't hold back a gasp of surprise when Ailbe's lovely brown eyes suddenly appeared to turn a sparkling shade of emerald green.

Ailbe stared at him intently for another few moments, and then her eyes slowly returned to her natural caramel brown color. "Whatever you like, Sean. Whatever you like," she said with a flirtatious smile, as she slowly stepped back from his car.

"That will be enough of your shameless flirting, young lady," Aengus said mildly. He was smiling, but Sean thought he detected a hidden warning in his tone.

Ailbe seemed to pick up on her grandfather's tone also, as her smile faded a bit. "Please plan to join us for a meal before you return to your real world," she said.

Though still a bit shaken, Sean smiled and said, "I'm not sure how long I'll be in town, but I will if I can."

While he was driving back to town, the image of her beautiful brown eyes changing to emerald green and then back to brown played over and over in his mind. He also wondered what she meant by "his real world". He finally tried to laugh it off as more of her teenage silliness and his own overactive imagination.

Instead of Ailbe's eyes, Sean tried to focus on the beautiful countryside he'd seen. During his tour of Rundimahair and the surrounding area, the property developer in him had selected several fine locations that would be perfect for development of a medium-sized strip mall. He could anchor it with a major-chain grocery store, since he hadn't seen one in town.

It was part of what he found charming, but also a little strange about Rundimahair. It was set up much like an Irish village from two or three-hundred years ago. Of course, they had modern conveniences such as electricity, telephones, and indoor plumbing, but it all seemed to be added on instead of built into the building's original floor plan. There wasn't a building of modern design anywhere in town.

Aengus riding around in a wagon right out of the old west was part of the strangeness he felt. Why wouldn't he be using a tractor, or some other motor driven vehicle, to rescue Gertie? He wondered if some folks in the outskirts of town might be like the Amish who disdained the use of modern conveniences. Rundimahair was definitely a charming but somewhat mysterious place.

⁂

The following morning, Ashling had been home when he came down for breakfast. He'd gladly accepted Ashling's offer to accompany her as she ran errands throughout the morning. It turned out to be a pleasant time, filled with agreeable conversation, as he got to know more residents and store owners in town.

Ashling had kept their personal conversation neutral and continued avoiding in-depth answers to his questions. Eventually, he gave up on seeking answers and just enjoyed her company.

One question he would really like an answer to was why everyone in town seemed to have an Irish accent. This continued to baffle him each time he thought of it. The older folks in town had the strongest accent, but even the younger adults and all the children spoke with an Irish lilt. It appeared that only Irish families settled down in the strange little town of Rundimahair.

When they'd returned to the walkway in front of Ashling's home, Sean thought he noticed some movement in the hedge that ran along the side yard. When he glanced at Ashling, he realized she'd seen it too and appeared tense or even angry.

"Did you see—" was all Sean could say before Ashling cut him off.

"Wait right here," she said forcefully, and hurried into the house without further explanation.

Sean was surprised by her sudden change in demeanor. She went from a friendly, sometimes teasing young woman to deadly serious in a matter of seconds.

His surprise continued when he saw a blur of motion rushing from the side hedge into the back yard. Either his eyes were playing tricks on him, or something had just rushed into the back yard quicker than his eye could follow. He wondered whether he should investigate what he'd seen or just stay where he was.

A sudden crashing noise and the distinct sound of breaking glass spurred Sean into motion. He rushed up to the front door only to find it locked. He ran around to the back door and saw that it was not only open but barely hanging on its hinges. The door's glass lite had been shattered as though something hit it with tremendous force.

"Ashling, are you all right?" he shouted, as he ran through the ruined doorway.

He turned and stepped through the café doors into the kitchen where all the noise was coming from. It was like stepping into a war zone. The refrigerator was open with much of the contents strewn about on the floor. Several of the upper cabinets had been torn from the wall, and others appeared to have been singed black by fire. The old wood stove was lying in pieces in the middle of the kitchen floor. Water was spraying out of the hole where the sink had been, and the sink was sitting on top of the dining room table.

"Ashling, where are you?" he shouted.

"Get out of here now, Sean!"

Sean heard her warning and turned toward the open door to the pantry. It sounded like her voice came from inside, but he had difficulty seeing anything clearly. The entire kitchen was filling with a mixture of blue-gray smoke that smelled faintly of burnt almonds.

Before he could enter the pantry, there was a fierce rush of hot air and smoke that bellowed out at him. Something fast and strong crashed into him, and he was knocked off his feet and sent sprawling into the cabinets on the other side of the kitchen. His head cracked hard against the edge of the countertop and he collapsed to the floor, as unconsciousness came flooding in on him.

Sean thought he heard Ashling urgently calling his name and struggled to open his eyes. What he saw wasn't Ashling; it was a grotesque, bird-like creature coming directly at him. The creature had long, razor-sharp teeth on display, as it closed in on him with its beak wide open. Just before it reached him, the creature was struck by what appeared to be a whirling ball of gas. The terrifying creature was blown to bits in an explosion of searing hot red and blue lights.

Sean had closed his eyes. When he opened his eyes again, the terrifying creature was nowhere in sight. The kitchen was a disaster area, although he could barely see anything through the smoky haze still lingering in the air following the explosion.

"Sean, are you all right," Ashling cried out as she knelt beside him.

He looked up to see her lovely face come into view, as the smoke quickly began to clear. Her hair was a mess, and her face was covered with dirt smudges. There also appeared to be several cuts on her face and one large gash on her forehead. Sean tried to lift his hand to the bloody gash but found he didn't have the strength.

"This is…the strangest dream I've ever…" Sean started to say, but lost track of his thoughts. "Such a lovely woman-even after slaying a dragon. I don't think I've ever seen such a…" Sean stopped mumbling as his consciousness was quickly slipping away.

"It's all right, Sean. Everything is going to be all right," she said soothingly, as she touched her hands to each of his temples.

He tried to respond, but as soon as she touched his temples, his pain and discomfort suddenly vanished. All he had time for was a quick smile before he sank into sweet oblivion.

***

Darkness had descended when Sean opened his eyes again. He was back in his pajamas and lying in bed. His inner clock was telling him something wasn't quite right about this, but he couldn't reason out what might be wrong.

Even though he was feeling dizzy and weak, he tried to sit up on the edge of his bed. The first attempt was a failure, and he slumped back against his pillow. The second try was only marginally better, but he did manage to achieve an upright, sitting position.

The past few days seemed to be a murky quagmire in his memory, as he struggled to clear his mind. Only brief flashes were revealed that didn't seem to have any connection to each other.

There was something about being attacked by a large animal—some kind of bird?

He could recall the accident that had brought him here and knew he was staying at the home of Eamon and Ashling Cahir. There was also a vague recollection of meeting Ailbe and Aengus, while rescuing their cow, Gertie. Had that been today or the day before?

The harder he tried to recall, the murkier his memory became. He finally gave up completely because the effort was giving him a splitting headache. It was time to head for the kitchen and a little midnight snack. His hunger pangs were almost as acute as the headache. Sean reasoned that food might cure both ailments.

He struggled to a standing position and realized he ached all over. Was he still this beat up from the accident? Again, it didn't seem right, but he couldn't come up with any other explanation.

He made it down to the kitchen, despite feeling like he'd been run over by a truck. The kitchen looked clean, neat, and organized, just as it always did. The gas cooking range looked so clean it could be brand new. When he glanced at the pantry door, he felt a sudden pang of unease. He glanced back at the gas range and thought it didn't seem to belong there, although he couldn't figure out why.

Just as he was about to open the refrigerator, he heard voices coming from the library. His first instinct was to grab an apple and head back to his room, but there was urgency in the muffled voices that piqued his curiosity. After a few moments of indecision, Sean finally tiptoed down the hallway and stopped just outside the library door.

He could hear what sounded like Eamon's voice, but he was speaking too softly to understand his words. Then Ashling spoke, and her voice was much clearer; the urgency he'd detected moments before was coming from her.

"I know, Da, but I can't keep healing him and erasing his memory. I've had to do it several times within a few days, and you know that can be dangerous and not always effective. As it is, I think he'll have some aches and pains and perhaps some vague recall of what happened when he wakes up in the morning."

Eamon spoke again, but Sean could only hear a word or phrase here and there. It sounded like, "worth the risk," but he couldn't be sure. Then he thought Eamon said, "That young gray must be one of Riley's experiments. Did you talk with him about it?"

Ashling's voice was louder when she said, "You can be sure I had a face-to-face discussion with him. I told him there would be no more dragon breeding without unanimous approval of the council. He's just not careful enough with his little pets."

"Aye, that's the truth of it. Even though he's a gifted breeder, he's gone too far this time," Eamon said in a louder tone." He continued talking, but Sean couldn't hear enough to make sense of it.

"We don't even know if he's the one, Da. I know you think he'll save us all, but I'm still not convinced of that. We really don't have any proof positive," Ashling said.

Sean could hear the growing frustration and worry in Ashling's voice. His mind was swimming with confusion, as he tried to come to grips with what she was saying. She had to be talking about him, but none of it made any sense. In fact, nothing made any sense since the accident had landed him in this strange little town.

It was time to get out of here. He didn't understand much about what was going on, but he was developing a very uneasy feeling about Eamon and Ashling. In truth, something wasn't right about the entire community of Rundimahair.

In his haste to be gone, Sean turned too quickly, and the dizziness that continued to plague him caused him to slump against the wall of the hallway. The old oak wall paneling creaked noisily, causing Sean to grimace. He hoped the noise didn't carry into the library. He stood very still for several moments, waiting to see if there would be a reaction from Eamon or Ashling. Slowly he began to relax when the library door stayed closed. He tiptoed quietly out of the hallway and into the kitchen, ready to make a rush for the stairway.

"Things just haven't gone well since the moment you set foot inside our little town, have they Sean?"

Sean cringed at the sound of Eamon's voice and looked up to see him standing on the other side of the saloon doors to the kitchen. He was smiling, but Eamon's gray eyes were filled with sadness. His first thought was to try to rush past the older man and run for the door.

"You've nothing to fear from the likes of us, Sean. We're your friends and you're safer here with us than anywhere else you might wish to go."

Sean forced himself to concentrate on what Eamon was saying. If only his thought process wasn't so muddled. One thing he did know for certain was that he didn't feel safe, despite Eamon's gentle words.

"Look Eamon, I don't really understand everything that is going on around here. There are definitely some weird vibes flying around your town, and the strangest vibes of all are coming from your daughter, Ashling. I don't think I want to know what the answers are anymore. I just want to gather my things together and get back to Portland. Do you have a problem with that?"

"Not at all, my young friend. When the time and circumstances are right, you will be free to go if that's what you choose," Eamon said.

"I don't know how you ended up standing there blocking my way, when a moment ago I thought I heard you talking to Ashling in the library. You sound like the voice of reason, but what you're really saying is that I'm not free to go now. To me, it feels like you're holding me against my will, and apparently, you can move invisibly at the speed of light. Just two more bizarre events to add to the list."

"We're not holding you against your will, Sean. We're actually protecting you from those who may do you harm," Eamon said.

"It's a waste of time trying to convince him of our good intentions, Father. Think how you would feel if you were wearing his shoes. Well, it's true he hasn't shoes on his feet at the moment, but you understand my meaning, I'm sure," Ashling said, as she stepped out of the hallway behind Sean.

He was pleased that he hadn't flinched at the sudden sound of her voice so close behind him. In truth, he was expecting Ashling to show herself at any moment. He turned slowly and locked eyes with her, trying to understand what her intentions were.

"So, you overheard parts of our conversation in the library; am I correct, Sean?" Ashling asked quietly.

"I came downstairs for a midnight snack and heard voices. I guess I was wondering who was up at this hour aside from me," Sean said. "Is that gas stove new?" he added without thinking, as he stared at it in confusion?

Ashling nodded her head slowly as she walked toward Sean. He stared into her beautiful green eyes that often sparkled with humor and intelligence. Her eyes were softer now and seemed to be filled with compassion and warmth. He was sure that this was the look that some of her patients saw when she was about to deliver bad news.

"You can see this is not going to work, Da," she said, looking at Eamon. He has to go back to his own world."

"Don't be too hasty with your decision, my dear girl," Eamon said, as he stepped through the saloon doors. "You may be condemning him to death and taking the last ray of hope away from our people."

She stared at her father for several long moments, before she sighed deeply and said, "It's my decision to make, Da. I'll give him another treatment before he goes to be sure he'll never recall being in Rundimahair."

"And what of our enemies? If they suspect he is the one we've been waiting for, then he's as good as dead."

"They've not laid eyes on him; of that I am certain," Ashling said firmly. "As long as his memory of us is completely gone, then he'll have nothing to fear."

"And if he's the one I suspect he is?" Eamon asked, his eyes filled with sadness.

"He's not, Da."

"Are you so certain of this, my darling girl?" Eamon asked.

Even Sean saw the hesitation in Ashling's eyes, for just a moment, before she regained her resolve and said, "I'm sure."

Eamon didn't respond, but only shook his head sorrowfully. Ashling looked as though her own heart was breaking, as she turned to Sean.

"I couldn't be sorrier no matter how hard I tried, Sean. It was a mistake to bring you here, although we had little choice at the time. What were we to do? We couldn't stand back and watch while you crashed into the ravine."

She took another step closer, and he waited for his fight or flight instinct to kick in. Instead of running, Sean felt the urge to step forward and embrace Ashling. She was indeed a beautiful woman, but it still seemed an odd inclination considering the awkward circumstances. Her next steps brought her into his personal space—only a couple of inches separating them.

"Ashling, I don't want to seem unreasonable here. You and your father have been very kind to me, but you have to admit there is more than a little weirdness going on around here."

"A fair statement if I ever heard one, Sean. But I promise you there will be no more of that to worry about."

Ashling stepped up against him and gently put her arms around his neck. With the two-inch heels she was wearing, and Sean in his bare feet, they were very nearly the same height. He felt mesmerized by her steady gaze and her tender touch. How could he have ever doubted her motives?

Without thinking about it, he put his arms around her waist and leaned in to kiss her gently on her soft, full lips. He felt her respond briefly by wrapping her arms tighter around him, as he pulled her into a tender embrace. It was only for a moment, but nothing had ever felt more wonderful and right.

Finally, she pulled back, although she kept her arms loosely around his neck. He looked into her soft, green eyes and saw the turmoil and sorrow there. "It's going to be all right," he said softly.

She sighed deeply and smiled sadly as she said, "Though you're not going to remember any of this; I want you to know that it has been our great pleasure to make your acquaintance. We'll not soon forget you."

While he was struggling to understand her meaning, Sean felt a gentle pressure at the base of his neck. Ashling was saying something, but he could no longer hear her clearly. A sense of euphoria swept over him, from head to toe, and he collapsed against her. Even as his conscious thought was sweeping away, Sean had just enough time to marvel at the pleasant combination of softness and strength of the woman who held him in her arms. His last conscious thought was that he would never forget Ashling Cahir for as long as he lived.

Chapter Five

When I dream, I dream Of Ireland's rolling hills
Of all its lovely, shimmery lakes and little babbling rills
O, Ireland! O, Ireland! We're never far apart
For you and all your beauty fill my mind and touch my heart.

~ Old Irish Saying ~

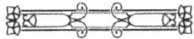

He is standing on the highest point of the rolling, tree-lined hills that surround the breathtakingly beautiful, green valley below. Small, lush meadows, sprinkled with multi-colored wildflowers, break up the thick tree growth on the valley floor. The two sparkling blue lakes, which are centered in the valley, are the true stars of Mother Nature's impressive show.

Despite his many travels, and the myriad wonders he has beheld, Sean is sure he has never been anywhere or beheld anything that could rival this stunning valley. There is more to it than just the dazzling beauty before him. He feels an almost spiritual essence emanating from the peaceful scene. The words "sacred ground" run through his mind, and this feels right.

At the far end of the valley, beyond the two lakes, is a group of stone buildings. At its center is a very tall circular stone tower with two small window openings very near the top. A church constructed of the same gray stone as the tower is nearby, with a small cemetery directly behind it. Several other buildings are laid out in loosely organized, close proximity, which is reminiscent of a long ago medieval European village. Without knowing how, Sean understands that this is a monastery—not a village.

A patchwork of grain fields lies to the east and north of the buildings, and a stone fence runs along the west side. This is obviously the monastery entrance, and he sees groups of men clad in homespun tan robes hurrying in and out at the main gate. By all appearances, this bustling community is as prosperous as it is peaceful and serene.

It is a beautiful sunny day in Ireland, and the sun's rays warm Sean pleasantly, as he contemplates hiking down to the monastery and paying a visit to the good people living there. Just as he begins his decent from the hilltop, a grouping of thick, dark clouds rolls over the hills, across the valley and quickly cover the sun.

He is suddenly filled with a sense of foreboding moments before a thunderous noise reaches him. When he sees the first wave of riders charge over the hills above the monastery, Sean realizes the noise is the thunder of thousands of horse's hooves. The riders are an embodiment of the apocalyptic destruction raining down on the peaceful valley below.

Without truly knowing how, Sean realizes the monastery was a source of pure light that was created by the Angels of the Sidhe. These angels were here on earth to protect humans from the demonic Tuatha race of immortals.

❖❖❖

Sean awoke from a deep sleep to the sound of someone shouting in impotent rage. His heart is racing and pounding against his chest. He sits up abruptly and realizes that he was the source of the shouting. It feels like he just awakened from a long, deep slumber. As the memories of the monastery quickly faded, Sean felt a sense of kinship with those who'd called the ancient monastery home.

His eyes darted from one location to the next as his mind struggled to make sense of his surroundings. While images of the beautiful Irish valley still played through his mind, he wondered how he knew it was in Ireland.

Slowly, his mind began to catalog the items in his room. The fog and confusion continued to lift as he realized that he was sitting up in his own bed. The familiar, luxurious appointments of his master bedroom suite surrounded him. The comforting feeling of knowing he was safe in his own home began to push back the anxiety that had overwhelmed him moments before.

Sean threw back the bed covers and tried to stand up too quickly. A rush of dizziness almost caused him to fall back onto the bed. After taking a few deep breaths and shaking his head, the wooziness began to fade away.

After taking a long hot shower and munching down two of his favorite granola bars, Sean felt almost normal again. He reached for his cell phone, which was plugged in, charging on the kitchen counter. Something about the cell phone being there seemed off, but he refused to ponder the weirdness that lingered in the back of his mind. Surely it was only the after-effects of his strange dream.

By the time Sean arrived at his downtown office building, he was slowly getting back into his everyday groove. His mind was clear and alert when he walked into the suite of offices his company occupied on the top floor of a ten-story building. Sean owned the entire building.

"How was the weekend on the Oregon Coast?" his office manager, Jennie, asked cheerfully.

His first thought was that it seemed like he'd been gone much longer than a weekend. Sean shook off the strange feeling and said, "Uneventful."

"Did you find anything worth pursuing at the real estate auction?" Jennie asked from the door to her spacious office, which was next to his.

There was that feeling again. It was like he'd just checked out for a few days with no real memory of where he'd been or what he'd done. He was fairly certain that he hadn't been at any real estate auction. Where had he been? No answers were forthcoming.

"Earth to Sean," Jennie said, laughing. "You seem a little bit out of it this morning.

Sean forced a smile and said, "The truth is I was feeling lousy by the time I got to the coast. I actually spent most of my time in bed trying to get over whatever was bugging me."

"Well, maybe you should be at home resting up. I can handle things for a few days," Jennie said.

Sean looked at her concerned smile and almost felt like he wasn't being completely honest with Jennie. Unfortunately, what he'd told her felt like the truth, or as much of it as he could recall. He was coming to realize that he honestly couldn't recall any details of what was apparently a lost weekend.

<hr>

Ashling was feeling uneasy after completing visits with her patients today. The truth was that even though it had been several weeks since they'd sent Sean home, she couldn't get him out of her mind.

She truly hoped he was back to his normal life by now. It would take time for the residual effects of the magic she'd had to use on him, to completely dissipate. After a month or so he shouldn't have any lingering ill effects, even though she'd had been forced to use very powerful magic on his mind. Ashling had been very careful, but it wasn't good to work such influential magic so often, especially in such a short period of time.

About a week after they'd sent him home, she'd linked minds with Sean during his sleep. It was clear that he was still troubled by vague dreams of his time in Rundimahair. It was nothing that could lead him back, but it troubled her that he still held on to even distant memories. All traces of his time there should have been washed away.

Even more troubling was the realization that he'd had several dreams about the distant past. The last time she'd touched his mind tracks, he was in the midst of a dream.

The dream was a shockingly accurate retelling of a long-ago tragedy among the humans, who were supposed to be protected by angels of the Sidhe. Instead of protecting the humans who worked and lived at the monastery, some of the angels had followed a woman named Danu and participated in the slaughter of innocent people.

Fortunately, the great Creator of all life cursed Danu and her followers. After the slaughter of the innocent humans that Sean had seen in his dream, Danu and her followers became known as the Tuatha immortals. While they could battle against the Angels of the Sidhe, the fallen angels of the Tuatha immortals could no longer harm humans in any way.

There was no way that Sean should have had access to memories of a tragic event which occurred thousands of years ago. The fact that he'd been blessed with such insight lent much credence to her father's belief about Sean. The belief that he was truly the one they'd been waiting for.

She wanted to check on him again to see what else was hidden in his mind, but she worried about the consequences. Ashling was the absolute best at searching through the myriad pathways of anyone's mind. She could wander through a person's mind without them ever knowing she was there. The problem was it always left an enchanted trail. It was nothing a normal human would ever notice, but others with immense magical gifts might possibly find those trails.

The malevolent forces she was protecting her people from might well have such gifts. Ashling was very good at covering her enchanted tracks. She had also learned that the malicious sorceress who now ruled the Tuatha immortals was adept at finding traces of magic-especially very powerful enchantments.

The dark sorcerer's name was Grainne, which meant dark blade or sword. Grainne was a descendant of Danu, who'd birthed the sorcerers known as the Tuatha race.

Almost from the very creation of the earth, Danu had used the powers of darkness to battle against the Sidhe. In the beginning, their success was very limited. The angelic powers of the Sidhe held secret powers the followers of Danu couldn't overcome.

For centuries, the Sidhe used their powers to protect the human race against the Tuatha immortals. As long as they held together, they were invulnerable to the dark powers of Danu and her people.

Unfortunately, Danu was very powerful and beautiful beyond description. She eventually seduced male members of the Sidhe to join her followers. Together, they begat children with the angelic powers of the Sidhe mixed with Danu's terrible, dark powers. The mix of powers eventually allowed them to destroy the monastery in Sean's dream.

Danu's warriors had been instructed to bring the ancient records to her before burning the monastery. Despite their best efforts, angelic fire flared up out of the hidden archives. All of the Sidhes magical history went up in flames, along with many of Danu's warriors.

Without those records, Danu and her followers were limited to a basic, very dark strain of sorcery. That didn't mean it wasn't incredibly strong and effective. It was nearly the equal of the original, pure enchantment with which Ashling was very gifted.

Danu's form of sorcery, mixed with the power of the fallen angels, was very deadly. It didn't delve into the many nuances of the higher enchantments, but in many ways it was an unstoppable source of pure evil and destruction. In truth, it was terrifying to contemplate how very powerful she and her mixed-race followers had become. Left unchecked, their dark sorcery could eventually destroy nations or even an entire world. This was why the Creator took away their ability to harm humans with their dark powers.

The Sidhe had eventually managed to banish Danu to outer darkness. Even though her dark, immortal soul would never die, Danu was consigned to a place of such despair and hopelessness that she would gladly have chosen eternal death over her imprisonment in outer darkness.

After pondering the terrible history between the Tuatha immortals and the angelic Sidhe, Ashling felt a sudden, urgent need to check on Sean again. Despite her reluctance, she did a quick mind link with him. He'd been home for over a month, and Ashling prayed his memories would be free of Rundimahair and her people. To her relief, his mind was clear and at peace while he slept. She didn't take time to delve deeply into his mind tracks but felt reassured that Sean was going to be able to move on with his life. Any possible lingering memories would surely disappear as time moved on.

⁂

It had been another tough week for Sean. On the one hand, his real estate business was booming. This company had been the main focus of his life since he came to work here as a teenager. What had started out as a part-time, after-school job had quickly become his hope for the future.

Sean begun a hands-on education, in wheeling and dealing in real estate, with the owner of the Oregon Development Corporation. His name was Bill Stanton. At the time, Sean was only sixteen and still in high school. Bill had hired him to run errands and help around the office as needed.

Sean's life to that point had not been ideal. He still had no idea who his absent father was. His mother had been a beautiful woman, who'd gotten pregnant when she was only nineteen. She was ill-equipped to care for a sickly infant because she too seemed to be sick most of the time. As Sean grew older, he realized that her sickness was mostly due to drug and alcohol dependency.

There were times when she could be a kind and thoughtful mom, but as Sean grew up, those happy moments became few and far between. It always seemed like his mom was a lost soul, who simply couldn't deal with the realities of life. She was always dreaming of a better life somewhere, but she could never find it.

Sean had been in and out of foster care for much of his life. When he was only nine, his mom disappeared for a year. He was placed in foster care with a good family who were always kind and patient with him.

His mom finally returned a year later, clean and sober. She worked very hard to get custody of her son again. Just after Sean turned eleven, she was granted full custody. Six months later, she was found dead from a drug overdose.

Grieving the loss of his mom, he was put back into the foster care system. This time the family he lived with was not nearly as kind and supportive.

They weren't abusive, and they kept him fed and clothed. However, to Sean, it was obvious they were in the foster care business for the money. They followed all the rules and cared for the four children who lived with them. What they couldn't provide was the love and comfort Sean had always hoped for.

The one thing that his foster parents had taught him was that if he wanted to get ahead in life, he needed a great education. Sean listened and was a straight-A student all through high school.

When Sean took the job with Bill Stanton, it had only been to earn money for things like cell phones and the more expensive type of clothes he wanted to wear.

Sean spent as much time as possible working for Bill's company. His incredible work ethic wasn't just directed at earning spending money. Sean began to feel needed and appreciated at work, which were two things he'd not seen much of in his young life.

During the summer months, Sean worked out on the construction sites and was a natural at learning the ins and outs of construction and development. Bill had even implemented some of his ideas for improving efficiency in their development process.

Bill Stanton and his wife, Eva, were not able to have children of their own. They'd come to terms with that over the years and put all their time and interest in their business. Eva worked in the office and she noticed that Sean was very bright. Just as he had learned quickly on the construction sites, he also seemed a natural at the business side of real estate development.

Without realizing it, Eva and Sean began to fulfill a need they both had. She began to think of Sean like a son, and he thought of her as the mother he should have had. The relationship with Bill was equally close for Sean. He admired and looked up to Bill immensely.

By the time he was eighteen, he was spending most of his time at the Stanton home. They'd even given him a suite of rooms that usually sat empty in their basement. When he graduated from high school, near the top of his class, he also graduated from foster care. It was a natural fit for him to move in full time with Bill and Eva.

The next three years of his life were by far the best. When he'd graduated from high school, he already had two years' worth of college credit. He graduated with a degree in business management by the age of twenty.

Not only were the Stanton's kind and generous with him, but they also traveled extensively with Sean. They showed him the world and taught him how to take advantage of opportunities. His understanding of business and his self-confidence grew immensely.

By the time Sean was twenty, he was a partner in the business. Bill and Eva were in their late fifties and relied more and more on him. Sean did all that he could to justify their trust and kindness. He had never been happier in his entire life.

Just after his twenty-first birthday, Bill and Eva decided they would spend a month in Italy. It was their favorite destination in Europe. With Sean running the business so well, they finally had time to enjoy other things in life. He was grateful he could give them the time and freedom they'd often lacked.

They kept in touch through video chats, and Sean could see that they were having the time of their lives. They had even learned to speak some of the language. The night before their flight home, they told Sean to be ready for all the gifts they were bringing.

It was the last time he spoke to the couple who had become the parents he'd always wished for. Their flight home encountered engine failure and went down over the ocean. It was in very deep waters and no passengers were ever recovered.

Sean grieved fiercely for the two people he'd grown to love most in this world. Just when he thought his life had turned a corner toward real happiness, fate had dealt him another cruel blow.

After the funeral services, his grief felt like a deep pit he couldn't climb out of. Not only had he lost his surrogate mom and dad, he'd also lost his mentors in the business world. When he was notified that the Stanton's attorney needed to meet with him, Sean assumed the worst. There was probably some relative somewhere who would take over the business, or it would be sold and the assets distributed according to their wishes.

Sean had met Stan's brother, who was eight years older than Stan. He also knew Eva had brothers and sisters who would be looking to inherit as well. He didn't mind someone else owing the business, as long as he could continue to work there. He hoped and even prayed that they wouldn't sell the business he'd grown to love.

The morning he met with Stan and Eva's lawyer; Sean was surprised to see he was the only one at the meeting. He'd expected all the heirs to be there.

"Good morning, Sean," the mostly gray-haired woman said kindly. "My name is Beverly, and I'm so sorry we had to meet for the first time under these circumstances. However, I am happy to finally meet you."

"A pleasure to meet you as well," he said numbly.

"You may be wondering why Bill and Eva's other heirs are not present."

"It crossed my mind," he acknowledged.

"Those were the terms of their will, Sean. As they instructed, I have met with the other six heirs individually. You are the last heir."

Sean knew they would leave him something, maybe even a small share of their fortune. He had no idea how much they were worth, and he really didn't care. Money could never replace what he'd lost.

The petite, older lawyer seemed to be a kind and compassionate woman. She proved that to be true when she said, "I know nothing could ever replace Bill and Eva in your life, Sean. They were very special people. To tell you the truth, I'm still wondering how I'll get along without them in my life. We've been friends since Eva and I attended law school together."

Sean looked up in surprise when Beverly began to tear up and had to stop and compose herself. He hadn't realized she was such a close friend to Bill and Eva.

"I'm sorry," Sean said. "I didn't realize you were that close to them. They truly were the finest people I ever knew."

After the attorney composed herself, she sniffled and said, "Yes, it's a rare privilege to meet people you can treasure as great friends."

"I wish I'd had more time with them," Sean said sadly.

The kind-hearted attorney sighed heavily and said, "Indeed so. I can tell you that your wish would be the same as theirs. They often told me that you had become the son they'd never been able to have. It's difficult to express how much love and joy you brought into their lives."

"It's impossible to explain how much I'd come to love and appreciate them," Sean said, as tears tracked down his cheeks.

After a few moments, while Sean composed himself, Beverly sighed and said, "It's time to get on with the business at hand."

Sean steeled his emotions, preparing to hear that he was out of a job now that someone else would own the company he loved. All he could do was nod at the attorney.

"They have divided up much of their assets amongst their family and loved ones," she said, back to using her professional attorney voice. "The house is going to be sold and the proceeds will be given to Eva's younger sister, who's having health issues of her own right now."

Sean listened as the attorney continued to explain much more than she probably needed to. It was almost like she was treating him as a member of the family. But Sean knew that no matter how much they'd meant to each other; he was never truly part of their family.

"Of course they left the real estate business to you, Sean."

He was thinking about his time with Bill and Eva and wasn't sure he heard her correctly. "What was that last thing you said?" he asked.

She looked up at him and smiled kindly. "I said that they left the real estate business to you, Sean."

It couldn't be true. He had to be dreaming. "They left it to me?" he asked incredulously.

"Who else would they leave it to? You've practically been running it by yourself the past year or so. You love the business as much as they did. You're the natural choice, Sean."

"But there's still so much I have to learn," he stammered, still in shock.

"Then you'll learn it as the new owner of the Oregon Development Corporation," She said, her smile widening. "I'll stay on as legal counsel, and Tera will still handle the taxes quarterly and at year end. The rest is up to you."

Since the day he'd inherited the business, Sean had worked very hard to justify Bill and Eva's faith in him. He'd put his heart and soul into his work and built the company larger every year. Now, at twenty-four, Sean was one of the most successful business men on the west coast.

While Sean was careful to stay on the right side of legal boundaries in business, he was known as a hard negotiator and a great salesman. Some who had dealt with him felt like he'd made promises during negotiation that weren't completely fulfilled in the final product.

Being a great salesman was something that came naturally to him and Bill had helped him refine it into an art form. Eva had always encouraged Bill to not stray across ethical boundaries, but occasionally he came close to crossing that line. Some people felt Sean had crossed that line more than once.

Jennie was aware of Sean's gift for charming potential clients and occasionally making a deal sound too good to be true. Not too surprisingly, he was particularly adept at charming female clients.

While she knew that Sean had the final say, Jennie had accepted the role of helping Sean not push too hard to make a deal happen or make promises he couldn't keep. On occasion, she felt like he went too far in charming and complementing women. It came so naturally to him that he didn't seem to notice when it got a little out of control. Jennie and Sean didn't realize it, but all of that was about to change dramatically.

Chapter Six

When Sean arrived at work on a bright and sunny Friday morning, he was feeling better than he had for weeks. It had been three months since he'd left Rundimahair, and he still had no real recollection of what occurred there.

The only strange lingering trouble was a series of odd dreams, which seemed to repeat every few nights. He could only occasionally remember a few small details of the dreams the next morning. Mostly it was a jumble of confusing images, which made little or no sense.

There were two images, which were most clear and consistent. The first was of him driving his SUV into a deep, rocky ravine during a terrible storm. The second image was much more pleasant. At the end of each dream, Sean always saw the face of an angel. Actually, it was the face of a beautiful young woman with thick, wavy, auburn hair and bright, warm green eyes. Usually she was smiling, which made her eyes even warmer and more compelling. Occasionally, he could recall great sadness in her eyes. It felt like she was about to do something she really didn't want to do.

Sean usually allowed the images of the beautiful woman to linger in his thoughts. This morning he let the images fade, so he could focus on a critical business meeting, which started in thirty minutes.

He stepped into Jennie's office to be sure everything was ready for the meeting. He wanted to be sure this all went according to plan. If all went well, they'd be signing a very lucrative real estate purchase contract before the meeting was over.

They'd been in negotiations with this seller for nearly a month, and this morning they were finally ready to close on the deal. If he was able to purchase the land at the price he had in mind, it would be one of the best deals he'd made in years.

The sellers owned a beautiful piece of land near Salem. It would be perfect for a combination project with retail on the ground floor and condos above. He already had the preliminary design finished.

His company would realize a tremendous profit once the work was complete. Of course, he didn't want the sellers to realize just how profitable it would be. If they understood the potential, he was sure they would ask for much more on the property sale.

This was an area where he and Jennie were occasionally at odds with each other. She was always looking for a good profit, but never to the point where they were taking unfair advantage of someone.

In Sean's mind, they disagreed on what was taking advantage of someone, and what was just good business. Jennie always wanted to give the seller the fair market value for their property. He didn't want to steal anyone's land, but he believed it was the seller's responsibility to figure out if the land was worth more than he was offering. It was his job to figure out the best way to earn the highest profit.

When he walked into her office, she was sitting behind her desk, gathering files together. He furrowed his brow when he looked closely at Jennie. She had dark circles under her eyes, and it appeared her makeup had been hastily applied.

It was his job to comfort her and help her to feel confident going into the meeting. He needed her focused and sharp. In his mind, he was about to compliment her on her professional appearance and tell her she looked ready to shine in the meeting.

"Wow, you look like you were on the losing end of a fight with the sandman," is what actually came out of his mouth.

Jennie looked at him with a shocked expression. She was used to him offering charming compliments, even when she didn't deserve them. She realized that he looked as shocked as she did that he had insulted her.

"Gee, thanks," she said dryly. "You try staying up most of the night with a two-year-old suffering from stomach flu. I'd like to see how good you'd look."

"I'm so sorry, Jennie. I don't know where that came from," he said honestly. "Who cares if you look like you haven't slept for days? You'll do fine in the meeting."

She could see the look of shock and frustration on his face, as he realized he'd just insulted her again. She rolled her eyes and said, "No more compliments, please."

He looked like he was going to say something else but decided against it at the last second. She stood up and said, "Maybe

I'd better do most of the talking in there, if this is your idea of charming banter."

Sean was a bit shaken when they entered the luxurious conference room where the property sellers waited. He'd have to make sure that the filter between his thoughts and his words was turned all the way up.

The meeting began very well, with the older couple showing a willingness to follow Sean's lead on the full value of their undeveloped land. He honestly explained all the risks and costs associated with the project.

Jennie skillfully supported all of his assertions and the couple nodded their agreement when the presentation was complete. It was clear to Jennie and Sean that the deal was going to go through.

The husband and wife stood along with Jennie and Sean. The husband reached out to shake Sean's hand. Their hands were only inches apart when the seller pulled his hand back and said, "Tell me one more time, Sean. Do you honestly feel that this is the best deal you can offer us on this property? As you know, it's been in our family for over fifty years. I know it's time to sell, but I just want to be sure we're doing right by our kids. When it's all said and done, this sale is for their future."

Sean smiled warmly, knowing they would accept his offer as soon as he assured him it was the best he could do. He put his hand on the elderly man's shoulder and said, "This is the price I'd like to pay for the property, but honestly, I can increase the price by fifty-thousand and still come out just fine."

The man quickly grabbed Sean's hand and shook it enthusiastically. "You've got yourself a deal, Sean. We knew we were doing the right thing in bringing this land to you. It's wonderful to work with a company that is grounded in integrity."

Sean managed to hold the smile on his face, as he realized what he'd just said. When he glanced at Jennie, her smile was almost as big as the sellers. She actually looked pleased that he'd just given away fifty-thousand dollars.

After the elderly couple left, Jennie turned and gave Sean a quick hug. When she let him go she said, "I don't know what is going on with you today, but I think I like this new side of your personality. Honesty and generosity–who knew you had it in you?"

Sean sighed, while a frown crossed his face. "This is a weird day. I'm thinking one thing, but something entirely different comes out when I open my mouth."

Jennie's smile slowly disappeared when she saw that he was serious. "Actually, that sounds a little worrisome," she said. "Maybe you've been working too hard lately."

He started to say something sarcastic, but this crazy behavior did have him worried. "Maybe you're right, Jen. It has been a long week. If you can handle things here, then I think I'll take the rest of the day off and enjoy a long weekend out of town."

"I think that's a great idea, as long as your long weekend doesn't entail searching for more property to buy. We've got more work than we can handle already, so go enjoy the weekend and do something fun."

"Fair enough. I'll find something to do beside work," Sean said.

"My cousin's best friend is single and looking. I could hook you up with a dinner date for tonight," Jennie said with a mischievous grin. She knew how much he disliked blind dates.

Sean started to answer when the image of the beautiful auburn-haired woman crossed his mind. Her beautiful green eyes sparkled with humor and her soft, full lips were turned up in a half smile.

"She doesn't have auburn hair and green eyes, does she?" he asked absentmindedly.

"Bleach blonde with brown eyes, but she's very pretty," Jennie said hopefully.

Sean shook off the dreamy image and said, "I think I'll head for the coast for a few days by myself. It'll give me a chance to clear my mind."

"Okay, but where'd the auburn hair and green eyes come from? I've never heard you mention that before."

"Just a silly dream I've had a few times lately. Maybe someone is trying to tell me something," he said, smiling.

"Sounds romantic," Jennie said, returning his smile. "Now get out of here and go see if you can find her this weekend."

⁂

Sean arrived at the Salmonberry Inn and beach house about four on Friday afternoon. It wasn't the trendiest or grandest place to stay on the Oregon coast, but it had always been his favorite. It was nestled into tall trees right across the street from the beach and just felt like home away from home.

The atmosphere was cozy and very friendly, and the food was simply the best. It was the perfect place for him to relax and get rid of whatever stress was causing his thoughts and words to be so jumbled. He couldn't afford anymore lapses, or his next mistake might cost him a lot more than fifty-thousand dollars. He hoped a relaxing weekend would cure what ailed him.

Sean enjoyed a very fine meal in the restaurant and was happy to see that there wasn't a big crowd at the inn tonight. He preferred a quieter atmosphere when he was in a reflective mood.

While he was finishing off an excellent bread pudding smothered in caramel sauce, a familiar, chubby hand rested on his shoulder. He looked up to see Chef Cesare smiling down at him.

"How are you, my friend? It's been too long since your last visit," Chef Cesare said.

Sean smiled broadly and patted the chubby hand on his shoulder. He truly liked Cesare very much. He was all Italian—full of warmth—and a four-star chef, in Sean's opinion.

"It's good to see you, Cesare," Sean said sincerely. I see the New York and LA restaurants haven't yet enticed you away from the Oregon coast."

"You know me better than that, Sean. They couldn't pay me enough to live in the big city. I'll be cooking right here until I'm old and gray."

"Good to know, Cesare. It's comforting to see some things don't change."

"Was everything to your satisfaction, my friend?"

Sean started to respond with an exaggerated compliment, but then remembered what had happened at the office this morning. Truthfully, the chicken had been the slightest bit dry, but nothing to really detract from a delicious meal.

"Delicious as always, my friend. If I lived closer to the coast, I would have gained twenty pounds just eating your amazing bread pudding," he finally said.

Cesare beamed from the honest praise and said, "You could use a few more pounds, Sean. You need to get married, so your sweetheart can fatten you up a little."

"I'll keep that in mind," Sean said, as Cesare waved farewell and moved on to a table across the room.

Sean was relieved that he hadn't blurted out something that would have hurt his friend's feelings. He wondered if he would have to spend the rest of his life having to think carefully before he spoke.

As he took a last bite of the decadent dessert, Sean was surprised to see someone sit down across the small table from him. Without looking up, he knew it was a woman by the smell of her perfume. The scent seemed familiar somehow. When he looked at her beautiful face, Sean was shocked beyond words to see the woman of his dreams staring back at him.

"Hello Sean. It's good to see you again," the beautiful, auburn-haired woman said.

He furrowed his brow and stared at her for a moment before he asked, "Do I know you?"

"Better than you might think," she said, smiling. Her bright green eyes sparkled, and a wave of feelings struck Sean. She was the beautiful woman who had haunted his dreams for months.

"I...I don't..." was all he could manage to say.

"This is going to take a bit of time to explain, Sean. It's not a conversation either of us wants to share with others. Let's go for a stroll along the beach," she said, as she stood and stepped away from the table.

He hesitated, realizing that her lovely Irish accent warmed his heart and seemed to fill an empty spot inside him that he just realized was there. Sean stared at her a moment longer while she waited patiently.

Finally, he nodded and said, "I could use a walk to work off that dessert. I'm happy to stroll on the beach with a beautiful woman, but I have to ask you where we have met before," Sean said.

"Oh, I'm that forgettable, am I, Sean?" she asked with that teasing smile.

"Actually, just the opposite is true. You are literally the girl of my dreams."

"There goes that silver-tongue of yours again, Sean. You were always quick with the compliments."

He smiled at what felt like a familiar reference, and said, "No, I think you actually are the girl of my dreams. I've been seeing your face in my dreams for months now. May I ask your name?"

"It's Ashling, Ashling Cahir," she said, giving him a sincere, lovely smile.

<hr />

Ashling took off her high-heeled shoes and carried them as they walked out onto the soft, warm sand. The sun was sitting low over the calm waters of the ocean while seagulls swooped down over the waves, seeking a tasty morsel for dinner.

Sean and Ashling walked in silence, neither of them quite sure how to begin a difficult conversation. For the moment he was content to walk in silence. With this beautiful woman beside him, Sean felt his recent worries slipping away.

After a few minutes passed, she stopped and turned toward him. "Sean, I know things have been difficult for you recently. I was sure that after a month or two you would forget all about your visit to our beloved Rundimahair," she said.

A confused look crossed Sean's face, as he said, "That does sound familiar, but I can't say I recall where I've heard the name before."

Ashling smiled at him and said, "You've been dreaming of it almost nightly over the past month."

His brow furrowed as he studied her beautiful face and warm smile. "I…yes, I have had some strange dreams about a quaint little village, but I don't know where or even what it is. I don't even know if it exists in the real world."

"Not everyone's reality is the same, Sean. Rundimahair exists, and you spent a fair bit of time there. True, it is that our fair town exists in a slightly different place than you're used to, but it exists right enough."

He was quiet for a moment, while he gazed intently into her beautiful green eyes. She seemed satisfied to let him work through his confusion.

Finally, he said, "If that's true, then why don't I remember it other than these confusing dreams?"

"Until now, you only recalled me vaguely in your dreams, but I'm real enough, am I not?" she said, with a twinkle in her eye.

He nodded and said, "But if I knew you so well and spent so much time in your little town, why do I only recall it in occasional dreams?"

She could clearly see the confusion and frustration on his face. Ashling felt guilt creep in regarding the way they'd handled Sean's unexpected visit to Rundimahair. She sighed deeply as she stepped forward and gently touched her hands to his temples.

Sean didn't flinch or back away because this felt familiar and very comforting. Suddenly, images of an old, beautiful Irish town began playing through his mind. Instantly, he knew he'd been there before.

While she held her hands gently to his temples, all the memories of his time in Rundimahair came rushing back. He remembered the accident and waking up in Eamon and Ashling's beautiful old home. Sean slowly began to recall all the good people he met during his stay in their lovely town.

Memories of strange occurrences were also becoming clear in his mind. Other memories of flying dragon-like creatures and little people digging in the back yard were still somewhat muddled.

She finally took her hands off his head and said, "I'm as sorry as a girl can be that things turned out the way they did, Sean. Normally, if I erase dangerous memories, there would be no trace left behind to trouble you."

"But for some reason, I could still recall some of it in my dreams," Sean said, feeling surprisingly calm. "Actually, I could only recall your face in the beginning. Then other images showed up. Lately, it has all faded except for the image of your smiling face and sparkling green eyes."

"Sure and true, you're still a silver-tongued devil, Sean. I think you recall my face because it was the last thing you saw before I erased your memories and sent you home."

"Or because I truly didn't want to forget you, Ashling."

She started to give him a sarcastic response, but she saw the sincerity in his eyes. Ashling also remembered that he could no longer speak anything but the truth.

"Since your flattering tongue can no longer speak anything but the truth, I'll take that as a fine and honest compliment, Sean."

He suddenly gripped her arm and asked, "How did you know about that? That just started happening this morning."

"I've been staying in touch through your subconscious since you left us, Sean."

"You've been spying on me?" he asked incredulously, as he let go of her and took a step back.

"Actually, I've been keeping you safe, Sean. I wanted to be sure you readjusted to your life without any long-term side effects troubling you."

"So, you've been watching me for all of these months?" he asked with a furrowed brow.

"Not in the way you seem to be thinking, Sean. I kept a loose connection between our subconscious thoughts and feelings. If it felt as though you were having some sort of difficulty, then I'd connect our mind tracks together to be sure you were fine and dandy."

"You seem to think that rummaging around inside someone's mind is just a normal, everyday occurrence, Ashling. Most folks I know wouldn't feel very comfortable if they knew you were peeking into their private thoughts."

"It's not like that, Sean. I only peek in if I feel you struggling with the after-effects of your time in Rundimahair."

"Still not a good thing," he said forcefully.

"Bye the bye, Sean, I can see the image in your head of an ugly witch stirring her evil brew in her big black pot. I suppose she's looking into the future to see what you're up to. Is that how you see me then?"

"Certainly not the ugly part, but the witch part might well apply," he said.

Ashling looked as though she was going to lose her fine Irish temper, but she managed to take a deep breath and calm down. "Very well, I see your point and I might feel the same if I was walking in your shoes."

"You think?" Sean asked sarcastically.

She stepped back closer to him and said, "Perhaps this will help. I'll let you have a wee peek into my mind, and perhaps you'll stop being as stubborn as a mule and try to understand."

"I'm not sure I want to look in there," he said, staring at her intently.

"Oh, you're definitely of the Irish blood, Sean Quinn. You're as hard-headed as me own father, so you are."

Sean noticed that her Irish accent became much more pronounced when she was angry. Even when he was upset with her, he couldn't help but smile. He found her accent so very charming.

"So, the thought of me as a witch makes you smile, does it? You're going to see the truth of it whether you like or not!" she said forcefully.

He was mesmerized by the fire in her beautiful eyes and didn't try to resist when she thumped him hard in the chest with her index finger. Seconds later, Sean realized he couldn't move. Whatever she'd done to him left him paralyzed from head to toe. He couldn't even speak.

Once he was immobilized, Ashling put her hands back on his temples and closed her eyes. For a moment, nothing happened. It was the calm before the storm.

Suddenly images began flowing through his mind. He quickly realized they weren't just images, but also Ashling's thoughts and feelings. He began to understand that she had only touched his mind when she absolutely had to—only when she thought he was in trouble.

Sean could now see that she'd safe-guarded his privacy as much as she possibly could. Above all, he could feel her genuine concern for his well-being. After a moment, he began to feel another background emotion coming from her. It was deep in the recesses of her mind, but he felt that Ashling was attracted to him. She was actually quite fond of him.

As though Ashling could sense his awareness of her feelings for him, she quickly withdrew her contact with his mind. It took Sean a few moments to recover and realize they were still on the beach in Lincoln City instead of in Rundimahair.

"Wow, that was a very serious rush!" he said enthusiastically. "How in the world do you do that?"

"It's magic!" she said, as she smiled at him with a sweet, innocent expression. "And I might just add for clarification that I'm not the only one standing here with the gift of magic running through their veins."

Chapter Seven

A toast to your coffin,
May it be made of 100-year-old oak,
And may we plant the oak tree together, tomorrow

~ Old Irish Saying ~

Sean had been very skeptical when Ashling claimed that not he too might be gifted with magic. He'd almost come to terms with the fact that she was a woman with magical gifts. The way she could read his mind, and the amazing medical cures he'd seen her perform in Rundimahair, had convinced him that she was someone very special. The part about him having such gifts was going to take a lot more convincing.

They were back in his room at the bed-and-breakfast, after walking on the beach until well after dark. She was still trying to explain how they knew that he too was magically gifted.

"The truth of it is, we didn't save you on that stormy night outside of Rundimahair," she explained. "We felt someone tap into the invisible, magical, protective sphere that surrounds our fair town. That should have been impossible, even if a very powerful wizard made the attempt."

"But that's my point, Ashling. I'm not Merlin the Magician or any other type of make-believe wizard," he said.

"What makes you think Merlin was make believe?" she asked with a teasing smile. He was Scottish instead of Irish, which is a sad misfortune for him. Still and all, he was a very powerful wizard in his day."

"I'm not even going to go there," Sean said. "Let's stick to one absurd notion at a time, shall we?"

"The only thing that's absurd is you trying to deny the truth that's as plain and true as you are stubborn. Bye the bye, that mile-wide stubborn streak in you only proves my point. Only an Irishman could be that rock-headed stubborn, and that's the truth of it, Sean Quinn."

"So, you're saying that I somehow touched a magical globe that surrounds Rundimahair and used its power to save me from going off into the ravine?"

Ashling sighed deeply and said, "The fact that you're sitting here being stubborn instead of dead at the bottom of that rocky ravine should easily prove my point."

Sean stared into her eyes intently and realized she was telling him what she believed to be the truth. "Maybe I struck your magic force-field with my SUV and it somehow turned on the magic that saved me and my car," he said.

She sighed deeply and said, "It doesn't work that way, Sean. Don't you think that we've exhausted our minds trying to explain what happened? Why do you think we let you stay in our town?"

"I've been wondering the same thing," Sean said. "You could have just let the accident take its course and I'd be dead and gone at the bottom of that ravine. That would have saved you all of this trouble."

"Sean Quinn!" she shouted. "How could you believe for one moment that we'd let you crash into that ravine? Sure, and it's true that you've been a major pain in our backsides since you showed up out of the clear blue sky, but that's beside the point."

"What is the point, Ashling?"

"The point is that we hold all life sacred. It is the most precious gift we've received from our loving Creator, and we would never willingly take someone's life."

"What about that dragon?" Sean asked.

"Dragon? What dragon are you jabbering on about ya' silly mortal?"

"I vaguely recall an ugly flying reptile soaring through your kitchen. The dreadful thing could breathe fire and had made a serious mess of your kitchen. If I'm not mistaken, you blew it to smithereens in a shower of sparkling, colored stars, or something like that."

Ashling rolled her eyes and said, "You weren't supposed to remember that part, which just proves my point. Only someone with powerful, latent magic in their blood would have ever recalled any of the memories I removed."

"Maybe so, but I'm just saying that you were willing enough to take that gross thing's life away," Sean said, smiling.

"May the good Lord preserve me from persistent fools," she muttered.

"That's not an answer," he replied stubbornly.

"For a man with magical, Irish blood flowing through your veins, you're sure and true as dense as a fence post, Sean."

"I don't think insults will help–" Sean started to say before she cut him off.

"If the shoe fits then wear it, you big eejit!" Ashling shouted.

Sean stared at her in surprise now that he was seeing her temper up close and personal. He wasn't sure why, but he just started to laugh.

"Oh, and what's so funny then?"

"For such a fine looking and dainty woman, you've got a fierce temper," he said, still chuckling.

She looked like she was going to take that temper to the next level, but somehow managed to rein it in. Ashling took a deep breath and said, "I'm afraid it's true that I inherited the fiery temper of the Cahir clan.

She looked so frustrated and contrite that Sean stepped forward and put his arms around her. He felt her stiffen briefly, before relaxing into his arms. After a moment, she put her arms around his waist and said, "Ah Sean, I couldn't be sorrier if I tried."

"Don't worry about it, Ashling. It's been an emotional discussion from the start. It's not like we're talking about the weather here. We're talking about things that didn't exist in my life until I met you."

She pulled back a little, looked up into his eyes and said, "I'm sure you rue the day you met this hot-tempered Irish girl. By the bye, I didn't slay that crazy little dragon, although he well and sure had it coming. I just banished him back to the realm he came from."

"So, you would never take a life under any circumstances?" Sean asked.

Ashling rested her head on his shoulder and sighed heavily. "I wish I could say I've never taken a life, Sean. The truth is that I have taken the lives of those who were trying to destroy our people."

He kissed the top of her head and said, "Then it was self-defense. Even the bible tells us we can defend ourselves and our loved ones. I see no fault in that."

She was quiet for several moments until he heard her weeping softly. Finally, she said, "What you said is true, Sean. Still and all, I wish it could have been otherwise."

After a few minutes passed, she stepped back and wiped her eyes. She stared at him intently, before finally saying, "I wish there were another explanation for what happened to you Sean. Believe me when I tell you that my Da and I looked for any other explanation for the past few months."

Sean held her gaze and slowly began nodding his head. "But you couldn't find one?" he asked.

Ashling shook her head and said, "It isn't just the accident, Sean. When I laid my hands on your head, I knew in my heart you had magic in your veins. What I didn't realize is just how powerfully our magic runs through you."

"If you say it's true, then I believe you. Tell me this if you can. How could I have not known about it until now? I've not had any other experiences like this until I met you," he said.

"This type of magic can lay dormant your entire life, Sean. Someone like you, who lives in the human world, could have easily lived and died without ever knowing what you were truly capable of."

"Unless something triggers it?" he asked.

"Or the Creator of us all decided he needed you in this fight, Sean."

"What fight are you talking about, Ashling?"

She hesitated for a moment before saying, "I think we've covered enough for one day, Sean. Let's save further enlightenment for another day."

He started to protest, but then realized he really didn't want to know more right now. Sean smiled and said, "Good call, Ashling. What you've told me gives me more than enough to think about."

"I agree, although there is one more thing I must warn you about."

"Why don't I like the sound of that?" he said warily.

"Trust me when I say knowing this will make your life much easier."

"So you say," he said, smiling.

Just as Ashling was about to explain, the door to their room suddenly burst open. Actually, the door was smashed into pieces which were flying all over the room.

"Get back, Sean!" Ashling shouted, as she used some of her magic to divert the chunks of door flying at them.

Sean was about to comply when two massive, misshapen creatures charged through the space where the door had been moments before. They were both at least seven-feet tall and built like gorillas on steroids. Their muscles were bulging, and they both radiated a deadly menace as they rushed him.

The ugliest of the two freaks pushed Sean to the floor and charged Ashling. It felt like he'd been hit by a battering ram, as he struggled to catch his breath. He managed to get to his feet, but before he could help Ashling, the other foul creature grabbed him from behind.

"Time to die, little wizard," the behemoth said, in a rough, scratchy growl.

Sean turned away from its grasp and realized that up close it was much more of a creature than a man. His face was deformed, and he had strange pointy ears. Not the kind of ears you see on elves in the movies. These were huge, misshapen things hanging on the side of his grotesquely large head.

The freak took a wild swing at him with a massive fist the size of a catcher's mitt. Despite the thing's size, he moved pretty quickly. Sean's thought was to move out of reach, but for some reason, he did just the opposite.

With worry for Ashling's safety his top priority, Sean stepped forward and tried to block the colossal punch coming at his head. He was only partially successful as the punch landed on his shoulder. The pain was tremendous, and Sean thought the punch might have broken some bones.

What happened next he would have little recollection of afterward. Sean felt a surge of power rushing through his entire body. It wasn't just an adrenalin charged fight-or-flight reaction. This felt more like his body was suddenly charged with a thousand volts of electricity. The growing fear of a slow and painful death was abruptly gone. He could hardly believe it, but Sean was actually looking forward to a good fight.

<hr>

Ashling used a very ancient spell to arrest the forward movement of the creature attacking her. She hadn't seen this type of beast before. Even so, her magic paralyzed it in mid-rush.

If she'd had more time, she might have tried to banish it back to where it had crawled out of its hole. With Sean under attack, she went for the quickest result. The spell began applying fierce pressure within the sphere she had the monster trapped in. In less than two minutes, the creature was crushed into a bloody pulp. She pushed it back into the netherworld where she could dispose of it later.

When Ashling turned to help Sean, she was shocked to see him engaging the creature in hand-to-hand combat. Even more surprising was that Sean was kicking the mountain of muscle's butt. She breathed a sigh of relief, realizing more of Sean's magic was coming to life.

She watched in amazement as Sean moved with inhuman speed. He struck the creature in the head four times, before it could even try to return a blow.

Next, he did a ninja-like flying drop kick that hit the behemoth in the throat. The ugly, man-like creature roared in anger and charged at him. Sean thrust his closed fist at the center of the beast's exposed chest.

Ashling watched in wonder, as Sean's fist punched through flesh and bone with little resistance. She knew it was a fatal blow and quickly encased the creature in a sphere that kept the bloody mess from splattering all over the room. She banished him to the same place as the other creature. Ashling would deal with them both later.

She suspected what was coming next, so she rushed in and put her arms around Sean, just as he collapsed. Ashling knew what it was like to experience the first flashes of magic. When the magic withdrew, it left the user completely exhausted and unconscious for hours.

With surprising strength, Ashling carried Sean effortlessly to the bed. She put him down gently, before sitting on the edge of the bed beside him and softly laying her hand on his right temple.

When she tapped into his physiology, Ashling realized he had a broken collarbone, several deep muscle and bone bruises, and a severe sprain to his right ankle. She could also see two deep cuts on his neck. After putting him into a deep sleep, she began repairing the damage. Ashling had never been more grateful for having the healing magic as one of her strongest gifts.

⚏▨◻▨⚏

Sean opened his eyes as bright sunlight touched his face. For a few moments he wasn't sure where he was. When he realized that a beautiful, auburn-haired woman was sleeping beside him, with her head on his shoulder, the crazy memories from last night came rushing back.

He recalled the two freakish, ugly twins who'd burst into their room with murder on their dimwitted minds. A ferocious fight followed, where Ashling crushed one creature and he somehow beat the heck out of the other freak.

He looked at the gentle beauty lying on his shoulder and smiled as he thought of the fierce warrior she had been the night before. Sean chuckled softly, as he thought that had to be the strangest first date he'd ever experienced.

As he looked around the room, he realized that it was now as clean and neat as when he'd checked in. He nodded his head and smiled, realizing that Ashling must have done some serious magical house cleaning. Even the entry door, which had been smashed to kindling wood, was back in its proper place.

When Sean moved slightly to get a bit more comfortable, memories of fierce pain coursing through his body returned. He was sure he had a broken shoulder and possibly serious internal injuries. How he could have continued to fight was another mystery.

The bigger surprise came when he realized that none of the pain or injuries he'd sustained last night still existed. He could move his shoulder with ease and his ankle was good as new. No bruises or residual pain at all. Gratitude for Ashling's amazing healing gifts filled his heart and mind. She was truly an amazing woman in so many ways.

One thing that her magic hadn't resolved was that he smelled as bad as an angry skunk. He recalled that the beast he'd fought had a similar unpleasant odor. Some of the stench must have rubbed off on him.

"Time to take a shower," he mumbled, as he carefully slid out from under Ashling's head, which had still been resting on his shoulder.

He managed to get to his feet and turn back to see if she was still asleep. His heart did a flip-flop at the sight of such a beautiful woman lying asleep on his bed.

Sean must have admired her beauty too long, since she finally said, "Were you hoping I'd join you in the shower, then?" She didn't open her eyes when she spoke, but there was a mischievous smile tugging at her soft lips.

"What? No, of course I wasn't thinking anything like that," he said indignantly, as he turned and headed for the shower.

"Sean, you should keep in mind that I can read your thoughts before you speak," she said, as she slowly opened her eyes.

"And you should keep in mind that these days I can only speak the truth, Ashling. The thought didn't enter my mind until you suggested it," Sean said with a 'got you' smile.

"She barked out an entirely unladylike laugh and said, "Either way, you'll be showering alone, so go wash that beastie smell off. I'll be kind enough to burn those very foul-smelling clothes for you. There's something about evil beast stink that just doesn't come out in the wash."

Sean smiled and muttered something about a crazy magical woman as he entered the bathroom. A few minutes later, he tossed his stinky clothes out into the hall. He wasn't sure if she was kidding or not, but he really hoped she did burn them. The stink was truly appalling.

When he came out of the bathroom, wearing a plush, white robe, he was surprised that she rushed over to embrace him. "Oh my, it's the Creator's truth how I do love the feel of these soft and fluffy robes," she said, as she snuggled close.

Sean was thinking the same thing about how much he enjoyed a cuddling embrace from this soft and beautiful woman. He also noticed that she smelled like a lovely flower garden on a fresh spring day.

Ashling looked up and said, "There are more efficient ways than showering daily to stay as clean as the day you were born. Still and all, some days it's hard to beat a nice hot shower before slipping into one of these wonderful, soft, terrycloth robes."

"That brings two things to mind," Sean said, smiling. "First, I look forward to you teaching me more of your awesome magic tricks."

"And second?" she asked playfully.

"Stop reading my mind, you nosy woman!" he said forcefully.

"Fair enough, Sean. I was still connected after our little brawl with the beasties last night."

"Shouldn't I be able to feel when you connect with my mind?" he asked.

"Only if I want you to," she said with a playful smile.

"Not fair! Will I be able to learn to read your mind?" he asked, with genuine curiosity.

"Same answer," she said, laughing.

"Only if you want me to," he said, rolling his eyes.

"The truth of it is that I don't know for sure if you'll one day share my gift of reading others, Sean. If I had to guess, you will likely be as good as I am and then some," she said seriously.

"I look forward to that day," he said.

"Be careful what you wish for, Sean. Hearing what goes on in other's minds can be as much of a curse as it is a gift. You'll often find things there that you wish you'd never discovered," she said with a sad expression.

Sean thought about what she said and the almost haunted look that momentarily crossed her face, before nodding and saying, "I can see your point, Ashling. Sometimes we're better off not knowing what those around us are thinking."

"Especially from those you long considered your very fine and good friends," she added sadly.

Sean considered what was best to say next, remembering he could now only speak the truth. Finally, he said, "I'll do my best to only think kind thoughts of you, Ashling. If I ever do think an angry or unkind thought toward you; please remember that it is only a momentary feeling. From what I've learned so far, I believe you are a fair and open minded woman, who prefers to think the best of others."

She seemed genuinely touched by his words, as she hugged him close and said, "And bear in mind, my new friend, that if I lose my temper on occasion and speak unkindly to you, it will only be a momentary outburst which I hope will pass quickly enough."

"Did you say 'if' you lose your temper?" he asked laughing. "From what I've seen so far, it should have been when you lose your temper."

She giggled pleasantly, with her head on his shoulder, as she said, "Tis an amazing occurrence that you've come to know me so well is such a short span of time, Sean."

I'm looking forward to knowing you much better, Ashling," Sean said. "I'm also hoping you'll come to know me well enough to explain why I can only speak the truth. Am I such a devious fellow that our Creator cursed me for my many weaknesses by forcing me to only speak the absolute truth?"

"Actually, there is some truth to that, Sean. When your magical gifts come to life, you are sure and truly part of the Sidhe. We are charged with helping mortals make correct choices throughout their lives.

"But I thought we were all born with free agency. Don't we have the right to choose between good and evil behavior while we're here on earth?

"Aye, that we do, Sean. The difference is you are not a mortal. You are here to help mortals make correct choices. Sadly, many of them still choose evil over good."

"Are you saying that because I have the blood of the Sidhe running through my veins that I have to always make the right choice or I'll be forced to?"

"If that were true, then we wouldn't have been fighting with Grainne for all these centuries. She had the right to choose to become the most evil and vile creature that ever lived on earth."

"I get that, but why does she get to choose and I don't?" Sean asked."

"What you're experiencing about only telling the truth is temporary, Sean," Ashling said. "We all go through it as part of our training once our powers come to life. Soon enough you'll be back to making all of your own choices. Even so, you'll always remember what it was like to be completely honest in all that you say and do. When your training is complete, you'll be free to do as you wish. Still and all, you'll never forget the difference between mostly honest and fair and truly, completely, living up to the potential you are blessed with."

Sean continued to stare at Ashling's eyes for a moment longer. Finally he said, "I've got to say that it's pretty overwhelming. I can see how experiencing the difference would be a life lesson I'll always remember."

"As will I, Sean," Ashling said. "That's enough deep thinking for now. It's time for us to be on our way."

"Back to Rundimahair?" Sean asked.

"Where else?" Ashling replied, smiling.

❖

"Couldn't you have just magically taken us from Lincoln City to Rundimahair?" Sean asked, as they drove down Highway 101.

"I could indeed, Sean. The truth of it is that each time I use magic, outside of Rundimahair, it leaves traces behind. There are those who seek to destroy our peaceful little community who might pick up on those traces—especially when the magic is filled with great power."

"Let me guess—your magic is more powerful than most," he said.

"Truth be told, there are only a handful still with us with powers so great, Sean."

"Your Da being one of them?" he asked.

"To be sure. In some ways, he is far and away the most powerful among us all. I pray daily that it will always be so."

"Okay, then we'll take the old-fashioned way to travel," Sean said.

"Young Sean, there are many more ancient ways to travel than in your wonderful SUV. The truth of it is that I love traveling by car, especially one with seats that will warm up your backside on a cold morning."

Sean burst out laughing for a moment and finally said, "You're a wonderful travelling companion, old Ashling."

Her face sobered as she asked, "Why do you call me old Ashling?"

He smiled and replied, "Because you're always calling me young Sean, when we're obviously close to the same age. Of course, I was only teasing. All you have to do is look in the mirror to realize you are a young, rare beauty, Ashling."

She stared out the front windshield at the cloudy morning for a moment without answering. Finally, she said, "I'm glad you think so, Sean. I truly am."

Though Sean didn't realize it, as time passed, she never again called him young Sean. It would be some time before he truly understood why.

The sun had broken through the typical Oregon coast, early morning cloud cover by the time they arrived at Rundimahair. Sean still wasn't sure how they ended up on the isolated side road that led to the small town.

One moment they were approaching the area where he'd had his accident; the next moment they were driving past the ancient myrtle wood sign that welcomed them to Rundimahair. "I take it that you whipped up some traveling magic that put us on this road," he said.

"You've been sitting beside me the entire trip, Sean. Surely you'd have realized if I were performing such a sophisticated bit of magic," she replied, smiling.

"There's nothing sure about it, Ashling. The only thing I know for sure is that you could be performing the greatest feats of magic the world has ever seen, and I wouldn't have a clue."

"It's good to be traveling with a humble man who realizes his many shortcomings," she said, chuckling.

"I'm not sure how humble I am, Ashling, but I do realize that I don't know diddly about magic."

"Truth be told, you likely would have realized I was up to something if I'd have opened the path with magic. For those of us who live here, traveling from the mortal world to our little bit of heaven on earth is automatic. My own dear father placed that magical miracle in place before I was even born."

"So, the residents of your town can come and go as they please without any trouble?" Sean asked.

"Heaven forbid! None of us are allowed to leave our beautiful valley without permission from the high council. You see, Sean, those who would do us harm are capable of tracking great feats of magic," she said.

"I know, it leaves a trail of some kind that they can follow. I still don't have any idea who your enemies are or how they could possibly find you here."

"All in good time, my friend. For now, it's enough to realize that we have to be very careful with our comings and goings through the enchanted shield that protects us."

"I'm fine with that. The truth is, I'm still struggling to come to terms with the fact that you are some type of magical female wizard. Add to that the possibility that I too could turn out to be a wizard. I'd say that I've got more than enough to ponder for now."

"I know it can be very overwhelming, Sean. I too struggled when I first came into my magic. The advantage I had over you is that I grew up in a magical world. My father and mother were the greatest wizards of their time. So please believe me when I tell you that I understand."

Sean nodded agreement, as he pondered another question. It was on the tip of his tongue to ask what had happened to her mother. He'd heard Ashling and Eamon mention her in passing, but she was obviously no longer with them. Before he spoke, he decided he'd wait for another day to broach that subject.

Even though he'd only spent a short period of time here, Sean felt an odd sense of homecoming, when they pulled into the driveway of Eamon and Ashling's home. He couldn't help but smile at the thought.

"It does feel good to be home, doesn't it, Sean?"

He was about to agree when he realized she had read his thoughts about this feeling like home.

"Hey, no mind-reading–remember?" he said, glaring at her.

"I said I wouldn't read your mind without your permission, barring a life-threatening emergency. Why would you doubt my word when you promised to trust me?"

Sean could feel the undercurrent of hurt feelings in Ashling's question. "If you didn't read my mind, then how did you know I was thinking about this place feeling like home?"

"To put it mildly, you sometimes broadcast your feelings like the public announcer at a Denver Broncos football game," she said patiently.

"Now I have two questions to ask," Sean said, smiling at her.

"I'm listening," she said, giving a small smile in return.

"What do you mean by broadcasting my thoughts?" he asked.

"And the second question?"

"How in the world do you know about the Denver Broncos?" he asked, shaking his head in amazement.

"I'll answer the second one first, since it is by far the easiest to explain. Over the past few years, I've spent a fair amount of time in the mortal world. One of the mortal women I became friends with was a huge Broncos fan. At first I thought it was a silly game, but I must confess that by the time I left Denver I too had become a loyal Bronco fan. 'Tis a shame Peyton was already married. Otherwise I may have put a love spell upon him when he retired."

He laughed and said, "I'm a Cowboys fan, but trust me when I say I can relate to being that loyal to your team."

"Good enough. Now to the other question. When your magical gifts begin to manifest, they are often a bit out of control. The ability to master your powers takes time and experience. In the meantime, try not to think any outrageous or inappropriate thoughts about anyone in town. If you do, believe me, many of them will hear you loud and clear."

"I may be better at it than you think, Ashling. When I was staying at your home, I may have had a few romantic thoughts about you that could be considered inappropriate by some people. Obviously, I was able to keep those thoughts to myself," he said proudly.

"A few of those thoughts were well beyond inappropriate, Sean," she said, laughing. "It's okay," she added. "A rare beauty like me hears them all the time."

Sean was sure he was turning beet red again, when he looked at her and said, "If you promise to never bring this subject up again, then I won't mention the obvious lack of humility on your part. Bragging about being a rare beauty, indeed."

"And yet it was just this morning when you were thinking those exact thoughts about me. You can see how it might be difficult to stay humble," she added, laughing.

"Okay, I surrender! You are a rare beauty, as anyone with eyes can see. Now, can we change the subject?

"If you insist," she replied. "Besides, my Da' is standing at the front door waving for us to come in."

They stepped out of the SUV, grabbed their overnight bags, and headed for the front door. When they were within speaking distance, Ashling waved and said, "It's good to be back, Da'."

"And I see you've brought some fine company to our humble abode," Eamon said. "Sean, it's a great pleasure to see you," he added, as he stepped forward and held out his hand.

"It's a pleasure to see you again as well, sir," Sean said sincerely, as he reached out to shake Eamon's hand.

Just before he could grasp Eamon's hand, Ashling's father disappeared from sight. When Sean turned to Ashling in confusion and shock, her luggage and coat were there beside him, but she too was gone.

Chapter Eight

Here's to lying, stealing, and cheating!
May you lie to save a friend;
May you steal the heart of the one you love;
and may you always cheat death.

~ Old Irish Saying ~

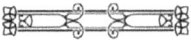

Sean remained standing where he was for several minutes, feeling like he'd turned to stone. He looked around, hoping some explanation might be forthcoming. Even better, he wished one, or both, Eamon and Ashling would reappear.

He stood there for another five minutes, unsure what to do next. When neither of them returned, he shook off his shock and forced himself to act. Sean grabbed Ashling's coat and luggage, along with his own, and hurried into the house.

The only thing he could think to do was try to find someone who might be able to help. His mind focused on all the folks he'd met in town without settling on anyone to ask for help. Suddenly, Ailbe's caramel-colored eyes came to mind, and he felt like she and her grandfather, Aengus, were the right folks to ask for help.

He drove out to their farmhouse at top speed, grateful there didn't appear to be any traditional police in Rundimahair. When he pulled into the driveway of their beautifully preserved farmhouse, he saw Ailbe jump up from her chair on the front porch.

By the time he was out of the car, Ailbe was there, throwing her arms around him. "It is you, Sean!" she said as she held him close. "I didn't expect to ever see you again once I heard you'd left town."

He couldn't help but smile at her exuberant nature as he said, "I didn't really expect to be back either, but here I am."

"Let the poor man go before you crush his ribs, Ailbe," her grandfather said from the porch.

Sean looked up to see Aengus smiling at him as he stood by the porch railing. "Good to see you again, young man," Aengus said.

When Sean was finally able to free himself from Ailbe's grip, he said, "It's a pleasure to see you again too, sir."

"I know I'm older than the hills, but I prefer to be called by my God-given name," Aengus said while he walked out to meet Sean.

"Aengus, it is," Sean said.

The look on Aengus' face sobered when he saw the concerned look in Sean's eyes. "I'm thinkin' you didn't drive out here for a social call. Am I right, Sean?"

"I'm afraid so," Sean said, as he followed Aengus and Ailbe into the house.

The interior of the home was furnished in surprisingly contemporary design. Somehow Sean was thinking it would look like something out of the late 1800s.

"It's Ashling, isn't it?," Ailbe said.

Sean looked over at the pretty teenager and saw her eyes were closed, and she appeared to be concentrating on something far away.

"It's Ashling and Eamon. When Ashling and I returned to their home, they both just disappeared right before my eyes."

Aengus cut in before Ailbe could respond, and said, "Am I correct to be thinkin' that you are now aware of their unusual abilities?"

"Yes, I've seen Ashling's magical gifts at work several times. The last time was when she was busy saving my life," Sean said.

Ailbe looked like she wanted to hear a lot more about that, but to her credit, she focused on the problem at hand. "Did she say anything at all before she left?"

"Nothing," Sean said. "I was reaching to shake Eamon's hand when he disappeared. When I turned to ask Ashling what happened, she was also gone."

"And so, you thought you'd come here?" Aengus asked.

"Actually, I was frantically thinking of who I'd met who might be able to help and Ailbe came to mind. I'm not sure why I thought a teenage girl might know what to do, but I decided to follow that feeling."

"Very interesting," Aengus said, softly. He was giving Sean a thoughtful look, as though he was trying to read his mind.

"You're right, Daideo," Ailbe said softly. "Sean's got the gift too. If I'm not mistaken, he'll one day be a mighty wizard."

Aengus looked at her for several moments before he said, "You're not often mistaken about such things, my dear girl."

"I think you were guided here because of Ailbe," Aengus said. "Ashling has been teaching her since she turned twelve. It seems that Ailbe has many of the same gifts Ashling does, though not at the same level."

"Not yet," Ailbe said, grinning. "Ashling tells me that one day I may be as strong in the gifts as her."

"May well be," Aengus said, smiling fondly at his granddaughter. "But keep in mind, my dear girl, what she often tells you; with great power comes great responsibility."

Ailbe rolled her eyes and said, "How can I forget, when she reminds me constantly?"

A soft warmth came into Aengus' normally cautious eyes as he said, "It's only because she loves you like you were her own young lass. She can see what you're able to become. She won't let you fall short of that potential. Our people need you too much to allow that."

Tears welled up in Ailbe's soft, brown eyes, as she said, "I know, Daideo, I know. I may be a silly girl at times, but I won't let you or Ashling down."

Sean felt awkward having to interrupt this tender exchange, but he felt a sense of urgency in trying to find Ashling and Eamon. "You think you can help find them?" he asked Ailbe.

"Is it all right?" she asked her grandfather.

"Do what you've got to do, Ailbe dear," he responded.

Suddenly, Ailbe threw her arms around Sean, and they both disappeared from the farmhouse living room. Aengus sighed deeply, while gazing up to the heavens, as he said, "You know she's all I have left. I'll be grateful if you can bring her back safe and sound," he whispered. "And the young fella too," he added hastily.

⚌▣ ▣⚌

It seemed to be no more than a few seconds before Sean found himself standing on a mountain top. Ailbe was still holding him close, as though she feared he might disappear too.

"What are we doing here?" he asked, as he gently pulled back from her embrace.

"Sorry to grip you so tight, Sean. I'm still new at much of this magic and I didn't want to lose you," Ailbe said sheepishly.

"Not a problem," Sean said, smiling. "I too would prefer you didn't drop me somewhere along the way. So, what now?"

"I'm not sure about that exactly," Ailbe said nervously. "I followed her magic pathway to this spot. I was hoping she'd be here."

Sean sighed and nodded, as he said, "Well I suppose–"

An earsplitting series of shrieks pierced the air. It sounded like it was coming from the other side of the mountain. "Take us there!" Sean said urgently.

This time Ailbe grabbed onto his hands tightly and they vanished, only to reappear on the back side of the mountain seconds later.

The reason Sean had told her to go to where the harsh shrieks were sounding, was because he'd heard them before. Actually, he'd only heard one before. That was in Ashling's kitchen when the dragon creature had been busy destroying everything in sight.

"These are much bigger than the one I saw in Ashling's kitchen," Sean said, looking at several much larger versions of the dragon, or whatever it was, which had nearly killed him.

"They're Tatsu," Ailbe said, looking fearful. "Female dragons are the worst, and that's no lie."

"Tatsu means female dragon?" Sean asked.

"It means a world full of trouble, is what it means," Ailbe said. "I have no notion at all about how to destroy the likes of these."

"Maybe we don't have to fight them," Sean said. We just need to find Ashling and Eamon and get out of here."

"We've already found them, Sean," she said, looking up into the sky. "You see that large one with the blue scales?"

"I do," Sean said.

"That's Eamon in his gifted, natural dragon form."

Sean was too stunned to speak. When he saw another, slightly smaller dragon with a fiery, red mane, he tried to articulate his worst fear. "Is that...it's not possible, but that looks like..." was all he could manage to say.

"Yes Sean, the one with the long red mane is Ashling," Ailbe said, confirming his fears.

Sean watched in dumbfounded silence, as the dragon form for Eamon and Ashling did aerial battle with a half-dozen dingy gray dragons. He saw three of the dragons lying on the side of the mountain, below where the airborne combat was continuing.

"It looks like they've taken out three of them already," Sean said hopefully.

Ailbe nodded grimly and said, "But there's still six more in the fight."

As if to signify the desperate nature of the battle going on above them, Sean saw a gray dragon singe Ashling's back, as it released a colossal belch of flames.

Eamon took advantage of the gray dragon's focus on attacking Ashling, roaring in from behind to snatch hold of its neck. He shook the gray dragon's neck back and forth in a frenzy of anger, snapping it like a twig. When he released the dragon, it fell to the mountainside, joining the other three dead grays.

Three of the remaining grays all attacked Eamon in unison. The last two charged at a clearly injured Ashling. Eamon couldn't come to her aid, since it was all he could do to hold off the three who were battling with him.

Ashling raked one of the gray's attacking her with a deadly blast of flames. It took out part of its left wing, making it difficult for the creature to stay airborne.

While she was occupied with trying to disable the injured gray, the second gray managed to take hold of her leg, just below the hip. It raked a deep tear into her flesh, and she couldn't shake the creature off.

When the injured gray saw Ashling was in trouble, it circled back and began belching flames at her. She was in deep trouble and could expect no help from Eamon.

In the moments before the second dragon could reach Ashling, Sean could see what was about to happen. Ashling was badly injured and would not be able to fight her way free of her attackers.

He felt a surge of anger blast through every core of his being. A feeling similar to the rush of power that he'd felt in the hotel room erupted inside him. The difference was that this feeling was a thousand times stronger.

"Sean, are you all right?" Ailbe asked when she saw his body going into contortions of pain. She watched in helpless awe, as huge lumps began to form all over his body. They were rippling and multiplying so fast that soon she couldn't recognize him.

She watched helplessly while Sean cried out in agony, as his human form morphed into something unrecognizable. Ailbe started to move to help him, but it was too late. "May the Creator preserve us!" she cried.

Sean didn't hear her cries, because he was suffering through agony that he didn't think was possible to survive. His entire body was exploding out of his skin and growing at a fantastic, impossible rate.

It all happened so quickly that he could hardly maintain consciousness. Suddenly, he felt his body expand outward and upward at a tremendous rate.

As quickly as it began, it was over. The pain subsided and was replaced with a feeling of unbelievable, raw power. He glanced at Ailbe and realized he was now at least five-times her height. She was staring at him with a mixture of awe and fear. In the next moment, Sean understood why.

He burst into the air at what felt like supersonic speed. All because he was flapping his arms. That's when it hit him. He looked at his arms and they were gone. In their place were massive, red wings. Sean was a dragon!

There was no time to contemplate what had just happened, because he was soaring through the air at unbelievable speed. Sean was on a collision course with the flame-belching gray, which was still bent on attacking Ashling.

He hit the large gray dragon from its blind side with tremendous force. The creature already had a damaged wing and couldn't do much to evade Sean's attack once it was hit.

From that moment on, Sean's human reasoning was gone. He could only feel unrelenting anger mixed with an overwhelming desire to protect Ashling. While the injured gray was trying to fly away, Sean bit down on its neck with his massive jaws. One vicious shake of his head and the gray's neck snapped.

Sean let the dead gray go and turned in a lightning fast and graceful arc. He soared downward, intent on destroying the gray who had its jaws locked on to Ashling's flank.

When the creature saw what Sean had done to the other dragon, it released the grip on Ashling and tried to flee. It was a hopeless effort.

When Sean was within thirty feet of the fleeing dragon, he released a stream of fire without conscious thought. The searing flames consumed the gray, turning it to dust.

He realized that Ashling was trying to fly over and help her father against the remaining two grays he was battling. She was moving slowly, and he could see she was in no condition to continue fighting.

With seemingly no effort, he put on a burst of speed that allowed him to shoot past her in seconds. One of the grays fighting Eamon saw him coming and turned to confront Sean. It was the creature's last mistake.

❧❦❧

Eamon finished off the huge gray he'd been battling just in time to see a magnificent, young red dragon bearing down on the last gray. He glanced at Ashling and saw that she too was watching the attack.

They both watched in stunned silence, as the powerful red released a stream of white-hot flame when it was still fifty-feet away from the gray. Eamon could hardly believe his eyes, as the huge gray dragon was incinerated in seconds.

The magnificent red circled back to Ashling's side, in the blink of an eye. With astonishing swiftness and grace, the red dropped underneath Ashling and took her weight on its back. Eamon watched gratefully as the red quickly spiraled to the ground and landed softly beside Ailbe. He hurried to join them.

125

When he realized Ailbe was there, Eamon understood who the great red was. Sean was turning out to be more–much more–than he or Ashling could have ever imagined.

⁂

Sean slowly opened his eyes to sunlight filtering through the window shades. His first conscious thought was that it felt like déjà vu to wake up in the Cahir's spare bedroom. His second, and more urgent, thought was that he'd never been so thirsty in his entire life. His throat felt so dry and parched he could barely swallow.

He climbed out of bed, intent on guzzling water right from the bathroom faucet. Sean made it two steps before he collapsed in a heap on the bedroom floor.

When he opened his eyes again, the sun was setting. It was apparent that hours had passed since he'd collapsed on the floor. Sean began to wonder if this would always be the case when he visited the Cahirs.

"Before you complain," Ashling said, as she charged into the room. "I was only reading your thoughts to make sure you didn't try to get up and then fall flat on your handsome face again."

"Water!" was all Sean managed to croak.

"If you weren't too lazy to turn your head, you'd see a quart of ice water right beside you on the night stand," Ashling said, smiling brightly.

Sean turned his head, struggling to ignore the massive pain. When he reached for the jug of water, he realized it wasn't just his head that ached. His entire body felt like it had been run over by a Sherman tank.

"Let me help you with that," Ashling said gently, as she hoisted the jug to his lips.

He was grateful for the straw in the jug, since he was certain he couldn't raise his head to drink. Sean guzzled the entire quart without taking a breath. His burning throat fell marginally better, but he thought he could drink another gallon without hesitating.

Ashling sat on the edge of the bed and held his hand. Even the gentle squeeze hurt like crazy. "Ouch" he mumbled.

"Sure, and true, you're the worst patient I've ever encountered, you big baby," Ashling said tenderly.

"Now I know why that dragon, in our kitchen, came after you. It no doubt could recognize you were dragon born–even while I was too ignorant to see the truth staring me right in the face."

"You were too busy being suspicious of me and trying to throw me out of your house," Sean managed to rasp out. Sean was immediately sorry for his jest when he saw the crestfallen look on Ashling's face.

"Though I know you're only teasing, you're right as rain about me. I was much too preoccupied with my unfounded suspicions to listen to my dear father. He told me all along you were someone very special. Da even suspected you could be the one spoken of in the writings of our beloved ancient of days."

She started to say more, but when she saw the worried look on his face, Ashling just smiled and bent over to kiss his unshaven cheek. "Who knew you could grow such a manly beard in only four days, my dear Sean."

"Four days?" he mumbled.

"Well, it's been four days since you tried to get out of bed on your own and fell flat on your face, so you did."

"How long...?" was all he could ask.

"I assume you're asking how long since you turned into a magnificent and amazingly fierce red dragon. If that is indeed the question, the answer is three long weeks."

"Weeks," he muttered.

"Truth be told, you're fortunate that you woke up at all, my dear Sean."

That was the second time she'd called him "her Sean". He liked the sound of it very much. "How did...I mean doesn't it seems impossible...so confused," he stammered.

"Don't try to understand it all right now, Sean. It's the Creator's own truth that Da and I can hardly fathom what we witnessed with our own eyes. Never in the long history of our blessed clan had anything like this taken place. You're a miracle, dear Shawn, and don't ever try to convince me otherwise. To do so would be a silly, hopeless cause and that's the sure and simple truth of it."

Sean tried to think clearly through the pain in his head. Three weeks had passed without him being aware of it. A thought struck him out of the blue. He gathered himself to try to explain his concern to Ashling.

"Save yourself the trouble, Sean. Until I teach you how to guard your thoughts, they are open to anyone with a touch of Irish magic, without the need for me to read your mind."

"Jennie," he rasped.

"Not to worry, Sean. Do you not recall when I explained that time in the mortal world is not the same as it is here? Though you've been gone for three weeks, it will seem like less than a day to Jennie. The only problem that might occur is if she tries to call you."

"That is going to take some time for me to wrap my head around," Sean rasped. "The three weeks that passed since I left Portland, is less than a day outside of Rundimahair?"

"Strange to you, but it's the Creator's truth," Ashling said. "It all depends on what plane of existence you're in. If you lived where our Creator lives, a thousand of our years is like a single day."

"I…it seems impossible," Sean stammered.

"Sorry Sean, I've given you too much too soon," Ashling said, smiling kindly. "Don't worry about Jennie. To her, you've only been gone a short while."

"It's not likely she'll call if it is only the first day I left Portland. She wanted me to get away from the stress and worry of work. Jennie won't call unless it is an emergency of some kind," Sean explained.

"Your voice is sounding stronger. I slipped a bit of home-grown remedy into your water. It always does the trick," she said, smiling.

He was going to complain, but he realized that his voice was stronger and his aching throat felt better too. It was past time to trust Ashling and her amazing healing gift.

"Thanks," he said.

"You're very welcome, I'm sure," Ashling said.

"Actually, it's time to trust me in all things, Sean," she said chuckling. "I have many amazing gifts you still know nothing about."

"I take it I'm still broadcasting my thoughts for all the magical world to hear," he said.

"Loud and clear," she said cheerfully. "Don't fret, we'll work on that in the days ahead."

"Sounds like a good plan," he said.

She smiled mischievously and said, "I'd worry more about those dreams of yours. We wouldn't want some of your dreams about you and me getting out for public consumption."

"What?" he asked miserably. "I don't even recall any dreams."

"Not surprising, my dear. Although I must say I won't soon forget some of your dreams of romance. It's not hard to believe that you're a red dragon. Even your dreams are very fiery."

"Just shoot me now, Ashling, before I die of humiliation," Sean grumbled miserably.

Ashling burst into happy laughter and said, "I'm just having a bit of fun with you, Sean. No one can see or hear your dreams unless they climb into your mind while you're dreaming."

"Which you promised faithfully not to do," Sean reminded her.

"I did indeed, so rest easy."

"At least this time I didn't blush like a school boy when you teased me," he said.

"Will wonders never cease," she said cheerfully.

"I love that smile," he said. "I figured I might as well say it out loud, since you'd hear my thoughts anyway."

"Very practical and very Irish of you, dear Sean," Ashling said.

Chapter Nine

May your troubles be less
And your blessings be more.
And nothing but happiness
Come through your door.

~ Old Irish Saying ~

"But we have no record of seeing vile, dark creatures like these since we brought Rundimahair here centuries ago," an average height woman with a shapely figure said. "How is it possible they were able to pass through our protective shields?"

The woman who spoke appeared to be in her thirties, and she seemed to wear a perpetual frown. Her name was Shannon Tiernay, and her shoulder-length, dark-black hair was full of soft curls. Shannon's large brown eyes were her best feature, although they were clouded with frustration and anger tonight.

This was an emergency meeting of the council of twelve, who were charged with keeping Rundimahair safe, prosperous, and fair for all. Among those in attendance were Ashling and Eamon, along with Ailbe's grandfather, Aengus.

For one of the few times in history, a thirteenth individual was attending the very private meeting. Because he had been a primary participant in the aerial battle of magical creatures, Sean Quinn was an honored guest.

"Dear Shannon, you almost make it sound like we invited them in for dinner," Aengus said, in his usual calm manner. "None of us are certain how they managed to find their way into Rundimahair."

"Is that so, Aengus?" Shannon asked doubtfully.

"Unless you've discovered a deep and dark secret you aren't sharing with the rest of the council," Aengus said patiently.

"I've no deep-dark secrets I'm keeping from everyone," she said indignantly. "Perhaps you're asking the wrong person about secrets being kept close to the vest," Shannon added, glaring at Ashling.

"If you've got any facts to share with the council, you'd best get them said, Shannon," Eamon said patiently. "Otherwise, we'll live without the insinuations and your usual huffy tone."

"Huffy or no, Eamon, perhaps I'm the only one with the courage to speak their mind," Shannon said indignantly.

"Sure, and it's true that you speak your mind often enough, dearie, but it's also true it's usually smoke and wind with nary a fact to be found in that head of yours," a heavy-set, older woman said impatiently.

"You'll not be talkin' to me in that tone, Margaret," Shannon shouted. "Just because you're happy to kiss their backsides and follow along with the council leadership, it doesn't mean I'll be kissin' along with you."

"I'm wondering, in my heart of hearts, if the lack of kissing-of any kind-is why you're such a sour old goat," Margaret said, smiling wickedly.

Fergus, the aged head of the council, banged his ancient gavel down on his desk and said, "Enough from both of you now. We're not here to reignite old disagreements. Let's get back to our purpose and keep it civil," he added forcefully. "Now is there anyone who has anything pertinent to the discussion at hand?"

"I'm sure I still have the floor!" Shannon shouted indignantly.

"You've had your say, such as it is," Fergus said while staring hard at Shannon. "Take your seat or I'll have you removed from the meeting, so I will."

"Well, I've never been treated in such a way!" Shannon huffed.

"Therein lies the problem," Margaret said quietly. Several quiet chuckles could be heard from council members sitting close by.

When Shannon continued to stand defiantly, Fergus sighed and said, "Take your seat or be escorted from the room, Shannon."

"Wait until my husband hears of this!" Shannon said furiously.

"Better him than us," Aengus said.

Shannon glared hatefully at Aengus as she grabbed her purse and coat. "You haven't heard the end of this," she said haughtily, as she stomped toward the exit doors.

"We all know that well enough," Eamon said, sighing deeply.

"Why not vote her off the council and be done with it," Margaret said wearily.

"You know very well that we cannot do any such thing, Margaret, dear," Fergus said. "Each of the founding clans must be represented on the council."

"But does it have to be the grumpiest, evil-minded sharpie in the entire O'Quin clan?" Margaret asked.

"Not if we had a say in it, Fergus said. "But you know as well as I that each clan chooses their own member on the council."

"Oh aye, we know that well enough," Margaret said. "I'm convinced they voted Shannon onto the council, years ago, just so she wouldn't have so much time to torment the rest of her clan."

Ashling nodded sympathetically and said, "Since we have the rare opportunity to have a discussion without her constant interruptions; I suggest we take advantage of it.

"Spot on with your observations as usual, Ashling," Fergus said. "Do we have any idea how those gray devils found us?"

"It's all guess work so far, but Da' and I have a theory," Ashling said.

"That's more than the rest of us ornery Irish folk have if you added all our opinions together. Say on, lovely Ashling," the eldest and presiding leader of the twelve said, in his usual gentle voice.

Ashling smiled at Fergus McCree, the longtime leader of the Council. He often said he was older than the hills surrounding Rundimahair, and Ashling thought it might be the truth. Fergus was long and lean with a full head of silver hair. His gray eyes were soft with age, but his mind was as sharp as ever. He usually let Eamon, Aengus and Ashling take the lead in council meetings, but when he did speak, it was always worth listening to.

Before she spoke, Ashling looked at the semi-circle of council members seated at their matching oak desks, in their gray, high-backed and well-cushioned chairs. Apart from the now absent Shannon Tiernay, she knew each of her fellow council members to be fair, open-minded people. They were also not the type to be easily frightened. She was grateful for this trait above all.

"You've all had the opportunity to meet our guest, Sean Quinn," Ashling said, gesturing toward Sean, sitting in the chairs reserved for townsfolk, when they were invited to council meetings.

Sean looked as though he was going to stand, but at the last moment decided to stay in his seat and nod solemnly at the council. Ashling could feel his nervous energy churning just below the surface. She smiled at him and nodded back, hoping to calm his nerves.

"You've also heard the tale of how he came to Rundimahair. In a feat we thought impossible, he managed to tap into the ancient, incredibly powerful spells which have protected us for centuries."

"Do we yet understand how a handsome young fellow barely out of his knickers managed such a stroke of magic?" Fergus asked softly.

"Truthfully, we don't a clue," she said. "If you'll bear with my lengthy story, I'll try to explain all that we know and all we don't yet understand."

"Carry on and forgive the interruption. We're all anxious to hear every detail," Fergus said, smiling.

"Nothing to forgive," Ashling said, returning his smile. "From the beginning, we suspected Sean had latent gifts of white magic coursing through his veins. After some of the experiences we've shared, there is no doubt that he is a tremendously gifted wizard. We're still working on his family history to discover where the magic came from."

"How can you be so sure?" one of the council members asked.

Ashling launched into a discussion of the fight with the foul beasts they'd battled at the bed-and- breakfast. She could see the interest and fascination of the council grow as her story concluded. It had been centuries since anyone with such powers had been found.

Next, she went on to discuss in detail what had taken place during the battle with the deadly gray dragons. She heard Margaret gasp when she explained how he'd destroyed the dragon intent on killing her.

By the time she'd explained Sean's heroic battle to help Eamon, everyone in the room was spellbound. After letting her tale sink into the council's minds, she finally said, "I'm sure you can see that Sean is a tremendously gifted and powerful wizard. When you consider that he is only just now becoming aware of his powers, it is not unreasonable to assume that his potential may well be nearly unlimited."

"Aye, it would be a fierce hard thing to argue with that," Aengus said. "The young fella sure and true has the gift and there's no doubt about it."

"Amen to that, Aengus," Margaret said solemnly. "How many generations have passed us by since the last red dragon appeared out of nowhere, roarin' and ready to go in a fight to the death with the grays?"

"To my recollection, which I readily admit is not as sharp as it could be these days, it's not happened in the long history of our race," Fergus said.

"Taint nothin' wrong with your recollection, dear Fergus," an aged woman named Mona said. "I've been a student of our race's history since I was no more than a wee little one at me mother's knee. I can promise you there is not the like of Sean in our long and troubled history."

Ashling nodded at the ancient woman and said, "I couldn't agree more, Mona. While we know that he is a young man with great potential; none of us can say for certain where the ceiling on his powers might be.

"It is my belief that Sean's presence is what brought the grays inside of our ancient, protective shield," Ashling continued. We all know that Grainne has her dragons out searching for us constantly. I feel that Grainne's gray dragons were searching in our area and were pulled into Rundimahair by the powers of the great Creator of us all."

"Why in heaven's name would the Creator do such a thing?" Fergus asked. "It could have been the end of us all!"

"Because it is the only way such a powerful red dragon could be called out," Ashling said. "When Albie brought Sean to the high mountains, it was meant to be."

"Because nothing but the possibility of you and Ashling dying, could call forth such a mighty red!" Fergus said.

"More likely it was the danger to his dear Ashling that caused his dragon self to roar into existence," Eamon said, smiling.

"I was thinking the same thing, so I was," Margaret said, glancing at Ashling.

It was Ashling's turn to blush as she glanced at Sean and then down at her feet. "Whatever the case may be, it was meant to bring Sean's magnificent red dragon to life. Not only that, but Grainne would be none the wiser. She would only know that a group of her gray dragons had disappeared without a trace."

"I couldn't agree more and while I readily admit that it's a fascinating topic of discussion; perhaps we should forego talkin' about Sean as though he isn't sitting right in front of us," Eamon said, smiling.

Ashling realized her mistake, as she looked at Sean sitting in the front row of seats below the dais. She nodded at Sean, who smiled in return. "My apologies, Sean. As usual, my Da's right as rain."

"No offense intended, and none taken, Ashling," Sean said, waving his hand dismissively. "I'm as interested in discovering how I fit into your history as you are."

"Very kind of you, Sean," Fergus said. "Can we assume you won't mind us asking a few questions? Before you answer, I must warn you that some of the questions may probe into your family history and personal life."

"Ashling's constantly asking me questions lately, so I've become somewhat used to being given the third degree. "I'll warn you ahead of time that I've not come across any relatives who could turn into fiery, red dragons at the drop of a hat."

Or dragons of any other color, may I assume?" Margaret asked, showing a broad smile.

Sean chuckled, enjoying the kindness the Council showed him under difficult circumstances. "Right you are, Margaret. No dragons of any color that I'm aware of."

"I'm wondering if any of your amazing gifts showed themselves in some small way before you found yourself in Rundimahair," Fergus asked.

Sean was silent for a few moments before saying, "Nothing earth shaking, but from time to time I think I did have what might be considered unusual occurrences."

"Please explain," Fergus said.

"There have been times in my life–going back as far as my teenage years–where I was sure I could hear someone's thoughts."

Sean saw several of the Council look at each other with raised eyebrows and expectant glances. Obviously, they were very interested in what he had to say.

"Do you mean you could actually hear what they were about to say, or know what they were thinking?" Eamon asked.

"The latter more than the former," Sean said. "I didn't hear their voices speaking to my mind just before they said the words out loud. It was more of a sense that came over me where I knew what they were feeling."

"That must have come in handy when you were thinking about asking a pretty young lass out during your schoolin' days," Fergus said, smiling.

"Once I began to trust those feelings, it was very handy, indeed. It was very comforting to know if a girl was thinking that she'd like to go out with me, before I even asked."

"Sure enough, Sean, such a gift could have saved me some humiliation in me younger days," Fergus replied.

"But there was more to the gift than helping out with your love life," Ashling said. "Explain how it had a darker side as well."

Sean nodded slowly while he gathered his thoughts and shifted direction. "Soon after I turned eighteen, my ability seemed to expand. I could actually feel if someone was very upset, or very happy without ever looking at them. Eventually, I refined the ability enough to know if someone was thinking dark, dangerous thoughts."

"And what did you do when you recognized such feelings in someone?" Fergus asked.

"At first I tried to ignore them, since I didn't want to believe some of the feelings I was picking up on. That all changed when I was in the last few months of my senior year of high school."

"Something forced you to take action?" Fergus asked.

Sean nodded and said, "I was walking to gym class with two of my friends when I felt very dark, angry thoughts close by. Vicious anger and a desire for revenge hit me so hard, I almost cried out in pain. I quickly looked around me and didn't see anything at first.

When I started walking forward again, I finally spotted a slender, pleasant-looking girl, glaring at a boy across the hall who was flirting with a pretty girl.

"You were able to pick her out of a crowded, school hallway?" Fergus asked.

"It was like she was sending out violent, radio waves that only I could tune into. Her feelings were so vehement that it physically hurt to accept them into my mind. I realized she wasn't just angry at him; she truly wanted to hurt him."

"What did you do?" Margaret asked, her eyes wide with interest.

"Just as we approached her locker, I saw her turn quickly and reach onto the top shelf. In that moment, somehow, I knew she was going for a gun. I stepped up so close behind her that she physically could not pull away from her locker or take the gun off the shelf. I expected her to resist, but she froze in place and stared straight into her locker. I put my arm on her shoulder, so a passerby might think we were boyfriend and girlfriend."

"That was quick thinking, Sean. Did she try to resist at all?" Fergus asked.

"Only for a moment, until she realized it was futile. I remember thinking that I might be able to help her if she didn't panic. To my astonishment, she slowly nodded her head, as though she'd heard my thoughts. For the first time in my life, I heard exactly what she was thinking."

"What was it?" Margaret asked excitedly.

"Somehow–mind to mind–I heard her say, 'I wasn't going to hurt him; I only wanted to scare him. He lied and cheated on me and then laughed in my face when I confronted him about it. I could see the confrontation clearly in my mind and felt sympathy for the girl."

"I suppose you notified the authorities," Margaret said.

"I probably would have, but when I pulled the gun out of her hand, I saw it was a very realistic, plastic gun. She had very angry thoughts in her mind, but I realized she hadn't intended to actually do him physical harm. She only wanted to humiliate him, just like he'd done to her."

"Still, it seems like she could have gone from thinking about humiliating him to actually doing him harm, if she was that angry and unstable," Margaret said.

Sean nodded and said, "I took the fake gun from her and told her I wanted her to report this to a student counselor or I would. She promised she would talk to Mrs. Williams, a very well-liked counselor at our school. I told her I'd give her until the next morning, and that I'd be watching closely."

"I assume she complied," Fergus said.

"She didn't show up at school the next day, or any day after that. Rumor was that she'd transferred to another school. I probably should have turned her in, but I had a strong notion we'd never see her again, which turned out to be the case," Sean said.

"Did anything like that every happen again?" Margaret asked.

"Nothing that dramatic, but from time to time, I realized I could feel or hear other people's thoughts," Sean said. "It troubled me at first, but it happened so infrequently that I just put it off as a weird physic anomaly. I'd read about similar things on the internet, and now I assumed I was just one of those peculiar people."

"You didn't tell anyone–not even your folks?" Margaret asked.

"What would I tell them? I couldn't just blurt out that I had awesome psychic abilities that seemed to show up occasionally. I did my best to ignore this weird ability and eventually it faded away."

"Use it or lose it," Aengus muttered.

"In Sean's case, I believe it's not so much lost as put away until needed," Ashling said. "I've picked up some vibes since I began working with Sean, that indicate his psychic sense is alive and well. A bit dusty from lack of use but the powers remain."

"That would jibe with other experiences we've had over the years," Aengus said.

"Indeed so, Aengus," Ashling replied.

"Any other unusual abilities you might have noticed, Sean?" Fergus asked.

"Only one that felt like it might have involved a touch of magic," Sean said.

"Say on," Fergus said, with a touch of eagerness in his scratchy voice.

"Coincidentally, it occurred less than fifty miles from here on Highway 101," Sean said. "It was a foggy, rainy Saturday afternoon in late September about two years ago."

"Nothing coincidental about it, Sean," Ashling said. "The proximity to our incredible magic power source had everything to do with what occurred. Being so close to such a marvelous magical power source, is what allowed you to trigger your own great powers."

"I can't argue with that," Sean said. "Looking back on it with the knowledge I've gained, I believe Ashling may be correct.

"Sorry to interrupt. Please continue, she said."

"I was hurrying to an investor meeting, related to a large parcel of land I later purchased and developed," Sean said. "As I came around a bend in the road, I was shocked to see an eighteen-wheel truck and trailer less than ten feet in front of me. I could see the driver slumped over the wheel, either asleep or unconscious."

"Does anyone else feel like someone with dark powers may have been trying to kill Sean before he grew into his powers?" Margaret asked.

"Sure, and true, Margaret, the same thought just occurred to me," Fergus said, as several others around the room nodded in agreement.

"If it's true that a sinister force meant me harm, another powerful force must have been defending me," Sean said. "In the blink of an eye, the huge truck was back in its own lane, as I drove safely past him. Despite my shock, I noticed the driver was sitting up straight in his seat, looking alert and refreshed."

"I pulled over to the side of the road, until I could stop shaking and tried to make sense of what had just occurred," Sean said. "Of course, I couldn't make any sense of it and eventually convinced myself that I'd imagined the entire incident."

"Let me assure you, Sean, the event was very real," Ashling said firmly. "While working with Sean to develop his magical gifts, I've seen so many of the experiences of his life–mind to mind. This particular experience had the stench of dark magic all over it."

"Are we to assume that he was able to tap into our shields on that occasion as well?" Fergus asked doubtfully.

"Highly unlikely," Ashling said. "He was too far away to be able to access its power base – especially at such a young age. I believe he sensed the power, without really understanding what it was."

"Then how could it...? Margaret stopped in mid-sentence and slapped both hands on her desk. "As you say Ashling, it must be he himself what did this!"

"Da' and I were thinking the same thing."

"So, you've already begun the search for his ancestors?" Fergus asked.

"I have, and It's not too surprising to find that his troubled mother is descended from our lineage."

Fergus and Eamon spoke almost in tandem, saying, "Why did ye not tell us?"

"I've only just learned the truth an hour before the meeting started," she said. "I wasn't sure you wanted to share it with the entire council just yet, so I thought I'd tell you two in private."

"Do you know where she joins with us then?" Eamon asked.

"She left our people at least a thousand years before we fled to the Oregon Coast. Her name was Orlagh. "I've not had time to read all of her family history here, but it was said that she was always fascinated with the human world. She disappeared without a trace one night and was never heard from again."

"How can you be so sure Sean is related to her?" Fergus asked.

Ashling appeared to be a bit embarrassed and hesitated before finally saying, "I borrowed a bit of Sean's DNA and put my gifts to good use in searching his family tree."

Fergus looked troubled for a few moments, before he finally said, "I approve of this risky and highly unorthodox approach to finding the answers we seek. I also realize that only you can find the answers we desperately search for. Be all that as it may, lovely Ashling, you'll be asking my permission before trying a stunt like that in the future. Am I making myself clear?"

For one of the few times in their long friendship, Ashling read disappointment in Fergus' eyes. She stepped in and hugged him close as she said, "Aye, clear and true, my dear, Fergus." She stepped back, but kept a firm grip on his hands, as she added, "I swear on the blood of me ancestors, it will never happen again."

"See that it doesn't, young lass," Fergus said, as he slowly smiled. "Pursue your search with all haste and keep Eamon and I informed. The three of us will discuss when and what to share with the entire council once we have more answers."

"That I will, Fergus. I should be able to find answers quickly enough, since one or more in Orlagh's family line must have been extraordinarily powerful to produce a wizard like Sean."

Chapter Ten

The test of the heart is trouble and it always comes with years.
And the smile that is worth the praises of earth
Is the smile that shines through the tears.

~ Old Irish Saying ~

Ashling was searching in earnest for the origins of the woman named Orlagh. She was convinced that the mystery woman had to be Sean's ancient ancestor. While tracing Orlagh's life story, she became increasing entranced by all she found. As the days passed, it almost become an obsession.

After working through a full weekend, Ashling was interrupted by Eamon standing at the open door to her office.

"I'd have sworn that door was closed and locked," Ashling said, when Eamon stepped into the room.

"Locked doors have never been much of a hindrance to your dear old Da'," Eamon said, smiling.

"True enough, but your darlin' daughter is trying to get something done–hence the locked door," Ashling said, trying to hide her annoyance.

"I can see you're working your fingers to the bone on that computer," Eamon said. "In truth, that's why I'm standing here."

"To watch me work?" Ashling said, without looking up.

"To encourage you to cease and desist for the night is more what I had in mind."

Ashling sighed heavily and stopped typing, as she said, "Was it not you and Fergus who gave me the directive to seek out Orlagh's history with all haste?"

"Aye, so we did, and you know as well as I do that we didn't mean working 'round the clock without a rest," Eamon said firmly.

Ashling heard the tone change in her Da's voice and understood it would do no good to argue further. "Very well, I'll stop after one more hour."

"It's past midnight and you'll stop now," Eamon said.

She'd never enjoyed having someone give her orders–even if he was her Da'. "I've not been a child for many long years, Father. I'll go to bed when I'm good and ready."

"You're right in thinking I shouldn't order you about as your father, and I've no intention of doing so," Eamon said calmly."

"So you say, but isn't that what you just did?" Ashling said with growing irritation.

"Nothing of the kind, dear girl. I ordered you to cease and desist as your direct superior on the council."

Ashling glared at him for several long moments, while she tried to think of a way around his order. All the while he was waiting patiently with a slight smile fixed in place. She finally gave up and rolled her eyes as she shut down the computer.

"Thank you, dear girl," he said softly, as she stood and walked toward him.

"Don't be complaining to me when the descendants of Danu crash through our shields because my Da' sent me off to bed before I could find the answers we need!" she said testily, as she tried to step around him."

Eamon grabbed her arm firmly and pulled her back to him. He looked her in the eye for several moments without speaking, while he struggled to control his own temper. Finally, he said, "You'll see things more clearly after a good night's rest, dear Ashling."

"So you say," she replied petulantly.

"Not only are you the spittin' image of your saintly mother, you also inherited her fiery temper," Eamon said, smiling kindly. "Still and all, I wouldn't change a thing about you, even if I could. I loved your dear mother, fierce temper and all. I love you too–all the more so because you're the only child we were blessed with."

Ashling wanted to stay angry, but when she saw the tears in his eyes, her anger melted away. She embraced her father and said, "It's true that I've always been grateful to be so much like Mom, but to tell it true, I could have done without inheriting her fiery temper."

"It helps keep you humble and, we all know you have very few things to feel humble about," Eamon said, chuckling.

She stepped back, looking into his warm eyes. Finally, she leaned in to kiss him on the cheek. "No wonder Mom married you, Da'. You're as full of the blarney as Sean is–maybe more so!"

"I think by the time he's my age, he'll be known far and wide as the king of all blarney," Eamon said, smiling. "Off to bed now, me darlin'."

Ashling began falling asleep as soon as she climbed under her covers. She had been burning the midnight oil for too many days in a row, and her mind and body desperately needed the rest.

She'd been putting in even longer hours since Sean had gone back to Portland a few days ago. It had been her idea to have him spend some time at work, while she was busy researching his family tree. It would keep anyone at his job from wondering where he was.

Even though time worked more slowly in Rundimahair, Sean would need to spend some time at his home and work in Portland.

The truth was, she was missing him a great deal more than she could have imagined. Her long hours of work helped pass the time until he returned. She struggled against the notion that she needed Sean in her life, but she could no longer deny that she was developing strong feelings for him. Ashling kept telling herself it wasn't a good idea to become too attached to him, but so far her heart was ignoring her warnings.

She drifted off to sleep, wishing Sean would be there when she came down for breakfast in the morning. Her thoughts of Sean gradually shifted to the search for his ancestors, while she fell into a deep, dream-filled sleep. In her vivid dreams, Orlagh's story began to come to life.

❦❦❦

Orlagh had lived in ancient Ireland nearly two-thousand years ago. Her people were descended from the Sidhe, an angelic race sent to earth to assist, guide and comfort humans through the challenges they would surely face due to their mortality.

For thousands of years, the Sidhe lived peacefully in the mountains of Ireland. Because of their nature as immortal beings, the Sidhe were not visible to humans unless they wished to be seen.

Their home was in the high peaks of Mt. Carrauntoohil, the highest peak in all of Ireland. The entrance to their city was under the calm waters of what is today known as Devil's Spy Glass lake. It was impossible for mortals to locate the entrance since it was ten feet underwater and protected by powerful enchantments. The

Sidhe also had a variety of magical shields which frightened away any local citizens who might venture too near the lake.

The Sidhe were experts in the use of what mortals came to call white magic. They used their powers to benefit mankind, helping them develop skills and invent tools, which allowed them to progress as a society. They also taught mortals that living as families was the surest road to happiness.

Though the Sidhe remained invisible to mortals, they often walked among them. While mortals slept, their immortal guides would plant thoughts and ideas in their minds. Often the idea had to be planted several times before it took root and began to grow. Many of the great inventions of mankind grew from suggestions the Sidhe planted in human minds.

During the days of Orlagh's youth, there began to be a division amongst the Sidhe. A mighty man among the Sidhe—named Donal—revolted against traditions the Sidhe had lived by for thousands of years. He was tall, agile, and well-muscled, as well as exceptionally handsome. Donal had also been blessed with the gift of eloquent, persuasive speech.

Donal, who was a direct descendant of Danu, used his gifts to draw some of the Sidhe to him. He began a campaign to make himself leader of the Sidhe. His secret ambition was to replace their current leader, Faolan.

Many of the Sidhe were distantly related to Danu since she had been a part of the Sidhe in ancient days. While a few were aware of Donal's kinship to Danu, most were unaware of how pure the blood line was. That bloodline gave him the same desire to rule over the Sidhe as Danu once had.

In the beginning, he kept his ambition to overthrow Faolan secret from others, because he knew that Faolan was beloved above all others by the Sidhe. He had been their leader since the very beginning and taught harmony and love for each other as guiding principles. Because of Faolan, the Sidhe had lived in harmony and stayed true to their calling as spiritual guides to the human race.

As time passed, Donal secretly convinced more of the Sidhe to follow him. He taught them that they were never meant to be servants of mankind. Donal's goal was to rule over humans and establish himself as king of the Sidhe.

Contention grew among the Sidhe, and many were misled by Donal's flattering words and promises of great power. He assured his followers that they were meant to be great leaders who would force the human race to serve them and obey their every command. He promised his followers that this would be for mankind's greater good, since the humans would be forced to obey the laws which Faolan had given.

Those who remained loyal to Faolan informed him of Donal's subtle treachery. For the good of the Sidhe, and mankind, Faolan removed Donal from the leadership council and forbade him from preaching against the council's teachings.

While he pretended to abide by Faolan's ruling, Donal secretly gathered his followers and revolted against Faolan's leadership. It was a terrible battle that was unlike anything the Sidhe had ever experienced.

The bitter, brutal rebellion lasted for many years. Eventually, Donal and his followers were defeated and cast out into the mortal world. While they were free to roam amongst the humans, they soon realized that they could not take the life of a human, nor could they rule over them.

From that day forward, Donal made it his mission to cause as much misery and sorrow as possible among mortals. His passion was to persuade them to ignore the teachings of Faolan and think only of their own power and wealth.

The followers of Donal persuaded mankind to think only of their desires and pleasures, while the Sidhe sought to persuade them to love one another and work hard for the common good. This great battle for the souls of mankind continues to this day.

While Donal, Faolan, and their followers were immortal, they were all eventually called back home to their Creator. Whether that was a joyous day depended upon whom they chose to follow.

Fergus and Eamon, along with all residents of Rundimahair, were direct descendants of Faolan. Like their ancestors, they were here to persuade mankind to live up to their great potential.

Donal's ancestors strove to cause wars and acrimony amongst humans. Their goal continued to be the destruction of the Sidhe and domination over humans.

Eventually, Ashling's dream followed the path of Orlagh's ancestors, who were among Donal's posterity. Orlagh was a direct descendent of Donal but had conflicted feelings about the darkness of her ancestor's teachings.

As time passed, she chose to live among the humans. She had always been drawn to mankind and eventually met a good man, who was a leader among mankind.

They lived in the human world together as man and wife until he died at eighty-eight. Soon after, Orlagh was called home to be judged by the Creator of us all.

She had lived a good life, having rejected the teachings of her ancestor, Donal. Her descendants had great hope that she would be viewed kindly on her judgement day.

Among her descendants was a beautiful woman named Kerry. All her days, Kerry struggled to decide where she belonged.

She lived among the humans, but the blood of her ancestor, Donal, called to her. Eventually, she chose another descendant of Donal as her husband, and they had three children.

Ultimately, her husband left her because of her reluctance to completely embrace the teachings of Donal. Her children would face the same struggle. Some chose to follow Faolan's teachings, and others let the darkness of Donal's example be their guiding star.

That battle between darkness and light raged in the heart of Sean's mother, causing her much sorrow and pain. Although she had the blood of Donal and Faolan running through her veins, she eventually let the darkness destroy her life.

She abandoned her son, Sean, to the mortal world, and was never heard from again. Having mixed blood running through her veins eventually drove her mad. She took her own mortal life through a drug overdose in her thirty-sixth year. Her spiritual being lived on and returned home to the waiting arms of her Creator.

❖

Ashling awoke early the next morning, feeling weary and sad. While she'd slept the night through, the troubling dream didn't allow for a deep, refreshing sleep. She now had the answers to Sean's family history, but she felt sorrow over his mother's troubled life.

While she showered and dressed for the day, Ashling wondered how she could explain her dream and Sean's mother's sad life story. Even though Sean could guess that her history would not be a happy one, it would still be difficult to be faced with the truth. Anyway one tried to justify it, there was no way around the fact that his own mother had abandoned him.

Ashling told her Da about her dream, without going into too many details. They decided to invite Fergus to their home for lunch to discuss it further. After going over the basic history of Orlagh's life, and her ancestors, they discussed their best course of action.

"It's a great blessing to have among us a dear girl who has the gift of dream sight," Fergus said, between bites of dessert. "If you throw in that she can also cook like the Creator's own personal chef; well, it hardly seems fair to the rest of womankind," he added with a charming grin.

"Aye, she's got her sainted mother's gift for creating heavenly culinary delights," Eamon said.

"How is it you've maintained your boyish figure all these years, with this type of cookin' in the house?" Fergus asked.

"I'm sure I don't know, since I eat like a starving grizzly bear most of the time," Eamon said with a smile.

"That he does," Ashling said, as she touched her father's hand. "The only man I've ever met who could eat like Da' is Sean. He can put away a month's worth of groceries in a single meal, so he can."

"Now I'm two times jealous, since Sean is as fit as a fiddle too," Fergus said.

"Look who's talkin'," Eamon said. "Yourself is as skinny as a lamppost."

"Maybe so, but I must watch what I eat, to stay in fighting shape," Fergus said, laughing.

I can see that is true," Eamon said in a teasing tone. "You've kept a close eye on both of your helpings of my dear Ashling's strawberry cheesecake, so you have."

They all shared a laugh together, enjoying Eamon's quick wit. When the laughter died down, Fergus said, "Thanks again for the very fine meal, dear Ashling. As much as it pains me to say so, I suppose we've put off talking about your amazing dream as long as we should. I know you've told us the basics of what you saw. Will you be kind enough now to give it to us in fine detail?"

Ashling nodded her agreement and proceeded to explain her fascinating dream in great detail. Both men listened carefully, only occasionally interrupting to request clarification. When she finished her story, all three of them sat back and sipped their tea.

"Tis a sad story to have to share with Sean," Eamon finally said. "No young fellow should ever have to hear his own mother left him on someone's doorstep, so to speak."

Fergus nodded his head and said, "Aye, you've got the truth of it there. To know your dear mother took her mortal life must feel like the ultimate rejection. In the end, all we can take with us is our hard-earned experience, and the blessed family ties we've developed in this life. To have the bond with your own mother lost in this way is a terrible tragedy."

"And poor Sean, with no other family ties at all," Eamon said.

"Not completely accurate, Da," Ashling said. "Bill and Eva Stanton may not have been his blood relatives, but they treated him more like their own flesh and blood son than many parents do the children born to them."

"You're truth telling there, Ashling," Fergus said. "The mortal world of today has progressed with technology at an amazing pace. Why, it's almost like magic to see what they can do with those miracle machines. Still and all, the family ties amongst the mortals have fallen into decay at a sorrowful pace. Mothers and fathers rejecting their own children is all too common. I'm grateful to the likes of Bill and Eva Stanton for stepping in where help was needed."

"Well said, Fergus," Ashling said. "While we can't undo his past, we can help Sean take hold of his future."

"At least we know where his amazing powers came from, since he inherited both dark and light Sidhe bloodlines through his mother. They may go back a fair piece, but his ancient ancestors passed down powers beyond belief," Eamon said.

"What you say is true, Da," Ashling said, but not all his blood lines are so ancient. You see, Orlagh also mated with a descendant of Donal. From what his DNA tells us, Sean may have more of the Tuatha blood in his veins than he does from Faolan."

"Say it isn't so," Fergus mumbled, while pondering this latest information.

"It doesn't mean he's doomed to follow the dark path of Donal," Ashling said. Remember, he also has much of Faolan's bloodline in his DNA. While his mixed blood may explain where his unusual powers come from, it doesn't mean he'll choose to use them for malevolent purposes. Please remember that we all came from the same bloodlines in the beginning."

"What you say may be true, Ashling," Fergus said. "Still and all, it should give us pause to consider the possibility."

"Especially when you consider that those of our beloved people, who've chosen to follow Donal's dark path over the millennia since his rebellion, were almost all of his ancestry," Eamon said.

"I'm not likely to forget, Da," Ashling said. "Do you not remember who was against bringing him into our midst in the beginning?"

"Aye, that I do, that I do, Daughter," Eamon said. "I'm the one who felt his coming among us was not by chance. Truth be told, I still feel that way. There's no doubt that Sean is someone special.

Still and all, we must keep an open mind about the future After all, he could be someone special but not to our cause."

"So we must keep an open mind and hope for the best," Fergus said. "Especially when we consider the enemy, who even now searches for our hidden location. She will stop at nothing to destroy us. If I didn't know much better, I'd suppose she might be the reincarnation of Donal or even Danu herself. If she ever finds out about Sean's abilities, she'll stop at nothing to turn him to their malicious purposes."

Eamon and Ashling both nodded in solemn agreement. As they continued their discussion and planning for the future, their common enemy was relentlessly pursuing their destruction.

⁂

Sean was sleeping deeply in his beautifully renovated home in the hills overlooking downtown Portland. He'd enjoyed his trip to Portland but was feeling anxious to return to Rundimahair. His plan was to leave early the next morning.

He'd spent much of the week in his office catching up on housing and development projects, which were underway or in the planning stages. Sean had always loved the excitement of his real estate business, but during this visit he'd found his usual enthusiasm lacking.

It had been good to work with Jennie and see they were doing well without his constant input and supervision. Before he'd met Ashling, it might have bothered Sean to realize he wasn't indispensable. Now the realization came as a great relief.

Jennie and the office staff didn't seem to find it unusual when he'd explained he'd be out of town for an extended period.

Her only response had been, "Be sure to keep your cell phone handy, in case I need to reach you."

It was nearly two in the morning when his deep sleep was interrupted by another strange dream. His subconscious was beginning to recognize what Ashling called her prophetic dreams. Most of his prophetic dreams were related to Ashling and Rundimahair. This dream was something entirely different.

Sean was in a tall, spacious building, which resembled an ancient castle. It had fallen into a state of ruin over thousands of years. Even in its dilapidated condition, there was an air of grand majesty about it.

The ancient fortress walls, which surrounded the castle, were still mostly intact. The castle itself was situated on a grassy hillock overlooking the sea. It was crumbling badly in parts, but was still a very impressive sight.

In his dream, Sean was suddenly standing just outside the crumbling stone walls of the castle. A gentle breeze touched his face. It was somewhat chilly, but not unpleasant. He could see through the crumbling castle walls to the grounds on the far side. Much of the interior walls had long ago fallen to ruin.

When he touched the cold, moss-covered stones, Sean felt a sudden burst of energy swirling around him. It was similar to the energy he knew shielded Rundimahair, but it was subtly different. Sean watched in fascination while a stone near what had once been the entryway began to glow in soft, blue hues. Instinctively, he stepped forward and cautiously put his right hand on the glowing stone.

Nothing happened for several moments, but slowly the stone began to turn warm under his hand. The soft, blue light began to glow brighter and the color seemed to intensify. Sean considered pulling his hand away as the stone grew hotter to the touch. A sense of urgency about maintaining contact with the stone forced him to keep his hand in place.

For several minutes he watched the blue light intensify and gradually encompass all the castle ruins. Before he could decide what to do next, the blue light exploded outward, forcing Sean to cover his eyes with his hands.

When nothing else happened, he slowly lowered his hands and opened his eyes. The ancient ruins had disappeared along with the vibrant blue light. Now he was standing at the opulent front entry doors of the largest, most beautiful building he'd ever seen.

While the structure resembled an ancient castle in some ways, it appeared more modern in design, while still maintaining its old-world charm. The new castle was made from rugged stone and was four stories high. There were large turrets at each corner, which towered twenty feet above the gray-tiled, steeply pitched roof. The beautiful, immense castle and grounds would easily encompass three city blocks in downtown New York.

There was attractive ornate stone and tile trim around the dozens of windows and doors. Sean had seen many beautiful structures in person, or online, but he'd not seen anything that could hold a candle to this beauty.

In addition to the building itself, there were acres of stunningly well-maintained grounds. Among the landscaping were many unusual trees and bushes of various sizes and shapes. They were carefully placed in what appeared to be several acres of immaculately maintained green lawns. It would take dozens of workers, countless riding mowers and hedge and tree trimmers to maintain the grounds so immaculately. That didn't even take into consideration the thousands of gallons of water and miles of sprinkler lines that kept everything a beautiful, vivid green.

The real estate investor, architect and builder sides of his nature gaped in awe at the massive feat of engineering. Even with today's technology, it would have taken years to complete.

In the far distance he could see dozens of buildings, which appeared to be a mixture of barracks and apartments. Beyond these buildings were at least twenty or more two and three-story buildings, neatly arranged in large circular patterns. He wasn't sure why, but he sensed a decidedly military vibe coming from this area.

Sean turned back to the beautiful castle-like building in front of him. The same compulsion that had encouraged him to place his hand on the glowing stone, now pushed him toward the massive front entry doors. The entryway was above him at the top of the stairs. Sean had to walk up at least two-dozen stairs just to reach it.

He took a moment to catch his breath, before raising the ornate, iron-knocker and pounding it against the steel-reinforced, thick oak doors. After waiting for several minutes, he was about to pound harder. Before he renewed knocking however, the door slowly swung open. He waited for a butler or maid to step into the open doorway, but after a moment he realized there was no one there.

Sean looked around outside and then peeked inside the palatial entryway. He finally came to the realization that he was the only person here. At least he was the only one within eyesight or hearing distance.

After a few moments' hesitation, he felt that same nagging sensation to move forward and explore the interior of the castle. He pushed the door open wide and stepped onto the polished flagstone entryway. He slowly closed the massive front door behind him.

The interior was also beautiful on a grand scale that must have cost millions to create. It was vast and open, with natural light flooding the interior from countless windows, doors, and skylights.

The plush furnishings were also expensive. It must have cost a fortune to furnish such a palatial interior. Sean was impressed, but also a bit put off by the gaudy display of immense wealth. It reminded him of some of the hotel-casinos he'd seen in Las Vegas. It was impressive in its own showy style, but it was too much for his tastes.

It took him nearly an hour to tour through the entire castle. He was feeling a little bored by the showy interior by the time he walked back downstairs.

When he was about to turn toward the large front doors, he heard what sounded like a trapped animal growling somewhere below him. He looked around for a set of stairs leading to what he assumed was a basement, but he couldn't find the stairway.

The roaring and growling almost sounded like an animal in pain. It also sounded like a powerful, potentially dangerous creature.

He thought it might be wise to head out the front doors and leave before someone arrived home and found him there. Just as he turned to leave, he heard the distinct ding that usually signaled the arrival of an elevator.

That same feeling, which touched his mind earlier, encouraged him to follow the sound. He walked down the hall and turned into a large open landing. At the far side of the landing was a set of large, stainless-steel elevator doors. A red light was blinking above the doors, as the familiar ding reverberated through the landing area again.

When he took a step toward the doors, they suddenly opened, revealing a large, posh elevator. He stepped inside and pushed the letter B, which he assumed meant he was going to the basement. The doors closed quickly and he felt a rush of speed while the elevator descended quickly.

When the doors opened again, he was looking at a long, wide hallway that was at least twenty feet across. On each side of the hallway were heavy, steel doors that looked like they were strong enough to stop a speeding tank from crashing through them.

The elevator dinged again, and Sean took that as his cue to step out into the hallway. There was a slight movement of air in the hallway, circulated by almost noiseless fans. They seemed to be circulating scented air which smelled like spring flowers.

As he walked quietly down the wide hall, he noticed an underlying scent that was very unpleasant. It resembled what he imagined was the odor of decomposing flesh. He knew that if he stayed down here very long, the smell would make him gag.

Suddenly, something large and very strong slammed into one of the doors on his left. It made the door shake from the impact, but the door was designed to resist such abuse.

What could only be described as a demonic wail came from inside the room behind the door. Whatever creature made the noise sounded like it was in pain and very, very angry.

Sean carefully touched the heavy latch on the door and said quietly, "Are you all right?"

The response was instantaneous and vicious. The creature began slamming against the door in rapid bursts of energy, all the while screaming its rage at Sean.

"Time to leave," was the thought that urgently filled his mind.

Sean fully agreed and hurried back to the elevator. He no longer wanted to know what was inside the basement rooms. In fact, he felt an urgent need to leave this strange place immediately.

When he stepped out of the elevator, Sean hurried back into the entry hallway. It was definitely time to get himself gone from here.

Just as he hurried toward the front doors, four very large, powerfully built men stepped through the entryway. Sean was now feeling scared and nervous as he watched them walk directly toward him.

The man in the middle was more intimidating than the other three which was saying quite a bit. They were all similar to a young Arnold Schwarzenegger. It wasn't just his massive size which caused this feeling. It was more a sense of sinister power radiating from him, although he was tall and incredibly muscular.

The four men walked toward him at a rapid pace, glaring with blank, menacing expressions. His fight-or-flight sense kicked into high gear, but he hoped he could talk his way out of trouble without things getting physical. There was no way he was going to win if this turned into a slugfest.

"Look, I understand that you're upset, and I apologize for walking into your home uninvited. I didn't break in though. I know it sounds strange, but the front door just opened on its own. Of course it didn't give me the right to just walk in, but I was curious to see what this amazing place looked like inside."

Sean realized he was babbling now, and from the look on their faces, they weren't listening anyway. They just continued to glare at him in a way that almost appeared like they were looking right through him.

He quickly stepped out of the way when they were almost in his face, but he brushed against the big man closest to him. Instead of turning this contact into a physical confrontation, the group just walked into what looked like a conference room and shut the door behind them.

Sean furrowed his brow as he looked at the place where his shoulder had contacted one of the men. Although Sean knew he'd bumped the big guy's arm, he realized that he hadn't felt a thing. Just as that was starting to creep him out, the strange whisper he'd been hearing on rare occasions spoke to him now.

"You are only here in spirit," passed through his mind. *"They cannot see or hear you."*

As he heard the voice in his head, Sean realized it wasn't really a whisper. It was hard to explain—even to himself. It seemed as though someone was talking softly inside his mind. It felt like an old friend he'd known for years but hadn't heard from for a very long time.

"Who are you?" Sean asked aloud.

"Your Guide, now please turn around. Grainne is why you are here," the voice murmured in his mind, in the same calm, quiet manner.

"Who or what is a Grainne?" Sean muttered, as he turned and looked toward the front door.

Sean's question was answered when a tall, stunningly beautiful, and curvaceous woman walked through the doorway. She appeared to be in her twenties, except for the look in her eyes. Those dark gray eyes seemed to express several lifetimes of experience.

She wore her thick, lustrous, dark-brown hair onto her shoulders. In her four-inch heels, she was near to his height. Her stride was quick and confident, and her form-fitting designer dress really accented her perfectly shaped figure.

Sean stood very still and hardly breathed as the striking woman sauntered past him. She too seemed oblivious to his presence. She'd marched by him like he wasn't even there.

The beautiful woman quickly approached the conference room, just as another dozen men and women hurried through the home's entrance door.

They all rushed past him and filed by the gorgeous woman holding the conference room door open. They smiled and greeted her with friendly respect, but Sean could see a certain uneasiness in their demeanor. The woman holding the door was definitely the one in charge.

"Thank you, Grainne," another attractive woman said, as she passed into the conference room. "It looks like we're all here."

"We'd all better be here," the woman she called Grainne said, smiling prettily.

She'd spoken in an open, friendly manner, but Sean sensed the steel in her voice. The one called Grainne was used to being obeyed.

Just as the last person was filing past her to enter the conference room, Sean took a couple of steps toward them. If he could get past her before she closed the door, he could hear what they had to say.

When Sean was within twenty feet of the door, Grainne suddenly turned and looked in his direction. He froze instantly. Something about the predatory look on her face terrified Sean.

"Do not move and do not look at her!" the voice in his mind said urgently. *"She shouldn't be able to sense your presence, but she has extraordinary powers of perception."*

Sean looked down at the lovely flagstone floor and tried to clear his mind of all conscious thought. Even without making eye contact with her, he felt sure Grainne was glaring at him.

His breathing became shallow, and he was preparing to turn and run for the entry door, as he heard her high heels move slowly across the floor. It sounded like she was heading right for him.

"Be still as death," the voice in his head whispered.

"Still as death?" Sean repeated in his mind. That wasn't a very comforting thought.

She was close enough for him to smell her lovely perfume. It was an alluring fragrance, which he was sure cost a fortune.

Sean's "run for your life" senses were now kicking into overdrive. Despite her great beauty, he felt a dark and deadly nature inside of Grainne.

He wanted to look up and see how close she was, but heeded the quiet voice and kept his head down. He was so still he could barely feel himself breathe. Then he saw her high-heeled shoes come into view, where he was staring at the floor.

She was only five feet away. Now she was three feet away. The urgent desire to make a run for it was nearly overwhelming. Sean swallowed hard and prepared to turn and sprint for the front door.

Just as he was ready to turn and run, a loud thud came from the front door. Immediately he felt Grainne turn her attention to the front door. He let his breath out in a slow, deliberate sigh.

"It's about time," Grainne said cheerfully, as she hurried past him and toward the front door.

"Hey, it's not easy to find chilled, Russian caviar on short notice," a young, female voice said.

"I knew you'd do it, Linda—you always do," Grainne said.

"It's true. I am the greatest assistant of all time!" the new arrival said, giggling.

Sean used the distraction to move away from the path they would walk to return to the conference room. As he slowly stepped sideways, he glanced up at the two women. The young woman that Grainne had called Linda was at least four inches shorter than Grainne and very slender. They were busy going through the packages that Linda had brought with her.

"How did you get all this up those stairs?" Grainne asked.

"With my usual creativity and style," Linda said, smiling.

Grainne chuckled and said, "You are a stylish woman for sure. Now use your leadership skills to get a couple of them to help you get this set up for lunch."

"Not to worry, Grainne," Linda said. "I'll grab Jeremy and Sylvia to help me. We'll have this set up in fifteen minutes."

While the two women headed back to the conference room door, Sean used the distraction to rush back to the front entry door. He turned and glanced back just as he was about to run through the open door. His heart lurched in his chest when he saw Grainne staring directly at him with a knowing smile on her face. He could almost feel a loose connection being established between them, which was the last thing he wanted. Sean rushed through the doors and didn't stop running until he was down the stairs and across the massive lawn.

Chapter Eleven

Do not resent growing old.
Many are denied the privilege.

~ Old Irish Saying ~

The oddly fascinating and terrifying vision hastened Sean's desire to return to Rundimahair. He now felt safer there than anywhere else. This was all still so new to him. At times it seemed like an unreal nightmare, but when he was with Ashling and her family and friends, it felt like a delightful dream come true.

After all that had taken place since his first encounter with Rundimahair, Sean understood the experiences weren't his imagination. Too much had transpired in the past month for him to doubt it. As bizarre as it might seem, this was becoming his new reality.

He'd continued making new arrangements, with his office assistant, Jennie, to be out of the office for an extended period. With that understanding and the different realities of time in Rundimahair, Sean was free to try to comprehend where he truly belonged and seek what Ashling called his true destiny.

He was packed and ready to leave early the next morning. Sean had loaded his SUV with everything he might need for the foreseeable future. He wanted to be on the road early and arrive in Rundimahair before lunchtime. The thought of having lunch with

Ashling brought a surprising shiver of pleasant anticipation. He knew that his affection for her was growing stronger, but he was still surprised to realize just how much he missed her.

In the early morning hours, Sean opened his eyes and was immediately alert and fully awake. He lay completely still and listened intently, but he only heard the deep silence of a home closed down for the night.

What had brought him out of a deep sleep? He could hear the quiet movement of heated air through the furnace duct vents. Other than that, the house seemed completely still. Perhaps it was the after-effects of another bizarre dream. Sean shrugged that notion off. He usually recalled at least part of dreams like the one he'd had the previous night.

He couldn't really explain the feeling he was experiencing now, but he could sense that something was wrong. Something was definitely off. Sean thought back to the battle he and Ashling experienced in the hotel room on the Oregon coast. Just before it began, he'd had a similar feeling nagging at his subconscious mind.

Without really understanding why, he rolled out of bed, wearing nothing but a pair of exercise shorts, and rushed to the other end of his spacious master bedroom. Mere moments later, two massive, freakish creatures crashed through his bedroom roof and landed on the bed he'd been lying in moments earlier. Along with them came a large section of the roof rafters and ceiling. Without knowing how he understood, he was certain that these were two of the creatures locked in the basement of Grainne's castle. Somehow, she'd managed to find him.

Before Sean could react, two smaller, cat-like animals dropped through the hole in his roof. Before they hit the bed, they seemed to disappear. He studied the darkness carefully, but without success. Whatever they were, there was no trace of them now.

He quickly shifted his attention to the huge and grotesque beasts struggling to get free of the roof debris and his broken bed. While they had a basic humanoid shape, their faces resembled disfigured gorillas. As they struggled to their feet, he could see they were barefoot, wearing only very large, bulky sweatshirts and sweatpants. In the moonlight shining through the large new hole in his roof, they appeared to be overly hairy. Their ruddy complexions were pale green and covered with oozing sores.

While he watched them closely, they began to circle away from each other until they were about ten feet apart. The hulkish forms seemed ready to attack, but instead they just stood there. They were apparently waiting for him to either attack or flee.

Sean felt the same strange sensation overtake him that he'd experienced on the Oregon Coast. The feeling of thousands of volts of electricity rushing through his veins hit him anew. Instead of a healthy sense of fear, he now felt calm and actually looked forward to a fight.

Sean was tired of waiting for them to charge him. He leapt into the air, covering ten feet in seconds. He landed a few feet in front of one beast, who looked confused and was slow to react. Sean began spinning around and landed a rapid series of brutal kicks to the side of the behemoth's face. He heard bones cracking along its cheek bone and eye socket. Sean leapt and landed softly close behind it.

He sensed the other beast coming at him from behind. Sean leapt high into the air again just as its plate-sized hand reached for his neck. With a perfectly executed backward somersault, he landed behind the charging creature. Before it could react, Sean side-swept a powerful kick at its right knee. The sound of bones breaking and ligaments tearing told Sean his attack had been successful.

With a bellow of savage anger and pain, the behemoth crashed to the floor, grabbing at his ruined knee. Despite the disparity in size, Sean realized he could deal with these brutes.

Just as he was about to put them out of their misery, Sean felt a stinging pain burning through his right hip. Instinctively, he leapt away, now feeling weakness in his right leg. Before he looked around, he realized that he'd forgotten about the cat-like creatures that disappeared earlier.

He completed two additional leaps across his large master bedroom, trying to give himself time to see what he was fighting. Just as he landed the second time, he felt another stinging pain burn a line across his stomach muscles.

Sean ignored the pain and lashed out with a series of leg kicks and brutal punches. The incredible speed and strength of his attack still amazed him.

To his surprise, he felt one of the kicks strike something hard. There was very little resistance. Whatever he was fighting was not very large or heavy. When he saw a short animal-like creature suddenly appear on the floor on his left side, he knew it had been invisible. It was completely indiscernible until he'd knocked it unconscious. That is how the creature had approached him unseen.

He took a moment to study the creature and realized it closely resembled a large bobcat, only its claws were at least six inches long and curled upward at the end. It was covered in gray fur and couldn't have weighed more than fifty pounds. These animals must rely heavily on their speed and invisibility.

He abruptly realized that there had been two of the beasts as he felt another raking scrape across his back. The second one had attacked him from behind. With instinctive, blazing speed, he leapt high in the air and came down ready to fight.

To his surprise, the second cat-like animal ignored him and was licking its unconscious twin. Sean grabbed a large chunk of roof rafter and hurled it at the preoccupied animal. It struck the conscious cat in the head with tremendous force. The odd angle of its twisted neck told Sean it was dead.

He barely had time to take a deep breath, before a huge, hairy hand grabbed his left arm and flung him at the far wall. Despite his great strength, Sean was stunned by the impact. His left shoulder was badly injured, making his left arm almost useless.

He struggled to get to his feet, as the beast with the broken eye socket charged at him from across the room. Blinding, hate-filled rage filled its dull black eyes.

Just as he was about to leap away from the creature, Sean felt another massive hand close around his right leg. He looked down to see the second beast glaring at him and smiling grimly through jagged teeth. It must have crawled across the room to reach him, since his injured knee made it impossible to walk or run.

Sean doubled over and slammed his right fist into that creepy smile. The injured beast let go of him and roared in pain. Sean was sure he'd broken the creature's jaw and half of his teeth.

Before he could redirect his attention, the other beast struck him a vicious blow to his back, which again slammed Sean up against the wall. Searing pain shot through his midsection when he tried to jump free of the two injured beasts. It felt like there was serious damage to his ribs where he'd been hit.

Even with his injuries, Sean managed to get to his feet and leap up and away from his attackers. When he landed, Sean felt a surge of dizziness and weakness coming on. Next came a burning pain from his abdomen. He looked at the claw marks on his stomach and realized he was in serious trouble. The deep cuts were already swelling and dripping with an ugly, black ooze.

"Those cats must have had poisonous claws," he mumbled to himself.

He looked at the two badly injured hulks stumbling toward him. The one with the broken face was holding up the one with the broken knee. Together, they were dragging themselves toward him. Even from this distance, Sean could see the anger and murderous intent in their black eyes.

Sean knew his only hope was escape. He was feeling weaker by the moment, as the poison worked its way through his system. He managed one, half effective leap, to put more distance between them. One more leap and he could break through a window and out of the house.

The creature who could still walk realized what Sean was planning and dropped his companion to the floor. Before Sean could muster the energy to make the leap, he felt a massive, powerful hand close around his foot and was effortlessly lifted into the air.

The only thing he could think to do was to turn into his dragon form. Sean desperately tried to recall how that had happened back in Rundimahair. Before he could do anything, he felt himself flying through the air again. This time he landed high up on the wall, then dropped to the floor. As he felt consciousness slipping away, Sean whispered Ashling's name over and over.

Ashling was standing in the kitchen, in her robe and pajamas, when she felt a sudden desperation fill her heart and mind. It was such a powerful feeling that it caused her to drop the glass of orange juice from her hand.

"Sean!" she shouted, while she touched her father's thoughts. Mind to mind, she quickly told Eamon that Sean was in mortal danger. Seconds later, she disappeared from the kitchen.

⸙

He barely managed to open his swollen eyes, as consciousness partially returned. He'd been tossed back and forth several times, as the beasts took turns beating him to a pulp. They seemed to be taking pleasure in dragging this out, after the painful injuries he'd inflicted on them.

The creature with the broken knee sat beside him now, grinning through his bloody, shattered teeth. If it weren't for the paralyzing poison rushing through his bloodstream, Sean would have broken its neck.

When the filthy beast raised its massive arm for a killing blow to Sean's head, it appeared to be the end. It was indeed the end, but not the one he'd expected.

He felt a searing hot wind rush by him, striking the beast with incredible force. As the heat began to sear his skin, a clear bubble of protection enveloped Sean, protecting him from the deadly heat.

The creature desperately tried to crawl away, but it was useless. While Sean watched in amazement, the brutal hulk melted down to a blob of disgusting green muck. Even through the protective shield, he felt enough of the heat to realize it was hotter than a blow torch.

A surge of relief touched his mind, as Ashling stepped into view next to his ruined bed. She raised her hand and a large, jagged beam lifted off the floor. Sean realized it was part of his ruined roof structure that was hurled across the room.

The heavy beam followed a path to where Ashling was now pointing. When Sean turned his head to follow the speeding beam, he was just in time to see it rip out a large section of the remaining creature's chest as it passed through him. Seconds later, the beast dropped to the floor and didn't move again.

Ashling hurried to kneel beside Sean as the protective shield dissipated. "Are you all right?" she asked anxiously, as she began to run her hands over his head and body. "Oh Sean," she whispered sorrowfully when she realized the extent of his injuries.

That was all the sorrow she allowed herself as she went to work mending the damage. Ashling touched the swollen, bloody claw marks on his stomach and she frowned but didn't speak.

When she waived her hand over the terrible wound, Sean saw a searing blue flame enter his body. He expected it to burn, but it was ice cold instead. The artic flame rushed through his veins quickly and cleanly, causing him to shiver. He gritted his teeth to avoid crying out from the pain. After thirty minutes of the magical torture, he gave up and screamed in agony.

Ashling seemed satisfied with the progress of his healing, and the freezing blue flame disappeared. Next came a comforting warmth surrounding him from head to toe. Soon the warmth penetrated the frigid cold, and Sean could finally breathe a sigh of relief.

Without a word, Ashling stood and began moving her arms and hands about like a magical orchestra conductor. Like a film moving in reverse, Sean watched in wonder, as the debris from the roof reassembled itself in proper order. In less than twenty minutes, all damage from the attack on his home was repaired.

Sean watched in satisfaction as the gruesome, evil, magical creatures were bound up in a blinding, white light. It began to swirl them around in circles with ever-increasing speed. Finally, the brilliant light began to fade and the remains of the deadly creatures were gone.

Before he could say a word, she lifted him to his feet, while chanting something in a rapid whisper. Seconds later they disappeared, only to reappear in Ashling and Eamon's kitchen.

"I see all is well," Eamon said, from where he sat at the kitchen table. "There must have been a fearsome, large mess to clean up if it took this long." His words were calm and casual, but Ashling could see the worry had taken a toll on her father.

"That it was, Father dear," Ashling said, as she sat heavily beside Eamon. "That it was."

"And yet, Sean doesn't seem much the worse for wear," Eamon said. "Sure and true, he's fortunate to have the best magical healer who ever drew breath as his runsearc."

Sean sat across from Eamon and Ashling as he asked, "Her what?"

"Her runsearc," Eamon said, smiling. If you went English, it would be something like, secret love."

"That is more than enough out of you, Father," Ashling said, with a furrowed brow. "I can tell you it was close to total disaster, so it was. Much too close for my liking. If I'd arrived five minutes later, it would have been too late."

Sean wanted to discuss the "secret love" comment but could see by Ashling's expression that now was not the time.

"I'm supposing the attackers were similar to what you confronted when you went to visit Sean at the bed-and-breakfast," Eamon said, between bites of bacon and eggs.

"Indeed they were. Only these ugly brutes seemed to have the added unpleasantness of poison claws to work with. Sean had several nasty claw marks on him–especially on his mid-section. The infection was already deep within him when I arrived. Thank the Creator that Sean called for help when he did."

"It wasn't the giant brutes who clawed me," Sean said, as he snatched a crispy piece of bacon. "It was the little cats who got me."

"Little cats?" Ashling asked, confused. "I didn't see any other dark magical creatures."

"They looked a lot like a bobcat, only a bit larger. They were kind of cute if you don't count the poisonous claws," Sean said, now munching on an English muffin.

"Help yourself to some breakfast, Sean," Eamon said, smiling. "It sounds like you earned it."

"Don't mind if I do," Sean said brightly.

"But I didn't see any catlike creatures while I was cleaning up the mess you made," Ashling said.

"To be fair, you made a bit of a mess yourself, when you arrived on the scene," Sean said. "Not that I'm blaming you. I appreciated the help."

Ashling rolled her eyes and said, "Still and all, I didn't see any kitties roaming around your house."

"That's because they were invisible," Sean explained. "At least they could become invisible at will. That's how they got close enough to tear into me. I didn't see them coming. When I was finally able to finish them off, they just disappeared."

Eamon looked puzzled, as Ashling sighed deeply and asked, "Where are these deadly creatures coming from all of a sudden?"

"I wish I knew," Eamon said. "We've seen variations on the giant beasties before, but I've not heard of the wildcat creatures in all my days."

"How did these ugly creatures keep finding Sean?" she asked. I might understand it when he's with me, but he should have been safe in Portland."

"Aye, that's a good question all right. With the spells we cast for his protection, he should have been safe as a baby in his mother's arms," Eamon said.

"It had to be Grainne," Sean said thoughtfully.

"Faith and Begorrah! Don't be speaking that name, Sean," Eamon said, looking around nervously.

"You know about her?" Sean asked, surprised.

"Shush now before she hears you!" Eamon said in a fierce whisper.

"Calm yourself, Da," Ashling said, putting her hand on his arm. "She'll not be hearing us while we sit in our own home, in the midst of Rundimahair."

"So you say, daughter, but I'm not so convinced as you be," Eamon said.

"We've spoken her name in grand councils for many a year and she's not found us yet," Ashling said calmly.

Eamon looked as though he was about to respond in anger, but finally managed to calm down. "What you say is true, Daughter, but there's no need in pushing our luck."

She patted his arm and said, "True enough, Da, true enough. Of greater concern to me is how Sean knew the name at all."

They both stared at Sean, waiting for an explanation. He was trying to recover from Eamon's near panic at the mere mention of a name. Finally, he took a couple of deep breaths and said, "I saw her in a dream, not long before I was attacked in my home."

"You saw a woman in a dream?" Ashling asked. "Please start from the beginning and tell us as much as you can recall."

"That's easy enough," Sean replied. "The truth is that I can recall the entire dream with great clarity."

"That's not a comforting thing to hear, Sean," Ashling said. "Please tell us both exactly what you remember."

For the next twenty minutes, Sean held Eamon and Ashling spellbound, while he recounted his vivid dream of the ancient castle. He told them about the strange ruins, and then went on to explain all about the massive, beautiful castle hidden within those ruins.

When he explained his close encounter with the cold beauty, Grainne, Sean noticed that Eamon's face went suddenly pale. Ashling held her composure, but he could sense the grave concern in her mind.

As soon as Sean ended his story, Eamon said, "Tis the dark queen he speaks of, and there be no doubt about it."

Sean noticed that when Eamon was troubled, his Irish accent and word usage became more pronounced. This was true with Ashling too, but to a lesser extent.

"Aye, there's no doubt of that," Ashling agreed. Still and all, the news could be worse."

"So you say, daughter. If the news could be worse then I don't wish to hear about it," Eamon said, shaking his head slowly.

"It's clear that she now knows Sean is a person of interest to us, and that his powers are potentially troublesome to her evil plans," Ashling said.

"And what could be worse news than that, may I ask?" Eamon asked.

"She could realize that he wasn't just a man with a strong gift for magical power. She might also have realized he could be the one to foil all of her grand, dark schemes."

"And how can you be sure the dark queen isn't aware of that?" Eamon asked.

"She didn't go after Sean herself, Da. She sent some dangerous goons after him for sure, but she didn't go and make sure the deed was done right. If she truly knew who Sean could become, she'd have been at his house last night, along with her deadly creatures."

Eamon appeared ready to dispute her logic, but then he paused. After a moment, he began to nod his head and said, "When you're right, you're right, dear Ashling. If she truly understood Sean's great potential, she'd have trusted no one but herself to crush such a threat."

After listening to their back-and-forth discussion, Sean wanted to dispute their conclusions. In the end, he realized they knew far more about Grainne than he did. Even so, he said, "I've got to say that the freaks she did send were bad enough. They were just about ready to finish me off when Ashling arrived to rescue me."

"No argument there, Sean," Eamon said. "You don't have enough experience fighting such fearsome demons yet. Once we've helped you reach your full potential, you'll handle such creatures with the same ease our dear Ashling did."

"If Grainne is as powerful as you say, then the sooner we get back to my training the better I'll like it," Sean said.

"The sad truth of it all is, there be no way to overstate the brutal powers that woman has at her disposal, Sean," Eamon said. "She's as bad as we've said, and much more besides."

Ashling stood abruptly and said, "Come along Sean, we'll get you settled in quickly and start our training again this afternoon. "After all you've told us, I've a sure and certain feeling that time may well be even shorter than we thought."

Chapter Twelve

He who loses money, loses much;
He who loses a friend, loses more;
He who loses faith, loses all.

~ Old Irish Saying ~

Summer brought warm breezes and pleasant temperatures to Rundimahair. The skies were brilliant blue, with only a few wispy, white clouds passing overhead. The temperature was just right–not too hot or too cold.

Ashling and Sean were lying close together, in a hillside meadow, high above the town. They were resting after another exhausting session, designed to help Sean develop his knowledge and use of magic.

Training had occupied the vast majority of their time and energy, since Ashling had rescued Sean from the creatures attacking him in his Portland home.

As the months passed, they brought about permanent changes to the life Sean had always known. He could never go back to being a real estate developer, focused mostly on success and making more and more money.

He was slowly coming to understand who he truly was and what he might accomplish. Being successful and wealthy no longer consumed his time and interest. Sean knew there were much greater goals to attain to in his new life.

He had decided to break ties with his real estate business and sell his home in Portland. It was no longer a safe place for him to live, and he vastly preferred his life in Rundimahair.

To her great surprise and delight, Sean sold his business and home to Jennie. He knew she had the talent and drive to be successful. She had also taught him a few good lessons about integrity in business. Sean knew this was the right thing to do.

He'd explained that he'd met someone special, and they were going to be traveling extensively over the next few years. Jennie was very pleased that he'd finally met the right woman.

Now he was free to begin his new life without having to check in with his business or make excuses about his absences.

There was a tinge of regret about leaving the life he'd built in Portland. He knew it would fade quickly because of the great excitement and anticipation he felt about his new life in Rundimahair. There was no longer any doubt in his heart or mind that this is where he truly belonged.

"Earth to Sean, come in please," Ashling said, as she rolled onto her side and tugged on his earlobe.

Sean surprised her by rolling onto his side and then rolling her onto her back. He smiled as he stared into her soft, green eyes. Before he could change his mind, he kissed her gently and then with more passion. She stroked the back of his neck with her fingernails and returned his kiss with equal passion.

After a few minutes of serious desire, Sean felt her hands gently pushing against his shoulders. Very reluctantly, he pulled back and sighed deeply.

"Time to get back to work," Ashling said gently.

"You're a slave driver," Sean said, smiling. "A beautiful slave driver, but a slave driver nonetheless."

"You think I've been working you too hard?" she asked. "This is nothing at all. In fact, I've been taking it easy on you, so I have," she added, smiling, as she got to her feet.

Sean was quickly on his feet and embraced Ashling as he said, "I enjoyed that last workout the most."

She laughed and said, "Who knows, there may be more where that came from, if you can transform into your dragon form at will by the end of the day."

He let go of Ashling and spun around in a circle several times. "I'm trying my best; I truly am. I've already transformed twice this week."

Ashling could hear the frustration in his voice, as he stuffed his hands into his pockets and sighed again. She knew he was giving it all he had, but she couldn't let up on his training. His ability to transform into his dragon-self, might one day be the difference between life and death.

"I know you're working hard, Sean. "You're getting closer every day, so we've got to keep working at it," she said.

"Yeah, I hear you," he said.

Suddenly, an idea struck her and without a word, she transformed into her dragon self. She let loose a ferocious roar and blew red hot flames into the air. Seconds later, she leapt into the sky and began to circle high above him.

Sean was enthralled by the power and grace of Ashling in her dragon form. He watched, mesmerized, as she pulled out of her circles and dropped into a steep dive. Seconds before she would have crashed into him, she arched up and sped away.

An elemental force inside him was triggered as he watched her dive at him before pulling up and shooting back into the sky like a guided missile. She was truly beautiful in her dragon form. Her scales were the same green as her eyes, and her long, flowing red mane was breathtaking. At that moment, he wanted nothing more than to be flying alongside her.

Sean felt the familiar explosion of raw power inside as he transformed to his dragon self almost effortlessly. Moments later, he was flying side-by-side with Ashling.

They flew companionably for several minutes before Ashling burst up and away from Sean. With blinding speed, she completed a graceful arch and nosedived directly at him. Sean launched himself upward, roaring his defiance, as he released multiple, long bursts of flame.

For several moments, it looked like a game of deadly, high-speed, dragon "chicken", each daring the other to turn away from the imminent, fiery collision. At the last possible moment, Sean executed a perfect barrel roll which allowed him to land on top of her. He nipped at her neck and shoulders, just enough to let her know he had won, and then rushed out across the sky.

Ashling felt exhilarated, as she watched him loose a series of fireballs into air. She could still hear his exultant roars, when he was only a red dot on the horizon.

Sean quickly circled back, ready to go again, but she was already heading for the ground, dropping in slow, graceful circles. He felt his heart ache as he watched Ashling's elegant landing. Whether in her human form or her dragon self, she truly entranced him.

Moments after Ashling's soft, graceful landing, Sean shot toward the ground like a fiery bullet, slamming his large, clawed feet into the earth beside her.

"That's how a fiery-red dragon comes in for a landing!" he shouted, as he turned back to human form."

He noticed that Ashling was laughing as she turned away from where Sean was standing. "What?" he asked.

"That's how you end up standing around buck naked in farmer O'Leary's field," she said, chuckling.

Sean gasped and quickly turned back into his dragon self. In a burst of speed, he rushed back toward Ashling's home.

"I've got to remember to transform to my human self, where I've got a little privacy," he muttered, after landing in her back yard and sprinting down the basement stairs.

⁂

"I should have explained that to you earlier," Ashling said later, while they shared a bounteous supper."

"You think so, Ashling?" Eamon said, smiling. "I know it's been a while since I had to teach you the facts of life about your dragon self. Still and all, you should have given poor Sean fair warning."

"Aye, that I should have, but he was showing off something awful. I thought it might do him some good to enjoy a good dose of humility," Ashling said, smiling.

"Well, perhaps that is so. I know I needed to be taken down a peg or two when I first came into my dragon-self," Eamon said. "There was nothing like landing in the middle of a village, while changing into my naked human self, to bring me back to reality."

"As I recall the story Mom told, there were more than a few young maidens who got an eye full on that grand day," Ashling said, laughing out loud.

"Oh aye," Eamon said, chuckling along with his daughter. "Don't be forgetting that your own sainted mother was among the gawking, young lasses."

All three of them burst into raucous laughter over Eamon's predicament. "I don't feel so bad now," Sean said. "At least there was only Ashling there to witness my humiliation."

It took Eamon a moment to stop laughing, but finally he said, "It's not that tricky once you get used to it. You just have to store extra outfits of clothing here and there around Rundimahair."

"And you don't land and transfer back to your human-self until you're sure there are no prying eyes about," Ashling said.

"Not to worry," Sean said. "I'll not be making that mistake again."

"On the bright side of things, I believe we've found a trigger for you to easily become your dragon self," Ashling said.

"Do you mean when you transformed and leapt into the air?" Sean asked.

"Indeed so," she agreed. "Now all we have to do is plant that memory deep in your mind, so you can use it anytime you need your dragon to appear."

"Is it that simple then?" Sean asked.

"It usually is," Eamon said. "Once you've planted the thought in your mind, the trigger seems to be instinctive after a few tries at it. The fact that you have more than a passing interest in my sweet daughter should help it work all the better."

Sean didn't bother denying his ever growing attraction for Ashling. No one would believe him, even if he tried denying the truth.

"Once I stash a few changes of clothing, here and there, I'll give it a go," Sean said.

The days passed by quickly, turning into weeks of very exhausting training for Sean and Ashling. Occasionally, Eamon would join them. His dark blue scales gave Eamon a very different and fierce look as he roared through the sky. On those rare days when Eamon could join them, they would push Sean even harder, as he learned to fight two powerful dragons at once.

It was obvious that they weren't using all their powers while attacking Sean together. He was grateful for their patience in training him. It was all he could do to keep up with them when they were fighting at half-speed. He thought it would take years to catch up to their knowledge and ability.

Whenever they bested him too easily, Ashling and Eamon were quick to remind him that they'd been at this for hundreds of years. Sean had only discovered his dragon form a few months ago.

As summer turned into fall, Ashling realized that Sean's potential as a warrior–whether in human or dragon form–was truly amazing. What had been considered impossible, in Ashling's long lifetime, now appeared inevitable. Sean would one day surpass her powers as a magician and as a dragon.

She had to admit to a touch of jealousy at the thought of anyone surpassing her great powers. Beyond any small resentment, Ashling felt tremendous gratitude and relief. Besides, she was sure he'd never surpass her matchless skills as a healer. That didn't appear to be one of his gifts.

With the warriors of her father's generation aging, Ashling had long felt the burden of picking up the mantle of power for her generation. Until now, no one in her generation had come close to matching her powers. This left her feeling alone in carrying on the fight against Grainne and her many powerful warriors. Sean's arrival gave Ashling new hope for the future.

⁂

While Sean was a beacon of new hope for the people of Rundimahair, he was becoming an unwanted distraction for Grainne. She didn't yet know who he was, but she knew enough to realize he could be a potential threat to her grand plans.

When she sensed his presence at her castle, in the high mountains of Scotland, Grainne felt a chill of unease pass through her mind. It was the first touch of what might be called fear that she'd experienced in centuries.

She could only sense his presence on the outer fringes of her consciousness. That alone was cause for concern. Other than Ashling, no one had been able to hide from her immense powers of perception for centuries.

Not since Eamon had stolen away from their long-time home in Scotland, had she been unable to find anyone she searched for. That had been nearly three hundred years ago. To this day, she still hadn't been able to find their hidden sanctuary.

She'd make progress, to be sure, but she was still unable to find the exact location of Rundimahair. Only the combined powers of the Grand Council could have kept the location a secret for so many years. In truth, she was now convinced that only Eamon and Ashling had powers great enough to foil her centuries–long search.

Grainne had narrowed her persistent search to somewhere in the western United States but hadn't been able to get any closer to their true location.

Now this strange young man had shown up at her enchanted stronghold in Scotland. Somehow, he'd been able to see through the many protective spells and find his way inside her fortress. He wasn't there in his physical form, which was some small comfort. But he'd managed to enter the forbidden halls of her castle in his spirit form. That should have been impossible.

She was also concerned by how difficult it had been for her to track him. Grainne had just barely sensed his presence at all, and that was because she'd sensed his movement. She'd almost convinced herself that she'd imagined it until she felt him rush for the door, while she was distracted with her assistant.

Grainne had smiled when she sensed his thoughts and was able to take his name out of his worried mind. She'd only been able to track his mind for a few seconds before it was blocked from her again. This young man was receiving help from powers Grainne hadn't sensed for centuries.

She still wasn't sure if what she'd sensed was possible. For just the instant that she'd made a connection with him, Grainne was shocked to feel the powers of Faolan and Donal coursing through his veins. It should have been impossible to have both bloodlines running through his veins.

To be sure that he would not become a thorn in her side, Grainne had sent some of her most deadly and powerful warriors to destroy Sean. It should have been easy, but somehow, he'd managed to destroy them all and escape.

When she had finally controlled her anger, and visited the site of the rare defeat, Grainne realized she'd achieved a victory of sorts. Even though Sean had escaped, he'd only managed it with help from someone Grainne knew well. Ashling had come to Sean's rescue.

It was the first time she'd sensed Ashling's presence in over three hundred years. It was very faint, but it was there. Grainne was now sure that she could narrow her search from the Western U.S. to the Pacific Northwest. Time was running out for the traitors who'd betrayed her and followed Eamon and Ashling into hiding.

Chapter Thirteen

May you get all your wishes but one,
So you always have something to strive for

~ Old Irish Saying ~

Young Ailbe hadn't been this excited in years. After endless hours of trying to convince her grandfather to purchase modern farming equipment, he'd finally relented.

"What kind of tractor will you be lookin' to buy, Granda?" Ailbe asked.

"There's only one kind of tractor worth spending hard earned money on, my dear Ailbe," Aengus said cheerfully.

"Let me guess—a John Deere, right?"

"Saint's be praised, you did hear some small piece of what I've been tryin' to teach you, lass."

"I've heard plenty of what you've had to say, Granda," she replied, giggling.

"Oh, aye and sure it's true that you've chosen to ignore the most of what I say."

"Not most of it, Granda. "Just the parts that make my life miserable."

"Fair enough, child. Here we are at Riley's Farm Equipment," Aengus said, in a cheerful tone. "Can you believe the size of this place? Sure, and it's true that we could grow our entire corn crop on the acres he's using to show off his farming equipment."

"Welcome to the twenty-first century, Granda," Ailbe said between giggles. "It's your first trip outside of Rundimahair since I was born."

"Which wasn't so long ago, dear child," Aengus said.

"And when was the last time you've been to Eugene, or any other mortal town?" she asked.

"Longer than I care to remember, Lass. If you were old and wise enough to truly understand the dangers around us, you might understand why such trips must be few and far between," Aengus said solemnly.

"Saints preserve us! My old eyes must be playing tricks on me this fine day. For a moment there I thought I saw me old friend, Aengus, driving onto my lot."

"Oh, it's me you blind old robber," Aengus said cheerfully. "I've come to see if they've thrown you in jail for charging three times what your little tractors are worth."

"Three times what they're worth?" Riley said, frowning. "If I sold them any cheaper, I'd be giving them away–so I would."

"Oh well, then, Riley. I wouldn't want to be taking bread out of your wee little one's mouths," Aengus said.

"I'm afraid they've not been little ones for some years gone by, Aengus. I see it's the same with young Ailbe. She gone and grown into a beautiful young lass," Riley said sincerely.

"That she has, Riley. I can barely believe it myself, but she'll be eighteen years next month," Aengus said with a touch of sorrow in his voice.

"Here now, they'll be no sorrow for our young ones growing up," Riley said, as he slapped Aengus on the shoulder. "If she wasn't so grown up, you'd have no one to drive your computerized tractor."

"I don't own such a contraption yet," Aengus said.

"It's only a matter of time, once you see the old friend discount I've set up for you," Riley said.

"Sure, and it's true that I like the sound of that," Aengus said. "Especially since we are very, very old friends!"

"That we are, Aengus, that we are," Riley said. "It's a dirty shame you didn't come see me before you bought that old wreck of a pickup you're driving."

"Me old cow got stuck in the muck once too often," Aengus said, smiling. "Ailbe and a friend of hers finally convinced me to buy a truck. I must admit it's more than fair to middlin' useful around the farm."

"It's true I did nag him something awful, but I was hoping he'd buy one that wasn't as old as him," Ailbe said, chuckling.

Riley laughed loud and hard and said, "One step at a time, me darlin'. The tractor he's taking home today is so new that the massive rubber tires have yet to touch dirt."

"We'll see about that," Aengus said cheerfully. When Ailbe saw the brand-new shiny tractor her Granda was eyeing, she knew Riley would send that very tractor home to their farm.

For the next hour, Riley showed Aengus and Ailbe a few of his best tractors. It was obvious that it would take Aengus some time to master the high-tech equipment on the John Deere that he finally selected. Fortunately, Ailbe picked up on the technology quickly and easily. It was no surprise to her that he'd selected the same tractor she'd guessed would be going back to the farm with them.

The paperwork would show that someone else had purchased the tractor, and that it was delivered to a small farm in Idaho. In reality, the new tractor had already been sent to Aengus' farm, via magical portal, created by Ashling and a few close friends. If anyone ever bothered to check, there would be no paperwork showing that Aengus had ever visited Riley's fine dealership or ever purchased a tractor there.

⁂

Ailbe had convinced Aengus to do some shopping, since they were on a rare trip to the mortal world. She'd talked a lot about stocking up for things they needed around the farm, but she spent most of her time in the stores with the latest clothing fashions for teenagers.

By the time they'd stocked up on all they needed, the camper on the back of their old truck was full to the brim. It would slow them down a bit on the way home, but it had been a nice end to a wonderful day.

"How will we get the tractor to the farm?" Ailbe asked as they drove out of town.

"Nothin' to be worrying yourself about, dearie," Aengus said. "Riley has his own magical ways of transporting equipment to secret destinations. He told me he's already shipped four tractors to Rundimahair so far this month."

"But none so fine as ours," Ailbe said.

"Truer words were never spoken, my dear girl," Aengus said with a smug grin.

They drove on through the night for another hour or more. Ailbe had drifted off to sleep in the passenger's seat. So it was that she didn't notice her Granda looking at the rearview mirror, almost as often as he looked at the road ahead.

"What is it that's troubling you?" she finally asked, after she stirred from her sleep.

"It looks like we've got company tailing us for the last hour," Aengus said grimly. "They seem very anxious to find out where our final destination might be."

Ailbe was sitting up and looking out the back window in a flash. "We can't lead them home, Granda."

"Not to worry, Ailbe. I veered off the road home once I was sure they were following us. "My greatest concern is that if they take us alive, it won't be long before they know that we are from the lost tribe. Even though I've changed course, we are only a hundred miles or so from home."

"And if they find out who we are, they'll be so close to Rundimahair that it will only be a matter of time until they find us," Ailbe said.

"So, it's either us or them," Aengus said grimly. "And you can bet your bottom dollar that they brought plenty of firepower.

"Aye, I'm afraid you're right," Ailbe said thoughtfully. "But I might know how we can even up the odds."

<hr/>

"It's Ailbe!" Ashling shouted to Eamon and Sean. "I knew someone was reaching out to me.

"What in the blazes could they be wanting at this late hour?" Eamon asked.

"Aengus and Ailbe went to Eugene to buy a tractor," Ashling said.

"Tell the truth, dear girl," Eamon said. Aengus wouldn't be caught dead using modern equipment."

"It's a long story, but it's true. They were on their way home when they realized they were being followed."

"Saints preserve us!" Eamon shouted. "How close are they?"

"They quickly changed direction, away from Rundimahair, once they realized they had company," Ashling explained. "But I fear they were only an hour from us when they changed direction."

"So even if they can lead them away," Eventually, Grainne will track back to where they were going. That will narrow her search area dangerously close to Rundimahair. I'm thinking that they may soon be right at our back door," Sean said.

"Perhaps not, if they don't live to tell the tale," Eamon said thoughtfully.

✦

Aengus and Ailbe had been forced to switch from one road to another, trying to evade whoever was following them. The problem with that strategy is it led them onto winding roads that forced them to keep their speed down.

"We haven't got a prayer of losing them on these back roads," Aengus said.

"We don't have to lose them, Granda. "Just try to stay ahead of them until help arrives."

"You're that sure that help is on the way?" Aengus asked.

"You know Eamon and Ashling better than I do," Ailbe said.

"Right you are girl. If they said help is coming, then it'll be here," Aengus said.

"It actually looks like they are farther back than they were a few minutes ago," Ailbe said, looking through the truck's rear window.

"I was thinking the same thing, but I don't understand why. We're barely keeping our speed above fifty on these winding roads," Aengus said.

When they came around a wide, slightly uphill turn in the road, Aengus said, "That's the why of it right there in front of us."

Ailbe turned to look through the front windshield and felt her hopes for escape sink. A half mile ahead was a highway patrol car, with red lights flashing, parked in the middle of the road. There was also an eighteen-wheeler truck lying on its side. The truck was blocking both narrow lanes of traffic.

"We're in the soup and the fire's getting hotter," Aengus grumbled.

"I hate to think what's hiding behind that truck," Ailbe said.

"Aye, they won't make a fair fight of it for sure," Aengus said. "You can bet your bottom dollar they've got us outnumbered ten to one."

"They're coming up fast behind us too," Ailbe said.

"They've got us trapped now, so there's no point in hanging back," Aengus said. "I know I've held you back on using your magical talents, my dear. It's not that I didn't want you to develop your gifts. I just wanted you to learn how to do things with your own two hands and not always rely on magic."

"I know, Granda, I know." Ailbe said, while patting his shoulder.

"Well then my dearie, they'll be no holding back from either of us this night. If it's magic you've got, then now's the time to use it!" Aengus shouted, as he accelerated to full speed and rammed his sturdy, old truck dead center into the highway patrol car.

The collision caused a huge fireball to explode all around the two vehicles. It quickly spread to the eighteen-wheeler, causing its large gas tank to explode moments later.

Ailbe and Aengus were no longer in the pickup when it struck the patrol car. She had the ability to move from one place to another in seconds, and she used it to great effect just before the collision. To anyone watching, it would seem that she had simply disappeared. In reality, she had moved to another location. If she was touching another person when she disappeared, they would simply go with her. She'd taken Aengus' hand in hers, just before disappearing.

"Good to know you can still move about at will," he said, once they reappeared, on a stone ledge, fifty feet to the left of the fiery crash.

"It does come in handy at times," Ailbe agreed. "I just wish I could push us farther away."

"That will come with time, dear girl. With Ashling as your teacher, I've no doubt you'll be moving from one continent to another before you reach your thirtieth birthday."

"I hope you're right, Granda, but I wish I didn't have to wait until I'm old," Ailbe said.

Aengus barked out a laugh and said, "Thirty is still a babe in arms, in our world, my dear girl. Now let's move on and see what we can do about avoiding a fight to the death with these creatures from the pit of hell."

"Keep in mind I can only push us through space a couple of times before my reserves of strength are worn down. It could be an hour before I can do it again. Maybe we should hold on to the second one for an emergency exit," Ailbe said.

"When you're right, you're right, Ailbe. Let's try to slip away on foot before they get that fiery wreck under control."

As they walked down the back side of the ledge, Ailbe asked, "Do you have any warrior powers that I don't know about?"

"Sad to say that I don't," Aengus said. "My powers always lent themselves to working with the earth under our feet. I could always grow almost anything, and I used my powers to grow them in abundance. I've always loved working on the land, but growing a carrot larger than any man has ever seen isn't much use in a battle."

"It depends on how big you grow it," Ailbe said, smiling.

"Then there's the problem of how long it takes to grow it," he said.

"So it is with me," she said. "Other than moving us from one place to another, most of my powers are more on the artistic side of things."

"I suppose we're not much good in a fight, but we do make the world a better place to live in. If only we could ever get everyone to stop fighting," Aengus said.

"Well said, Granda," she replied. "Although there is one other skill that Ashling has been helping me develop."

"And that might be…?"

"Communication over distance. It's a bit like moving myself about. Only it's my mind's thoughts that travel."

"How far can you communicate with your mind then?" he asked.

"To be perfectly honest, I don't know. I've communicated, mind to mind, with Ashling quite a bit. The best we've done so far it's from one side of Rundimahair to the other."

"Very impressive, my dear girl. I had no idea you could do such a wonderful thing. I suppose you tried to contact her once we knew we were being followed."

"Oh aye, I've tried many times, but I don't think I was successful.

"You don't think you were?"

"For a moment or two I thought I'd touched her mind, while we were still in the truck. I could even see her sitting in her kitchen. It was only a for a couple of seconds that I could feel her mind touch mine."

"Do you suppose you should try again?"

"Here's the rub with that, Granda. When I try to use my mind-to-mind communication, it weakens my ability to move us physically from one space to another."

"And we might need that ability if things get too difficult out here," he said, nodding his head. "Very well, then. Let's keep moving and put as much distance as we can between us and them."

⁂

When Ashling, Sean and Eamon arrived at the crash site, Ailbe and Aengus were nowhere in sight. There was a smoldering fire still burning around the remains of a large truck and two other vehicles. There were also several bodies, or at least the burned-out remains of bodies. Two of them appeared to be human corpses. In the back of the truck there were a dozen more. They were obviously the remains of the grotesque creatures Grainne had created to do her bidding.

"It appears that Aengus rammed his truck into the police car and the truck," Eamon said, thoughtfully.

"But there are no bodies in his pickup," Sean said.

"These tracks make it clear that whoever was following them was able to avoid the deadly fireball from the crash. A vehicle moved off into the brush this way. That tells me that Ailbe and Aengus are still alive and fleeing on foot."

"It looks like they were going to try to trap them on the road and force them to stop," Sean said. "But Aengus surprised them by slamming his truck into the police car at high speed. How could they have survived that?"

"Ailbe has been working on her powers to quickly move from one location to another," Ashling said. "I suspect that she took hold of Aengus and moved them away just before they rammed the police car."

"I didn't realize she'd developed that power so well," Sean said.

"She and I have been working on it very hard for the past couple of months. I knew it would be a power that would come in very handy if a battle ever occurred," Ashling said.

"Maybe they are already back at Rundimahair," Eamon said hopefully.

"I wish that could be so, Da. Unfortunately, she hasn't progressed that far. She can move a mile or two at a time. She's also still limited on how often she can use this power. It takes a tremendous toll on her physically and mentally."

"Then she moved them out of the truck and off into the distance," Sean said. "But she was reluctant to move them again in case they needed a quick escape later."

"That's the way I see it," Eamon said. They are somewhere out there on foot, and whoever survived the crash will still be after them."

"Why can't you reach her mind to mind?," Sean asked.

"I'm not sure, but I suspect that when she moved them both out of danger, it taxed all of her powers a great deal. We had only just begun to work on her ability to move others with her. If she moved them any distance at all, she's fortunate if she didn't pass out from the effort," Ashling said.

"We can only hope that as her mind recovers from the strain, that you'll be able to reach her mind to mind," Eamon said.

"In the meantime, let's follow the vehicle tracks into the brush. They are the best hope of knowing which direction Ailbe and Aengus are running," Sean said.

⚜

It was only a couple of hours from sunrise when Aengus and Ailbe stopped to rest for a few minutes. They'd climbed to the top of a small hill and leaned back against the trunks of two fir trees.

"Do you think they are still on our trail?" Albie asked.

"I'd like to believe we've lost them, but it's pure wishful thinking. These creatures have been bred for generations as trackers. They aren't going to be easily mislead or outmaneuvered. My guess is they are just keeping us on the run until the warriors arrive."

"Makes sense," Ailbe agreed. "That way we're worn down and exhausted when the fighting begins."

"It wasn't going to be much of a fight to begin with. I think they're just enjoying keeping us on the run. They might as well just show up and get to business," Aengus said quietly.

As if in answer to his soft-spoken summons, a dozen grotesquely misshapen warriors dropped to the ground around them. A quick glance showed Ailbe that they were completely surrounded. Ailbe locked eyes with Aengus and could see that he was worn out. She had two options left to her, and she had to make a choice in seconds.

She could grab Aengus and move them somewhere farther away. It would remove the immediate danger but would only be postponing the inevitable conclusion. The enemy would certainly find them much faster next time.

Her second choice was to throw all of her restored energy into a last-ditch mental cry for help. If Ashling had picked up on her last call, she would be close by. They might be able to arrive to time to save them.

In the end, she knew there was only one choice. She jumped to her feet and rushed toward Aengus. One of the creatures managed to get his slimy paw on her foot, causing her to fall face first at Aengus' feet. She reached out and touched his leg, hoping and praying she'd made the correct choice.

"Stay behind me, Ailbe," Aengus said, as he got to his feet. "If you've got enough energy left to take yourself away, then I'm begging you to do it now. I'd give up anything to see you safe and far away from these crazed killers."

"I've got nothing left to take either of us away, Granda. Even if I did, I'd not be able to leave you here to fight the devil and his followers alone."

They were standing atop the tree-covered hill, side by side. Twelve massive, deformed dark warriors had them surrounded. As they slowly closed the circle around them, Ailbe took hold of her grandfather's hand and hoped the end would come quickly.

Before the creatures could completely close the circle, a blur of vicious, soaring power rushed past her. It struck the warrior closest to her with so much force that it was decapitated from the blow. Before the bloody behemoth hit the ground, two more of the monsters fell in a bloody heap.

Ailbe stood in shocked silence, when she recognized Sean standing over the dead creatures with a bloody, curved sword in his hand. Before she could react, she felt something very powerful sweep her and Aengus to the far side of the battle zone.

They both stared in joyous wonder at the familiar face of their old friend and leader, Eamon. "Here, take this and use both barrels. Aim it at their ugly faces if they come at ye," he said.

Eamon pushed a double-barreled shotgun into Aengus' hands. He also handed him a handful of shotgun shells. Sean smiled just before he turned back to the fight. "Aengus, if your jaw drops any closer to the ground, you'll likely trip over it. Surely you didn't think we'd leave you to have all the fun."

Before Aengus could gather his wits well enough to answer, Eamon drew a large deadly blade and returned to the fight.

Ailbe's eyes were locked on Sean during the deadly struggle. He moved like a whirlwind full of raw power. At times he moved so quickly that she couldn't be sure it was Sean she was looking at. It was truly just a blur of magical motion that cut back and forth across the hill top.

Ashling and Eamon were not far behind with their own efforts. Even though they were outnumbered four-to-one, they cut through the hideous warriors with deadly grace and speed.

One of the creatures managed to break free and rush at Aengus and Albie, probably hoping to at least kill the two they'd followed all night. Aengus waited calmly until the ugly giant was almost upon them, before bringing up the massive shotgun. He triggered both barrels, at point blank range, into the savage's face. The force of the double shot took most of its head off, while knocking it flat on its back. He watched it closely while reloading the shotgun. This one was out of the fight for good.

Aengus turned to look at Ailbe, wanting to be sure she was all right. She looked pale but managed a smile. He smiled back and said, "I know I shouldn't have enjoyed that so much, but that was much more than passing satisfying."

"I couldn't agree more, Granda. Thanks for watching out for me."

The one-sided battle was over quickly, with only the dark warriors to pay the price for starting a fight they couldn't finish. It seemed as though Ashling, Sean and Eamon were almost unhappy when it ended so quickly.

"I suppose we could wait around to see if another dozen or so come by to check on their fallen comrades," Ailbe said sarcastically. "It almost appears that you three wanted a better fight than you got."

Eamon smiled and said, "Sure and it's true that the lucky man who marries your dear Ailbe will have his hands full. Outside of my own dear, Ashling, I don't know if I've ever heard such a quick and biting tongue."

Ailbe ran forward and threw her arms around Eamon, as she said, "Sorry Eamon, Aengus often tells me that my mouth runs well ahead of my brain. The result is that I often speak first and think about what I said when it is too late."

Eamon looked up at his old friend's granddaughter and said, "Well said Ailbe. I must admit I've been guilty of that often enough—especially in me younger days."

"I've seen and heard enough from both of you over the years to stand witness that you both were guilty of letting your tongue run well ahead of your brain. Now do you suppose we could stop jawing long enough to burn the evidence and get well away from here before help arrives?" Ashling asked.

"Took the words right out of my mouth, so you did," Eamon said, while sheathing his sword.

An hour later they were on their way back to Rundimahair. The hilltop looked like a stray lightning bolt had kindled a flash fire before burning itself out. Not an unusual occurrence in this neck of the woods.

Ashling was relieved when they arrived home safely, but she wasn't naïve enough to think they'd gotten away scot free. Grainne knew who was driving Aengus' truck, and she knew where he must come from. Their deadly enemy had now narrowed her search down to a single state–or two at best–and time was running out for their beloved Rundimahair.

Chapter Fourteen

May the leprechauns be near you
To spread luck along your way.

~ Old Irish Saying ~

"Either they truly do have the ancient luck of the Irish running through their veins, or you are an abject simpleton who doesn't possess the brain power to put his pants on the right way around," Grainne said with deceptive cheerfulness. "Which is it?" she asked, smiling, even while her eyes narrowed dangerously.

Barock, one of Grainne's finest captains, knew that look very well. He'd seen her use it on others who'd failed to carry out her commands. He also knew that if he didn't tread carefully, his fate might be as terrifying as others who'd let her down.

"Well Grainne," he said calmly, as he looked down at his blue jeans. "The zipper's in the front, so I do know which way my paints go on. That means that they did have some good luck when our warriors attacked them."

The smile disappeared from her face, and her beautiful, dark eyes were as cold as ice. "And what form did that luck take, Barock?"

"They were lucky no one informed me that the girl was a mover," he said calmly.

"The teenager was a mover?" she asked, new interest sparkling in her eyes.

"Apparently not very strong yet. It was just enough to push her and the old guy for several miles, when we had them trapped. By the time our trackers caught their scent again, hours had passed."

"What about the old fellow?" Grainne asked.

"Nothing that would help them in a fight. Our trackers said his powers centered on working the land," Barock said with contempt.

Grainne walked up behind him and put her hand on his shoulder. Instantly Barock could feel sizzling heat where she touched him. His first instinct was to knock her dainty hand away from his shoulder, but he knew better. If he slapped her hand away, he would die a slow, burning death.

"I know you don't have much use for powers that are not related to fighting, Barock. But without those who can bring forth all manner of food to feed our hungry warriors, those always starving beasts would die very quickly. All magic is important to us in one way or the other."

Sweat began to bead up on Barock's face as the white-hot heat, from the palm of her hand, began to burn through his favorite leather jacket. He knew that in another minute it would be burning through his skin. He shifted his massive frame slightly and said, "When you're right, you're right."

Grainne watched him stay calm, even while sweat began pouring off his face. She couldn't help but admire his calm and cool attitude when death could be mere minutes away. He was a giant brute with thick, corded muscles, just like all her warriors. Unlike most of them, he had a sharp mind to go with the brute strength.

She let the heat sizzling from the palm of her hand just touch the bare skin of his shoulder. Slowly, she pulled her hand back. Ugly red welts bubbled up on his thick, gray skin, but he didn't move a muscle.

"You missed one other thing about the old man," Grainne said as she turned to glare at him.

"I'm listening," he said through gritted teeth.

"He was smart enough to keep the shotgun hidden until he was ready to shoot. He also…" she stopped, waiting for him to fill in the missing thought.

"He knew to shoot for the face," Barock said. "The one place on our warriors where a bullet could do instant damage."

"Exactly!" she shouted. "They aren't supposed to know about that vulnerability, but he shot him right between the eyes."

"The guy might be a farmer, but I never said he was stupid," Barock said. All you got to do is look at our warriors to figure that a head shot is the best move. Even a scatter gun isn't going to kill them with a body shot. He had time to watch the fight before he was attacked. He could see that the head was the vulnerable spot."

Grainne stared at him for several moments before she slowly nodded her head. "I came to the same conclusion. This is a weakness we need to overcome. Otherwise, our enemies won't even need magic to fight our warriors. They can just use the same weapon a lowly human would fight with."

Barock nodded and said, "There was another important point that was missed in this fight."

She had started to walk away but turned to look at him again. "I'm listening," Grainne said softly.

"We weren't fighting a little girl and a farmer out there," he said grimly.

"Someone's grandmother showed up as well?" she asked sarcastically.

"They were much older than that and a whole lot meaner," he said, anger building in his voice.

"Still listening," she said calmly.

"It was Eamon and that devil brat of his!" he shouted; all control now gone. "Eamon and Ashling are the ones that destroyed my warriors!"

"You lie!" she shouted, rushing toward him.

"See for yourself, Your Majesty. Two of our trackers survived the carnage, and it's all recorded in their mind tracks."

Grainne turned to the closest surviving tracker. The creature was badly burned, but still walking. She touched its head with her fingertips and instantly the battle scene filled her own mind.

She watched in stunned silence, while she saw the devastation that Eamon and Ashling unleashed on her best warriors. While that was fascinating in its own right, what really grabbed her attention was the young man fighting with them.

He wasn't an ancient of days who still looked young. This man was no older than his mid-twenties. Despite being so young, he fought with a wild abandon that was mesmerizing.

"It can't be," she whispered when she got a closer look at him. But it was the young man she thought she'd sensed inside her castle. "How could he know where to find our sanctuary?"

Even though this was very troubling to her, she also realized something that made her smile. If Ashling and her father were here, along with this mystery boy, then their own sanctuary must be close at hand.

Grainne put her hand on the still bubbling burn she'd inflicted on Barock's shoulder. In seconds, the wound healed over and disappeared.

She handed him two five hundred-dollar bills and said, "Go buy yourself a new leather jacket, Barock. "This one is ruined."

Barock smiled thinly and said, "As you wish."

When Grainne was alone, she narrowed her eyes and whispered, "It won't be long now, Ashling. I'll find Rundimahair and I'll destroy you and anyone else who dares stand in my way."

<hr />

"At least we brought young Ailbe and her Granda home safe and sound," Eamon said.

"Not to mention beating the ugly off those seriously gross beasties of hers," Sean said. "Where do those things come from anyway?"

"Believe it or not, they were once as fair and good as the residents of Rundimahair. We all were part of the same race in the beginning. We were sent to earth to watch over and help the mortals develop as the Creator wished them to," Ashling said.

"It was Grainne who got some of you to rebel?" Sean asked.

"It was a close ancestor of hers named Donal. He managed to take many of our brothers and sisters with him when he left. Eventually they lost the light that made them special. Over the centuries, many of them were mutated into the disgusting savages we were fighting. Grainne has accelerated the mutation, making them more grotesque and infinitely more dangerous."

"Not all of her followers have the curse upon them. Many others were recruited from the mortal world, which seems to exempt them from the curse," Eamon said.

"I thought they couldn't compel humans to do their will," Sean said.

"She doesn't compel them to follow her," Eamon said. "Her promises of wealth and fame are enough to lure them into her clutches. If they come of their own free will, then they have no protection against her powers."

"Then what about Grainne?" Sean asked. She looks like any normal young human female."

"Grainne is another story altogether. Somehow she has managed to elude the curse."

"Or she's figured out a way to hide the physical effect of the curse," Ashling said. "Many believe that she is one of the most powerful beings of light ever created, so she may well have the power to control the less desirable side effects of the curse."

"Don't be forgetting that just as many–or perhaps a few more–believe that you are the most powerful of us all," Eamon said.

Ashling shrugged and said, "It appears it won't be too long until we'll have to find out one way or the other."

"My money's on Ashling," Sean said, smiling.

"You haven't witnessed what Grainne is capable of," Ashling said grimly.

"True, but you've got a secret weapon that she doesn't have," Sean said.

"I assume we're talking about you," Ashling said, with a tolerant smile.

"Especially when we work together," Sean said.

"I second that notion," Eamon said, smiling. "The way you two fought together was nothin' short of amazing. Tis even more incredible when you realize you've only just started working together."

Ashling nodded in agreement, but she also felt uncomfortable discussing it. There was no doubt that they fit together naturally on any battlefield. During the recent battle, their reactions were very well timed and in perfect harmony. Any stranger watching would indeed believe they'd been fighting side by side for many years.

"Let's just hope we don't have to put our fighting prowess to the test against Grainne and her warriors for some time to come," Ashling said. "She has weapons of darkness that you've yet to see."

"You say that like you have seen them," Sean said.

The pause in the conversation was so long that Sean thought she might not respond. Finally she said, "I've not seen the details of all her growing powers, but I've seen enough to know I'm in no hurry to face them."

As he stared into Ashling's troubled green eyes, Sean felt his over confidence melt away. If a woman with the powers and gifts that Ashling possessed was worried, then he was going to worry twice as much.

The days and weeks that followed were spent organizing the residents of Rundimahair into fighting units. Actually, most were already divided into battle brigades, but it had been too long since they'd been put to the test. The younger residents had yet to be assigned.

Eamon and the Council realized they'd been lax in keeping everyone in fighting shape, since it had been centuries since they last fought for their very lives. They were now dedicated to making up for lost time.

The key to organizing an effective fighting force was in the blending and sharing of the right powers. Today they were focusing on cataloging the powers and gifts of their younger generations. Everyone from eighteen years of age and older would be part of the greatest fighting force they'd ever assembled.

Today, Ashling and Sean were training young men and women between the ages of eighteen and thirty. Much of the early training would involve helping them recognize powers and gifts they might have.

"We've been too slow to push our younger generation, Sean," Ashling said, as they watched training begin.

"I don't know about that, Ashling. Some of them look like they've got some serious powers."

"That's the point," Ashling said. "We have a very gifted younger generation, but they are nowhere near their potential."

"Can't change the past, so let's look to the future," Sean said.

Ashling glanced at Sean with furrowed brows but finally smiled and said, "Well said. We enjoyed so many years of peace that we've almost forgotten what it's like to be facing war in the near future. We can't get those years back, but we'll make the best of the time we do have."

"You're wise beyond your years," Sean said, smiling. "And that's a ton of wisdom, because you are really, really old."

Ashling smiled sweetly and then punched his shoulder hard enough to knock him off balance. Sean managed to keep from toppling to the ground as he regained his balance.

"Oh, I think I touched a sensitive spot. A little defensive about our age, are we?" he said, laughing.

"Age is meaningless to our race, Sean. By our standard of aging I'm still a young woman and you are still a brat in diapers," Ashling said.

Sean chuckled and said, "Fair enough, young lady. I'll make sure to never bring the subject up again."

"Probably for the best," she replied. "You do have a young girl closer to your age who has a serious teenage crush on you. Maybe you should set your sights on a youngster like that," Ashling said, arching one eyebrow.

"You mean, Albie?" Sean asked.

"Oh, so you can read her mind too," Ashling said.

"No, I leave the mind reading to you."

"I guess she's not one for hiding her feelings," Ashling said.

"You think?" Sean asked, smiling. "The first time we met she was making her interest very clear, and that was with Aengus right there beside her."

"Well then, there you go, Sean. You've got your future young wife all picked out."

"I was very careful to not encourage her at all," he said a bit defensively. "She's a sweet girl, but too young for me. I prefer a more mature woman but one still young enough to be interested in love and romance."

"I hope you find the young lass you're looking for then," Ashling said, sweetly.

"Judging by all the kissing and hugging you've thrown my way, I believe I've already found her," Sean said, chuckling.

Their romantic bantering was interrupted when a group of trainees began shouting for help. Sean and Ashling rushed to the small group gathered together. They were standing around an eighteen-year-old young man lying on the ground.

"What happened?" Ashling asked, as she knelt beside the young man writhing in agony.

"I'm not sure," a lovely, blonde-haired girl said through her tears. "We were sparring with clubs and I managed to hit him twice. The first hit was on his shoulder and wasn't that strong. He swung a hard blow at me and I moved behind him while he was off balance. I punched his kidney, and he went crazy."

A young, slender boy next to her said, "She's right, he just went berserk. David was shouting and screaming and then just fell on the ground and started rolling around."

Ashling had been examining David, while she listened to the girl and boy's explanation. "It's all right, Susan," she said to the distraught young girl. You didn't do anything wrong."

"Sean, please get everyone back at least fifty feet. I think I know what the problem is," Ashling said.

"You heard the boss lady!" Sean shouted, as he started motioning for everyone to get back. They responded quickly, seemingly anxious to get away from the struggling boy.

Ashling had already turned her attention back to David and placed her hands on his temples. She listened to his troubled thoughts for a few moments and nodded her head slowly.

She quickly began pounding on his chest and legs, while shouting angry words, in a language no one else understood. Ashling slapped his face multiple times while she continued shouting.

After a few moments, David began shouting, which quickly turned into a guttural growl. It appeared to the onlookers like he was having some type of seizure.

Slowly, his muscles began to ripple and twist as he cried out in pain and agony. Ashling touched his mind tracks, trying to control what was coming.

"Sean, I need you over here now!" she said urgently.

He rushed to her side and asked, "What is going on?"

"No time to explain. I need you to transform into your dragon-self right now!"

He was dying to ask more questions, but when Ashling spoke in this tone of voice, he did what she asked immediately.

Sean focused hard for several moments before he felt the change coming. He quickly morphed into his dragon-self and let loose a mighty roar. This is what always happened with the change. It was as if his dragon persona was celebrating its release from confinement.

As Sean's dragon-self flapped its massive wings and stomped around with thunderous steps, Ashling watched David very closely. His muscles continued to ripple and twist and turn even faster, while he screamed over and over. Slowly, the screams began to sound more like an angry roar.

"Okay Sean, give us a gust of fire!" Ashling said.

Sean raised his mighty dragon head and released a fearsome burst of white-hot flame into the air. The young trainees reacted in several different ways.

Some of them stood their ground and watched what was happening with fixed fascination. Others backed away and were silent, keeping a close eye on the massive red dragon which Sean had become. A few of them cowered and turned to run away as fast at their legs would carry them. Even though she was preoccupied with helping David, Ashling made a mental list of those who turned and ran. They would require special mental training before they ever went into battle.

David was now writhing on the ground in what appeared to be complete agony. His muscles bulged massively, and his skin seemed to turning a dark brown.

"Now Sean!", Ashling shouted, "Into the air with you!"

Sean burst into the air, rolling and twisting and turning as he flew. He released a series of fiery bursts as he roared his challenge to any and all dragons.

The effect on David was immediate. His young body convulsed as he twisted and turned even harder. When Sean roared out another fierce challenge, David's transformation finally erupted. To almost everyone's amazement, the young man burst into the air and began flapping his new wings.

"I knew it!" Ashling shouted, I knew it!"

The young trainees all gathered back around Ashling and watched in wonder as a long, slender dragon joined Sean in the sky. He was slow and a bit awkward, but he was flying!

"He's going to be a brownie," Ashling said.

"A what?" one of the trainees asked.

"He's a brown dragon!" Ashling said, smiling brightly. Not counting Sean, he's the first dragon to morph since we moved Rundimahair to America almost three hundred years ago."

"That is so cool," Susan said, smiling. "David's a dragon!"

<hr>

After flying together for several minutes, Sean recognized the symptoms of fatigue in David. He remembered them well from his own first time flying.

Suddenly, David began to revert back to human form. Sean saw what was happening and quickly flew under David, as the boy passed out and began to fall.

Sean slowly glided to the ground about fifty feet from where the trainees were gathered. Ashling quickly dismissed the children and asked them to be back at nine the next morning. She grabbed a blanket from the medical supplies on hand and rushed to David's side.

"That was totally amazing," Sean said, after Ashling had examined David and covered him with the blanket.

"You have no idea how amazing it truly is, Sean!" she said, as she watched him approach, while pulling a white t-shirt over his head. Apparently he'd heeded her advice about keeping a stash of clothes nearby for emergencies.

"I thought you said we weren't likely to see anymore dragons born to our people," Sean said.

"It had been so long since we'd had a new dragon that we all thought we'd see no more," Ashling said, with tears of joy in her eyes.

"This is a big deal, right?" he asked, as he knelt beside Ashling.

"Dragons were always what gave us the advantage over Grainne and her followers," Ashling said. "Without more of them, our chances of surviving a full out war with her were slim."

"So now our chances just got better," Sean said, with growing excitement. "I can't wait to start training David, and any others who might be born."

"You and I both," she said, smiling at him.

"So how come I came out full on red and he's kind of light brown. Is it because he's younger?" Sean asked.

She shook her head and said, "No, it's just a different breed than a red. Your red breed is the rarest of all dragons—and the most powerful."

"Oh, so David is not going to be as powerful as I am?"

"Don't get yourself all arrogant about it," Ashling said, laughing.

"No, it's not like that," Sean said, smiling as he took her hand in his. "I was just hoping for a really powerful guy to help us defeat the crazy woman."

"Yes, another red would have been amazing but don't discount our new brownie here. He's going to be a powerful dragon in his own right."

"Really? You call them brownies? That's kind of demeaning, isn't it?" Sean said.

"It's just what they're called when they are first born," she explained. "No one but a red dragon had better ever call David a brownie. As you know, dragon's tempers can be somewhat unpredictable."

"Especially those girl dragons," Sean said, laughing. Of course, that's the same with humans too."

"What do humans call guys like you?" Ashling asked. "Oh yeah, ignorant rednecks."

"Is that girl dragon humor?" Sean asked, as he slowly backed away.

"You're so lucky I have to get David back to town, Sean. Now close your ignorant yap before you say anything else offensive. I need you to fly our newest dragon home. After he's had a chance to rest up, and understand what happened, we'll announce it to everyone."

That's going to be awesome!" Sean said. "We finally have something to celebrate."

"It will be, but I'll be doing the announcing. I don't want you putting your big foot in your mouth again and getting everyone mad at you," Ashling said.

"Fair enough, darlin'," Sean said, laughing. "I do all the hard work and you get all the glory."

A small ball of dragon fire singed the seat of Sean's jeans. He glared at Ashling and asked, "How'd you do that?"

"Do what?" she asked innocently.

"Try to burn my favorite jeans."

"Oh, that. I was just reminding you to take those clothes off before you take David back to town," she said innocently. "You don't want to go through two sets of clothes in one morning."

"Good point. I've gone through a few outfits already since we started training. What I want to know is how you did that fire trick when you aren't in your dragon form."

"It's a little advanced for someone who's still a rookie dragon. When we start our class for teaching all of our new dragons, I'll teach you lots of tricks you don't know yet," Ashling said, smiling.

"There's only me and David, when it comes to teaching our new dragons," Sean said, while rolling his eyes. You've already been teaching me for a while, so I should be ready."

"There's only you two so far," she replied. "I have a feeling that we're going to be seeing more in the near future."

Sean was about to demand to hear more when he saw a gleam in her eye. She knew more, but she wasn't going to tell him anything until she was good and ready.

"Are you just going to stare at me all day or will you help David back to town?" she asked innocently.

"Fine, turn around so I can undress before I light up my dragon self. "Will you bring my clothes with you?"

Before she could answer, she heard an ear-shattering roar. When she turned back to where Sean had been standing, only his discarded clothes were there.

Ashling heard two mighty roars as she turned her gaze upward. There were Sean and David flying side by side toward town.

"You're going to regret flying again so quickly, David," she murmured. Her eyes widened when Sean did a series of arching rolls, leaving beautiful, circular trails of fire in the sky. "Ah well, Ashling said, smiling. "Boys will be boys and that's the truth of it."

Chapter Fifteen

Count your joys instead of your woes;
Count your friends instead of your foes.

~ Old Irish Saying ~

Grainne was not a happy woman. It had been a month since her troops had attacked Aengus and Ailbe. In that time there had been no significant progress in pinpointing where Rundimahair was located.

They'd been able to ascertain that it was somewhere in the Northwestern section of the United States—most likely Oregon, Washington, or Idaho. After the battle in central Oregon, she'd been sure her sworn enemies were in that state.

The problem was that none of the follow-up investigation in Oregon had provided any evidence they were hiding there. Reluctantly, she'd widened the search to include Washington and Idaho.

She wouldn't have included Idaho, since she felt they were more likely along the coast, but several reports they'd heard indicated two families living in Idaho were considered quite strange. More than once police had been called about strange lights and fire in the sky above their farms.

However, the last report led to a dead end. After an altercation with their nearest neighbors, both families had disappeared without a trace. When the police searched through their abandoned homes, it appeared that the only things they took were some clothes and personal effects.

There were no photos or personal mail. They left a lot of nice furniture behind, but there was nothing to indicate who they were or where they'd gone.

Her researchers believed they may have been families who'd left Rundimahair because of hard feelings. After being out in the mortal world for a few years, they suspected they'd gone home and made peace with their leaders.

She'd have them continue to search Idaho for other signs that Eamon's people–or anyone like them–were in Idaho. If they could find even one disgruntled follower who'd left Rundimahair, they could extract the location from them by any means necessary.

The problem was, they weren't finding anyone or anything. Not only was Idaho a dead end, Oregon and Washington gave up no leads at all.

When Grainne became too frustrated with the slow progress, she had to stop and remind herself of what happened in central Oregon. There was no doubt that Ashling, Eamon and their new wonder-kid, had been there.

It was possible they'd passed through time and space from somewhere far away. Grainne's gut feeling didn't buy it. She'd let some of her people follow up in Washington and Idaho, but she was using her best trackers in Oregon.

"We've got something in Idaho near the border of Utah!" one of her trackers shouted as she interrupted her musings by rushing into Grainne's office.

Normally, Grainne would have punished a tracker who dared enter her private office without permission. But the young woman's excitement was contagious, so she let it pass. "What have you got?" Grainne asked calmly.

"Someone connected to one of the families in Idaho is currently living in Utah."

"You have an address?" Grainne asked.

"Yes and no," the young woman said.

Grainne gave her a hard, impatient look and the tracker hurried to add, "It's not a street address, but we know where he is."

When the tracker paused again, Grainne seemed to flash across the room in a second. She pushed the terrified tracker up against the wall with her hand wrapped around her slender throat. She squeezed hard until the tracker's face began to turn beat red, while she gasped for air.

"When you bring a report to me, I expect it to be delivered quickly and completely, in clear, concise language," Grainne whispered in her ear. "You think you can do that?"

The terrified tracker began nodding her head vigorously. She knew she was seconds away from death if Grainne didn't release her strangle hold.

"Where is he?" Grainne asked quietly, as she released her death grip on the woman's throat.

"In jail, he's in the county jail!" the tracker managed to squeak, while gulping air into her lungs.

Grainne suddenly lashed out and struck the tracker hard in the temple. She collapsed in a heap. She was still breathing, but she'd wake up with a terrible headache.

"I'll handle this one myself," she said softly to the unconscious woman. "You stay here and rest."

Grainne noticed that the others currently working in the command center were keeping their heads down and focusing on the computer screen in front of them. She could sense their fear and unease, which was all right with her. It was good for her worker bees to stay motivated to do their best.

She made a showy display of standing up and extending her arms to the ceiling. Dark gray mist began to circle into the air around her until she was completely enveloped.

The clouds began to circle around her, slowly at first, then quickly gathering speed. Seconds later, the swirling mist slowed and finally dissipated completely. Grainne was no longer in her office.

While she streaked through time and space, she knew her sudden departure had been unnecessarily dramatic. She could have easily just disappeared in the blink of an eye, but she enjoyed being a little showy at times. Besides, it helped remind her subjects who was in charge.

Less than two minutes after she left her office, Grainne suddenly appeared in front of an occupied cell in a somewhat rundown jail in rural Idaho. The two officers on duty were momentarily stunned to see a beautiful woman appear inside their jail. Finally they leapt to their feet and reached for their pistols.

Grainne turned to them and said in a soft, pleasing voice, "Relax boys. Everything is going to be fine. In fact, you haven't felt this calm and peaceful in your entire lives. Why don't you both sit down in your comfortable chairs and lay your weary heads on the desk?"

She watched as a confused expression crossed the faces of the two deputies. Slowly, they began to relax and take their hands away from their pistols. They still had a slightly confused look on their faces, but it finally evolved into weary smiles.

They began to yawn as they sat in their chairs and rested their heads on their desks. Within a few seconds they were both in a deep, contented sleep.

Grainne smiled as she turned to the old man sitting on the small bed in his cell. "Sorry to arrive unannounced," she said calmly. "I didn't have your cell phone number to call ahead."

"Not to worry," the old timer said as he leaned forward to rest his elbows on his knees. "It's not like I don't know who you are."

"And who am I?" she asked.

"Anyone who ever lived in Rundimahair, knows very well who you are. You're the one and only Grainne," he said, smiling.

She nodded slightly and asked, "You know my name, so it's only fair that I know yours."

"I've gone by many names in my long life. Since I left Rundimahair, I've mostly gone by the name of Milton–Milt for short."

Grainne felt a thrill of expectation since the old man had twice mentioned he'd lived in Rundimahair. She forced herself to remain calm, as she said, "I've been looking for you for a long, long time."

"Well, maybe not me exactly," Milt said. "But I reckon you've been hot on the trail of my people for hundreds of years."

She was slightly puzzled by his calm demeanor and decided it might be because he was a rebel to his own people. Maybe he didn't care what happened to them anymore.

"I'm hoping you can help me with a project I'm working on," she said.

"I figured that's what you had in mind," he said as his smile slowly disappeared. "I reckon you know that me and my family and friends are deserters from our own kind. You probably figure we might be willing to switch sides."

"That would be the easy way, Milt. If you fight me, I'll still get what I need. The thing is, the way I extract the information would be needlessly painful for you and your loved ones," she said coldly.

Milt sighed deeply and looked into Grainne's cold gray eyes as he slowly nodded his head. "I kind of figured that would be the case," he said, suddenly looking very tired. "The thing is, there ain't no one else for you to threaten since I'm the last, lonely survivor of our little group of runaways. One way or the other, we've all met with an untimely end, except for me."

"Sorry to hear that, Milt. I was hoping to bring you all back home with me," she said.

He nodded and said, "We thought we knew everything back in the day. We ran off from our friends and family just so we could be free to live any old way we wanted to."

"We have that in common, Milt. I broke away from my people way before you ever thought about it. I won't say it wasn't painful, in many ways, but it was totally worth it in the end."

He nodded and said, "I wish I could say the same thing, Grainne. For the most part, my life has been full of sorrow and regret since I walked away from Rundimahair. Eamon and Ashling warned us that the consequences of leaving would be grim and permanent. The thing is that we just didn't want to listen. There were times when I hated Eamon but darned if he wasn't right about consequences. He didn't do anything to try to punish us when we left, we ended up punishing each other."

"It doesn't have to be that way for you, Milt. Come join with us and let me show you just how great life can be again," she said softly.

He stared into her demanding gray eyes for a long time before he said, "And all I have to do to join your eternal, joy-filled life is to betray everyone in Rundimahair. Believe it or not, I still got family there."

"The same family that cast you away for daring to disagree with the almighty Eamon?" she asked.

"That's how I thought of it at the time, but the truth is that me and my rebellious friends just wanted to do everything our way and we didn't much care if that hurt anyone else. They didn't cast me away. It was me who did the casting," Milt said.

"You can have a new family now, Milt. A family that understands not everyone has to be forced to think the same way."

"Where were you forty years ago when I might have believed you?" he said sadly. "The truth is, I don't much feel like a rebel anymore. I'd give anything to go back home and live out my days in peace there."

"But you can't go home, Milt. You've got one choice and that is to come with me," she said, her impatience beginning to show.

"Thought you might say something along those lines eventually, Grainne. I appreciate the offer, but the truth is I left myself one other choice."

Grainne abandoned any pretense of kindness or patience and said, "I don't have all day to debate philosophy. You're coming with me now, one way or another."

"There's the old witch I remember from the old days. You left because you wanted to be in charge of everything and everybody," Milt said.

"I still do, Milt! Now, are you coming the easy way or the hard way?"

"I think I'll choose my way, Grainne. I wish I could say it was nice seeing you again," Milt said, smiling, as red smoke began puffing from his eyes, ears and mouth.

It took her a moment to accept what she was witnessing before she screamed, "No you don't, Milt!"

She quickly engulfed him in what appeared to be a sheet of clear plastic. Whatever she was planning was going to be too little too late.

Milt laid back onto the bunk and smiled through the pain. Grainne saw his eyes melt away first, and then his entire face began to disintegrate. It looked like he'd dunked his head in acid, but Grainne knew what she was witnessing. Milt had built in a self-destruct fail safe for the day he might be captured by Grainne or some of her warriors.

He may not have made many good choices in his long life, but this one made up for a lot of the bad ones. Milt willingly suffered an agonizing death to be sure he'd never divulge the location of Rundimahair. He kept his final promise to never betray his estranged family.

"You ignorant fool!" Grainne shouted at the top of her voice. "I could have given you everything you ever wanted."

As the rest of his human body disintegrated before her eyes, she let her anger loose. Hurricane-force winds, coupled with massive strikes of gray lightning, erupted in an outward spiral.

The entire jail, along with the buildings on either side, were blasted into rubble. All electrical power was blacked out for a mile in any direction.

Grainne stood in the epicenter of the destruction she'd unleashed, still seething at being denied her greatest desire. Milt had the location of Rundimahair in his ancient mind, but had chosen an excruciatingly painful death rather than share it with her.

As she rose up out of the rubble, she wondered again how Eamon and Ashling were able to instill such incredible loyalty in their people. Even those who rebelled and left Rundimahair ultimately remained fiercely loyal to them.

While she streaked through space toward home, she realized that recruiting them to her side was a waste of time. The only way to win was to destroy them all–down to the last man, woman, and child. Only then would she find the peace she longed for and the absolute power she so desperately craved.

⁂

Training continued at a hurried but careful pace with the upcoming generation of gifted children and young adults. While the results were mostly gratifying, there were also disappointments, and there was much to do before they would be battle ready.

Testing had revealed that many of their students had the potential for gifts and powers that everyone had been unaware of until now. More than once, Ashling berated herself noisily because she'd neglected doing more in-depth testing on their youth in the past.

One evening she was bemoaning her failures when Eamon had heard enough. "Daughter of mine, hear me well. I won't listen

233

to another word from you on this subject. We all allowed ourselves to enjoy the years of peace and prosperity."

"But I knew better, Da," she replied earnestly.

"And I didn't? Saints preserve us, Ashling, we all knew better. And it's not like we didn't take precautions against being discovered."

"It appears that wasn't enough," Ashling said.

"It does appear so, my dear daughter. The point I'm trying to make is that we gave our all when we moved our beloved homeland to America. It was just a young, mostly undiscovered land, far from our own homeland. It took all we had to give to accomplish such a great task. We hoped it would be enough to keep us safe forever."

"Or at least three hundred years," Ashling said, nodding.

"Aye, that is true, my dear. With centuries of peace and plenty, I suppose we allowed ourselves to believe it would last forever. We should have been doing more and we both know it."

"That's what I've been saying," Ashling said.

"And I couldn't agree with you more if I tried. My point is that berating yourself day after day is not helping. In truth, it's hurting us. Our full attention needs to be on training our young'uns up so they can join with us in defending our new homeland."

Ashling sighed heavily and slowly nodded. "You're speaking truth, Da'. Sean's already reminded me that it's too late to change the past. My blubbering over lost opportunity is only slowing down our training."

"That's my girl," Eamon said, as he pulled her into a gentle embrace. "You and Sean keep working with our youth, and the rest of the council will keep working on the more experienced among us."

"You mean the old fogeys among us?" Ashling asked sweetly.

Eamon let her go and stepped back, as he said, "I prefer the term, experienced, my dear."

She laughed and said, "Me too, Da. After all, I'm one of those "experienced" folk myself."

"You don't look a day over one hundred and fifty," he said, ducking nimbly when she threw a couch pillow at him.

⚏⊠⊠⚏

"Your sweet, old grandma can move faster than that!" Sean shouted from where he stood on the ground.

David, in his dragon form, evidently heard Sean's snide remark. He quickly turned a graceful arch upward, before nose diving toward Sean at incredible speed. Just before he collided with Sean, David leveled off and singed the ground next to Sean with a decent-sized fireball.

"Not bad," Sean shouted, as David turned and shot back into the air with another burst of speed.

"He's really progressing fast," someone said from behind Sean.

He turned and wasn't a bit surprised to see it was Susan talking. Sean smiled and said, "That he is, Susan."

"I bet no one else has learned to be a great dragon as fast as him," she said, as her eyes followed his flight across the sky.

"He's a special young fellow, no doubt about that," Sean said.

Susan's brow furrowed as she stepped up beside Sean and asked, "Then why are you always so hard on him?"

"For the same reason Ashling is hard on me in my training," Sean said, smiling. "She wants to push me to be my very best, and I want to push David to be even better."

Susan was quiet for a moment before nodding her head, as she said, "I get what you're saying but isn't there a gentler way to bring out the best in him?"

"This isn't teaching them to play soccer or basketball," Ashling said, as she came to stand beside Sean.

Susan look startled to see Ashling, and looked at the ground as she replied, "I understand that, but can't we bring out our best in a more encouraging way,

Ashling sighed as she stepped over to stand by Susan. She put her arm around her shoulder and said, "We do encourage David, along with the rest of you. Everyone responds to encouragement differently. With you, all I have to do is suggest you try something and I know you're going to bust a gut doing all you can and then some."

Susan looked up at Ashling and slowly nodded her head. "You're saying that David doesn't necessarily do it that way."

"As much time as you've spent with David, I'm quite sure you know that is true. He needs to be pushed and challenged, from time to time, if we're going to make him the best dragon he can be."

"I know you're right, Ashling," Susan said softly. "It just seems a little mean-spirited sometimes."

"The rebels who are searching for us are as mean spirited as they come, Susan. It's going to take the best each of us has to offer to defeat them. We're in for the fight of our lives. How would Sean or I feel if we lost one of you in battle because we hadn't done our very best to prepare you?"

Tears began to well up in Susan's lovely blue eyes. She stepped forward and embraced Ashling without speaking. When she finally gained control of her emotions, she said, "I understand, Ashling."

"Good, because I'm going to push you just as hard as I can too," Ashling said.

Susan smiled and looked at Sean, as she said, "You yell at David all you want. I want him to be the best dragon that ever lived."

Once Susan had returned to the group of trainees, Sean said, "It's not fair that we have to be training these young kids to fight for their lives. They should be out having fun and enjoying life at their age."

"I agree, Sean," Ashling said. "If it wasn't for that psycho-woman, Grainne, we'd all be enjoying a more peaceful life back in Ireland."

Sean sighed heavily and said, "Yeah, reality is a bummer."

Ashling smiled as she stepped in close and put her arms around Sean. "Just the bad parts of reality are a bummer. Having the man I love at my side every day is actually a pretty great part of reality."

"That's a fair point," Sean agreed, as he put his arms around her and pulled her close. He kissed her long and tenderly.

A fireball landed ten feet from Scan and Ashling, as David flashed by. "Get a room!" he shouted, as he arched back into the sky.

The children laughed at David's remark, while pointing at Sean and Ashling. Sean reluctantly stepped back out of their embrace and said, "Have you noticed it's a bit of a challenge to find any privacy around here?"

"What did you expect when you signed on to teach a bunch of young'uns?" Ashling said with a patient smile.

Sean nodded and said, "I guess they're not so bad. I'd just like to find a moment or two of privacy to be with my girl."

"So that's how it is, is it? I'm your girl now?" Ashling asked innocently.

"For now and always," Sean replied.

His reply touched her heart deeply. Ignoring the children a moment longer, she leaned in and kissed him again. "I'll see what I can do to find a moment or two of privacy after dinner tonight," she said.

"Now there's a promise than can put the fire in a man's blood, so it will," Sean said, imitating her Irish accent, as he smiled brightly.

"So it should, Sean," Ashling replied with a teasing smile.

<hr />

In the early hours before sunrise, Sean's sleep was troubled by dark dreams. In truth, this felt more like a vision than a dream as he stood on beautiful, green, rolling hills overlooking ancient ruins.

He recognized the old castle ruins immediately. Hidden inside the crumbling walls was Grainne's sanctuary. Sean was unsure what sort of dark magic kept her people hidden from the eyes of the world. He assumed it was the dark magic version of what had kept Rundimahair hidden from Grainne for hundreds of years.

Just as he was about to walk down the hill, Sean felt his dragon begin to stir inside. Unbidden, he quickly burst into his dragon-self and arched up into the night sky. Other than the first time, he'd never turned into his dragon without any conscious effort on his part.

He flew over the old castle ruins, which he could see clearly, even though it was still dark. Not only could he see in the dark, but Sean could also see Grainne's hidden castle and grounds, which she'd created inside the ruins. He wondered if all dragons could see the normally invisible structures, or if it was it just him?

Sean landed softly on the castle tower, which was at least sixty-feet high, and sat just inside the tall, gated entrance. The main building, which he'd explored on his first visit, was in the center of the huge compound. Dozens of other large buildings sat along the back of the compound, spread out evenly.

In between the impressively designed buildings were spacious, open grounds, with beautiful gardens and large areas of luscious green lawn. It may have been created by dark magic, but it was a remarkably lovely sanctuary.

What puzzled Sean was the relatively small size of the compound. It was less than a third of the size of Rundimahair. Of course, Rundimahair was spread out with lots of land for farming, while Grainne's hidden lair looked more like a military compound. He wondered if she had more followers hidden elsewhere.

He silently soared over the compound, trying to commit it all to memory. Here and there Sean saw groups of guards on patrol. They didn't look up and seemed completely unaware as he flew over their heads. When two gray dragons flew past him, they didn't show any awareness of his presence.

Sean finally landed behind one of the buildings set against the rear wall of the compound. He wanted to change back into his human form, but for some reason he couldn't trigger the change.

While he struggled to complete the change, he heard the now familiar voice in his head saying, *"They can't see you in your dragon self. Some of her followers will see other dragons, but none will see you. Grainne may sense your presence in human form, but she will not sense your dragon. There is much to do, for you will attack her home base at the end of the ninth month."*

Once the voice had finished speaking, Sean's eyes opened and he realized he was still lying in bed. It had all been a vision. Sean locked in his mind the memory of everything he'd seen. It was obviously information they would desperately need.

Suddenly the door to his bedroom swung open and Ashling burst into his room. She rushed to the corner of his bed and sat down. Sean noticed she had a look of excited expectation on her face, but also a touch of irritation.

"First, tell me every detail of your vision. Second, tell me why you're having the visions now instead of me," Ashling said.

"Isn't there a rule about knocking before you enter a gentleman's bedroom? And I feel compelled to point out that your hair is a bit unruly at the moment," Sean said, smiling.

"My hair looks fine and quit being a baby. I've been in your bedroom before," Ashling said, as she ran her fingers through her hair.

"I could have been standing around in my underwear," Sean said in pretended outrage.

"Nothing I haven't seen before while you change back and forth from your dragon self," Ashling said, with a low chuckle.

"All right then, I'll get up", he said, as he sat up quickly.

When she saw bare skin to his waist, when he threw back the covers, she started to turn away. Then she caught sight of his Batman pajamas and relaxed as she said, "Batman-very stylish."

"Hey, Batman is cool," he said defensively. "Besides, they were a gift from a friend."

Ashling couldn't help but appreciate that Sean had filled out and added a lot of muscle. His upper body was lean, hard, and trim. "Put a shirt on you naked heathen," she said.

"You like it" he said, as he grabbed a t-shirt off his dresser and put it on.

"Yes, I do," she agreed. "Now tell me about the vision."

"How did you even know I had a vision? You ran in here a few seconds after it was over."

"I know everything. Now tell me the details of the vision."

"If you know everything, then I don't need to tell you the details. You already know," Sean said, smiling.

Ashling rolled her eyes and smiled as she said, "Tell me everything."

Sean yawned mightily and then began telling her everything he recalled about the vision. When he was finished, they were both silent for a few moments. She needed time to ponder all he'd said.

"This isn't where all of her people live," Ashling finally said. "It isn't nearly large enough to hold them all."

"That was the feeling I got too. This was more like a military base," Sean agreed.

"I've always believed that the majority of Grainne's people are still in Ireland. From what we've learned over the years, she has several bases like the one you saw in your vision. Although this is by far the largest," Ashling said.

"I suppose she's always suspected that you fled to America when you left Ireland," Sean said. "That's why her best warriors are over here."

"Unfortunately, that is true. What we need to do now is plan a strategy around your visions. They will be the key to our success in the coming battles."

"Not to upset you or anything, but why is it I am getting the visions since my dragon appeared? It was always you before," Sean said.

"To tell you the truth, that kind of bothered me too. Why bother to change the conduit for visions now? I suppose that as long as the visions come, it doesn't really matter who receives them."

"Probably has to do with my brilliant mind," Sean said, smiling.

"You wish," Ashling said, punching him on his shoulder.

"What is it with you and hitting people?"

"I don't hit people–just you," she said, leaning in to give Sean a kiss.

The kiss led to an embrace and gradually, much more passionate kissing. Ashling leaned into Sean until he gradually lay down on the bed, with Ashling on top of him. She felt a stir of passion and love that almost frightened her with its intensity.

They stopped kissing for a moment and just looked into each other's eyes. "This could get serious," Sean said, barely above a whisper.

"It already is Sean," Ashling said, leaning forward for another kiss.

Sean closed his eyes as their lips touched, and then something totally unexpected occurred. He felt Ashling's weight suddenly lift off him. He opened his eyes to see if she decided to calm things down a bit. To his great surprise and concern, Ashling wasn't in the room.

Sean knew she hadn't run out of his room because she hadn't made a sound. He'd also opened his eyes seconds after her weight lifted off him. He still got to his feet and rushed to the door.

When he swung the door open and rushed into the hall, Ashling was nowhere in sight, nor could he hear the sound of running feet–hers or anyone else's.

Chapter Sixteen

Count your smiles instead of your tears;
Count your courage instead of your fears.

~ Old Irish Saying ~

"It's been a long, long time, Lady Ashling," an aged voice said from the thick, black darkness.

Ashling was silent for a moment, while she composed herself. She knew this was outer darkness, where only the vilest spirits dwelled. It had been over a hundred years since she'd been here, and it was the same dark spirit that had called her from the mortal world a century ago.

"It has been a long time since you invited me to join you here," Ashling calmly replied.

"I'm sure the decades have passed much more pleasantly for you than for me," the scratchy, aged voice said.

"No doubt, grandmother," Ashling said. "We all make choices and sooner or later we all live with the consequences."

"You were always good with words, dear Granddaughter. It's one of the many things I admire most about you."

Ashling could hear the bitter tone in her aged relative's voice. She wasn't Ashling's grandmother. The old hag was her great grandmother, many times removed. Her given name was Cassiday.

Cassiday had been gifted with many talents and powers when she was called to go to the mortal world. At that time, only Grainne could match her powers.

Many generations later, Ashling was born into the mortal world. When she grew into her teen years, Ashling's powers began to blossom and grow. By the time she reached her thirtieth year, Ashling's powers rivaled both powerful women.

Grainne had long ago rebelled against the light and chose the powers of darkness as her path. When she realized how great Cassiday's powers would become, Grainne began a long, challenging process, which eventually corrupted Cassiday completely.

Cassiday was always drawn to the powers of darkness. For a time she managed to stay away from completely embracing them. She loved her daughter and grandchildren enough to keep her from falling completely away from the light. She also knew if she embraced the darkness, her family would be lost to her.

When Grainne openly recruited her to join the followers of Donal, Cassiday resisted for many long years. In the end, her desire to gain more and more power took control of her.

She joined Grainne with the promise that she would stand with her in defeating and ruling all of the Sidhe. This included Eamon, Ashling and all of the descendants of Orlagh who'd remained faithful to the true mission of the Sidhe.

"It must have taken many years and cost you much to be able to call me here again," Ashling said.

Cassiday was silent for a moment before she said, "You'll never know how high a price I paid to summon you. I know I'll never be able to do so again."

"That's good to know," Ashling said. "It's not my favorite place to visit."

"I remember a time when you loved to visit your dear old grandmother," Cassiday said bitterly.

Ashling could hear the undertone of sorrow in her grandmother's voice. "I remember a time when I loved you and you were worthy of that love," she said.

She knew the words stung, but she was long past worrying about being gentle with her evil ancestor. The fact that she dared to call her to the misery that was outer darkness, showed that her selfish instincts still ruled her mind.

"It was your choices that put you here for eternity, Cassiday. We tried everything to keep you from following Grainne. You chose her and the powers of darkness over your own family. You have no one to blame but yourself."

"How dare you talk to me this way!" Cassiday shouted as a blue flame began to glow in the dark.

Ashling watched as Cassiday let her dragon self loose. She could see the outline of the woman she'd once loved and admired. It was sad to see what she had become.

Her dragon-self was now black instead of the beautiful blue dragon she'd once been. Her flames were deep blue now and barely cast any light at all.

Ashling let her own dragon self loose and roared, as she released a mighty burst of hot, red flames. She heard creatures scurrying in the surrounding darkness, screeching in terror, as they desperately tried to escape the flames.

Cassiday released her dragon-self and hung her head in despair. She didn't even have the courage to look at Ashling's mighty dragon self.

"You're right, Ashling, I have no one to blame but myself for being trapped here. I brought you here with the last of my powers to seek your help. I know I don't deserve it, but I wish to serve the Sidhe again."

Ashling was shocked to hear such words from her grandmother. She'd been lost in bitter evil for so long it was nearly impossible to believe what she'd just heard.

"I know I can never come home again, after all that I've done wrong. But if I could help you defeat Grainne and her followers, perhaps the council would take me from outer darkness and let me serve my ancestors who've gone before me."

Ashling searched through Cassiday's open mind and realized that she was very sincere. Her grandmother was no longer strong enough to keep Ashling from reading her true intent. "I can't make a promise like that, Cassiday," she said quietly as she let go of her dragon self.

"Please keep enough fire to light the darkness around us. It has been so long since I saw anything but the dark."

Ashling's feelings softened somewhat toward her grandmother when she heard the desperate, pleading tone of her voice. She allowed a gentle light to continue emanating from her dragon self. "Tell me what you have in mind and I will see what I can do on your behalf. But hear me well, Grandmother. If this is some kind of treachery on your part, you will find out there are worse places to spend eternity than outer darkness."

"You know I speak the truth, Granddaughter!" Cassiday said in a shrill, panicked voice. "It is Grainne I will betray, not my family."

Ashling listened to the desperate thoughts running through Cassiday's mind, and she knew her grandmother did indeed speak the truth. Her time in outer darkness had finally broken the evil inclinations that put her here.

In a gentler tone, she said, "Tell me everything and tell it quickly. Time is short for Rundimahair. Grainne and her followers are many and they seek our complete and utter destruction."

"Yes, her ambition to rule all of the Sidhe is a dangerous obsession. I may have a way we can use that against her," Cassiday said hopefully.

"Tell me now, Grandmother. I can feel the powers you used to bring me here fading quickly. I won't stay much longer," Ashling said.

Cassiday began outlining her plan quickly, desperate to finish before Ashling was taken away. She knew this was her last chance to leave this eternal sorrow called outer darkness.

⁂

Sean was just about to start pounding on Eamon's bedroom door when he felt a rush of warm air behind him. He turned to see Ashling standing in the kitchen, looking as though she was about to collapse.

"Ashling!" he cried out as he rushed forward and took her in his arms. "Where have you been?"

"I'll explain it all later, my dear. Right now, just help me to my bed so I can sleep for a day or two," she said wearily.

Although he was full of unanswered questions, Sean could see she was on the verge of collapse. Without another word, he picked her up and carried her off to bed.

The next morning, in a turnabout from the normal breakfast routine in the Cahir household, it was Sean cooking over-easy eggs, bacon and toasting English muffins. Just as he was setting everything on the table, Eamon came in from some early morning work in the garden.

"Saints be praised! Do my old eyes deceive me? Sean with his apron on and cooking up a storm in the kitchen while Ashling sleeps 'til noon," Eamon said, smiling.

"Any more of that and you'll be making your own breakfast, old fella," Sean said, chuckling.

"Old fella is it," Eamon said as he sat in his usual chair at the head of the table. "I suppose I can't be arguing the truth of that young son. It looks like you're no slouch in the kitchen yourself," he added as he began filling his plate.

"I do my best," Sean said. "After what Ashling went through last night, I felt this was the least I could do."

"And don't think it's not appreciated," Ashling said, as she came into the kitchen, still wearing her pajamas, robe, and slippers.

Sean looked up and smiled since it was as rare as a full eclipse to see Ashling dressed so casually. He was impressed that she was still a rare beauty, even without the makeup and stylish clothes.

"So, what did Cassiday have to say for her no-good black-soul self?" Eamon asked.

Ashling looked up in surprise, as she loaded her plate with food, and asked, "How did you know?"

"There's only a rare few who could pull you into outer darkness against your will," Eamon said. "I can still feel it's dark presence on you now."

Ashling slowly nodded as she began eating with enthusiasm. "A fine spread you've laid out for breakfast, Sean. Thank you kindly, my dear," she said sincerely.

He beamed and smiled widely at her praise. "It's just a little something to build up your strength, Ashling. I could see from your condition last night that it had been a terrible ordeal."

"So, what did the old crow want?" Eamon asked.

"I have to say, I did not believe she still had the power to pull me into the darkness. Truth be told, it was almost more than she could bear. To hold me there for a few short minutes took a terrible toll on her emaciated mind and body. Despite all of the terrible things she's guilty of, I couldn't help but feel some compassion for her."

"Aye, you're a far better person than your stubborn father, my dear child. I can find no room for anything but disgust for that one. She turned against her own family, so she did. More than a few of them were murdered in cold blood by that she-devil. No, you'll not be seeing me shed a tear for her. Whatever pains she is suffering were brought on by her own evil deeds."

Ashling ate heartily while she listened to her Da. When he finished, she said, "I understand how you feel, Da, I really do. I'll not be forgetting or forgiving either, but I can still feel pity for such a wasted life."

"Will you tell us what she wanted?" Sean asked quickly before Eamon could let loose on another tirade.

"To put both of your minds at ease, let me start by saying that I scoured her dark mind so severely that she was crying out from the pain of it," Ashling said. "I had to know whether she was speaking the truth, and I know her words were indeed true."

"That's good enough for me," Eamon said solemnly.

"Me as well," Sean said, putting his hand over hers.

"Cassiday knows better than any of us how desperate Grainne is to destroy us. She has a plan to use that terrible ambition against her. Cassiday is also certain that Grainne won't be able to read her real intent because such discernment can only come from the light."

"Aye, she can read the minds of many who are not pure at heart," Eamon said. "But it may be possible for Cassiday to hold her thoughts deep in her mind tracks where Grainne would struggle to find them."

"That is her hope," Ashling said. She'll hide her true intentions under layers of bitterness and hate that she has built up over the years. We're hoping that Grainne will not try to look beyond those thoughts and pry any deeper. To find her true intent, she would have to destroy Cassiday's mind completely. Of course she's more than willing to do that to get what she wants, but she'll want to keep Cassiday alive until she believes she's actually found Rundimahair."

"So that's her dirty scheme," Eamon said. "It's a good one at that. Grainne will be so desperate to find us that she'll jump at the chance. It may well allow Cassiday to deceive her. But eventually Grainne will see through the ruse and destroy her."

"We only need her to believe she's found us long enough for us to attack her largest stronghold. Our plan is to destroy her fortress while she is chasing an illusion," Ashling said.

"And are we sure we know where to find her dark palace?" Eamon asked.

"May I touch your mind, Sean?" Ashling asked, pointing at his head.

"Be my guest," he replied, although he was still nervous about other people searching through his mind.

"I'll be gentle," she assured him.

Ashling closed her eyes and quickly joined minds with her father and Sean. She took Eamon through the memories Sean had from his spiritual journey into the bowels of Grainne's Ireland fortress.

When they were done, and she withdrew the contact that she and Eamon had shared, Eamon could only shake his head in wonder.

"Do you know how rare and wonderful a gift you have there, Sean?" Eamon asked.

"Ashling has told me it's a rare gift. To me it feels strange but also wonderful to be able to travel as my spirit self. Somehow, it seemed to work better and keep me safer while in my dragon form."

Eamon nodded and said, "That would hold true with what we know about our dragon-self. We are stronger in mind, body, and spirit in our dragon form. You're a special young man, Sean. I've always known this. But I had no idea your powers would grow so fast and deep."

"Perhaps so, but I'd still be shaking in my boots if I had to fight against Grainne one-on-one. When she sensed my presence in her castle, the first time I was there in spirit form, I thought for sure I was a goner," Sean said.

"She's a scary one, to be sure," Eamon said. "I don't know of anyone who could stand against her alone, excepting my own dear Ashling. Even then, I would never allow such a battle to occur. The one disadvantage Ashling would have is that she fights with honor and integrity as any great warrior should."

"You're saying Grainne may have the advantage because she'll use any evil trick ever conceived to destroy Ashling?" Sean asked grimly.

"Oh aye, she'd do that and more if she could," Eamon said. "It's hard to believe that someone who was once an honored leader of the Sidhe, is now the darkest, vilest creature who ever drew breath."

"I'm not above using a dirty trick or two if I must," Ashling said. "How we're planning to use Cassiday as a sacrifice, to distract Grainne, is not truly noble."

There was silence in the room for several moments before Eamon finally said, "There's truth in what you say, Ashling. I would only say that we're fighting a war not of our own choosing. If Grainne would turn away from her desire to destroy us, we could all live in peace. It is her dark ambition that forced us into a war for our very survival."

"Very true," Sean said. "Then we must add to that the fact that Cassiday came to us with this plan. We may be agreeing to use her to our benefit, but it is also to her benefit. Even if there's only a minute chance that she may be freed from her dark prison, she's willing to live with those odds."

"Well said, Sean," Ashling said. "When I pushed through her mind tracks, I knew that she'd rather see her soul destroyed than suffer eternity in outer darkness. After spending a few minutes in that dark place, I'm not sure I blame her."

"We're in agreement then," Eamon said firmly. "It is time to gather our people to council. We must prepare them for what is coming."

"Hope for the best and prepare for the worst," Ashling said.

"Exactly so," Eamon said.

"Are you going to change first?" Sean asked, smiling. "Even preparing for the worst may not be enough if they have to see you in your pajamas and that frumpy robe."

Ashling narrowed her eyes at Sean but couldn't hold back her laughter. Soon, Eamon and Sean joined in. They all seemed to realize that if this might be their last chance to laugh about anything for some time to come.

Grainne didn't usually sleep more than a few hours each night. Some nights she didn't sleep at all. It had been that way ever since she'd turned her back on her family, friends, and community nearly a millennium ago. Most nights she didn't mind not sleeping, but tonight she was feeling uneasy about the past. She'd much rather sleep than relive those dark days.

She'd joined forces with the followers of Danu and betrayed everyone who'd ever loved or cared about her. In the end, she'd even been forced to destroy her own family to prove her loyalty.

A man called Roderick had been the leader of Danu's Tuatha clan at the time. He'd laughed and howled like a mad wolf, when she burned down the home she'd been born in.

Grainne had been in her dragon self at the time, and the dark dragon seemed to lust after blood and death with a vengeance. By the time she came to her senses, she'd burned down the entire community she'd been raised in. Her parents, brothers and sisters, extended family and close friends had all perished that night.

Roderick couldn't resist the mayhem and joined her in his dragon form. He was the one who'd burned down everything in sight for miles around.

He'd welcomed her into the rebel community with open arms. She'd played the part of a loyal new member for two years. It took her that long to build up her own following among the Danu rebels.

When she was sure they could win, she'd ambushed Roderick and his soldiers on their way home from a raid on the Sidhe. They were tired and beat up from an unexpectedly difficult battle.

Grainne and her followers quietly surrounded them when Roderick had ordered his troops to stop and rest for the night. She waited until they were all asleep and then attacked from all sides.

The night sentries were killed silently before they attacked the sleeping soldiers. On quiet feet they crept into their unsuspecting camp and used their swords to slay them while they slept.

Grainne called out Roderick's name when she was leaning over him, watching him sleep. He was obviously fatigued from the battle because it took him several moments to finally open his eyes.

"Grainne," he said in a sleepy voice. "What are you doing here?"

"Taking my place as the rightful leader of Danu's Tuatha rebels," she said in a pleasant, soft voice. After a deep sigh, she added, "You're tired, so I'll let you rest now."

Roderick realized what was happening when the sounds of dying soldier's screams reached his ears. "How dare you!" was all he could shout before she plunged a long, black dagger into his throat. He grabbed the blade and tried to pull it out, but it only cut through his hands.

He realized she had somehow taken his dagger, which had once belonged to Danu. The sword, which was forged from the same dark magic steel, lay uselessly by his side in its scabbard.

She waited until the last spark of life left his now dull eyes before she pulled the dagger out. There were other ways to kill an immortal, but this had been the most satisfying.

Most of the time, Grainne could keep the visions of killing her family away from her mind. On rare nights like these, the cries and screams of her dying parents and siblings could still haunt her.

Suddenly she felt something else interrupt the night terrors she was experiencing. After a moment, she realized someone was trying to communicate mind-to-mind. It was extremely rare for anyone to come close to touching her mind tracks, but this one had unusual gifts for communicating mind-to-mind.

While keeping a strict guard up, she allowed a hint of the seeker's mind to touch hers. Instantly she recognized who it was. It had been a long time, but she would never forget Cassiday. It was a testament to the woman's power that she could even faintly touch her mind from outer darkness.

"What do you seek, old friend?" Grainne asked, mind-to-mind.

Grainne waited for a response, but it felt like static on an old telephone line. Finally, she heard a very soft, almost imperceptible message playing over and over in her mind.

"...found Rundi...I know...I can lead you...come to me...found Rundimahair!"

Grainne instantly threw back her covers and sat up in bed. Could it be possible that Cassiday had somehow located her hidden enemy? The odds against it were astronomical, but if anyone, other than herself, could locate their enemy it would be Cassiday.

She had extrasensory powers second only to her own. In some ways, Cassiday was even stronger. The fact that she was able to push through any type of message-from outer darkness-only proved her powers were still formidable in short bursts.

257

It would mean going through the terrible journey from here to outer darkness. Even someone with Grainne's great powers feared what waited there. It wasn't likely, but still possible that she could be trapped there. Was it worth the risk for what was likely the rantings of a deranged mind?

There were many enemies she'd destroyed who'd lost their souls to outer darkness. She was sure that Donal and Roderick were there, along with others she'd killed on her way to taking over the Danu's rebels. If they realized she was there and banded together against her... the thought made her shiver with disgust.

"Too dangerous. It's not worth the risk," she mumbled, as she lay back in bed. "Cassiday is likely in league with my enemies there, and they are waiting for me to fall into their trap."

Grainne rolled onto her side and closed her eyes, intent on forgetting about it altogether. Just as she was about to fall asleep, she heard it again. *"Grainne...time is short...come now or never..."*

⁂

Despite her very fierce, confident demeanor, Grainne couldn't help the shiver of fear and disgust that struck her. It had been centuries since she'd first entered the realm of outer darkness. It was one of the very few things that could still strike dread in her heart and mind.

Her fear arose from the fact that in outer darkness, she had little control. It was the great Creator of everyone and everything who had fashioned this dismal place. It was set aside for those who'd become so evil that there was no longer any hope of redemption for them. Grainne felt a shiver of fear and revulsion when she realized that description fit her perfectly.

It was why she'd set herself up to never leave the realm of the mortal world. If her physical body was ever destroyed, there was no doubt that her black spirit would spend endless eternities suffering in outer darkness. Being forced to pay for her terrible sins was the one thing that she truly feared.

Grainne forced herself to refocus on why she was here. She had to find Cassiday, finish their business quickly and leave this mournful plane of existence. When she forced her fears and uncertainties away, and focused on Cassiday, Grainne felt her presence immediately.

It only took her a couple of minutes to reach her. She'd ignored the other dark creatures lurking in the murky shadows. They all knew who she was and were wise enough to shy away from her as she passed by.

It was a shock to see how shriveled and emaciated Cassiday had become. Even though the sprits here were immortal by nature, the darkness had eaten away at them, leaving a sunken shell of what they had once been.

"I'm here, Cassiday. Let's get this over with as quickly as possible," Grainne said. She impatiently nudged Cassiday with her foot. Like many of the troubled spirits here, Cassiday was sitting on the hard ground, slumped against a rocky wall.

It took a few moments for Cassiday to gather her wits about her and struggle to her feet. "Sorry, I didn't sense your approach. The senses become dull and numb after existing in profound darkness forever," she said quietly.

"It hasn't been forever yet, Cassiday. If you are trying to deceive me in any way; I'll make sure that your suffering is compounded beyond your wildest fears."

Cassiday dropped to her knees and groveled at Grainne's feet, as she said, "No one knows better than me that I could not mislead you, even if I wanted to."

Without any warning, Grainne pushed into Cassiday's mind tracks with vicious power. The emaciated spirit, cringing at her feet, cried out in fear and pain. Grainne only pushed harder until she reached the core of Cassiday's mind tracks. It only took a few minutes to find what she was looking for. Grainne couldn't help but smile, even in this dark and sorrowful place.

"You see now that I spoke the truth," Cassiday said shakily. "Keep your part of our bargain."

"I see that you believe it is true," Grainne said. "If your information turns out to be good, then I will see what I can do to help you."

"But you said you would take me away from this place," Cassiday whimpered miserably.

"You should know by now that I lie much more often than I tell the truth. There is no way to leave this place once the Creator sends you here. There are things I can do to make your existence here more tolerable, if your information turns out to be true."

Cassiday began to wail and howl like a mortally wounded animal. Grainne pulled away from the grip she had on her leg and disappeared. She couldn't stand another moment in this place, and she vowed that she'd never return.

"It appears that Grainne believes what she took from Cassiday's mind," Ashling said, as she joined Eamon and Sean in the living room.

"How will we know for certain?" Eamon asked.

"When she attacks the false location we've established," Ashling said.

"But we hope to attack her own compound," Sean said. "We can't wait to see if she attacks the false location."

"We're not going to wait, Sean," Ashling said. "We're going to attack while she is gone on her wild goose chase."

"So we're that certain that she will attack?" Sean asked.

"She'll be there," Eamon agreed. "She's been waiting for this opportunity for centuries. Grainne wants to destroy us so badly that she'll never let this chance pass her by."

"I hope we're ready," Sean said.

"We've got to be ready, Sean," Ashling said solemnly. "Our time for preparation is at an end."

"May the Creator of us all be with us," Eamon said. "Let's gather our people together and do what must be done."

"As you wish, Commander," Ashling said.

Eamon smiled sadly and said, "I've always preferred Father over Commander."

"As do I, Father. Sadly, the time has come for you to put on the mantle of commander-in-chief. This calling must take precedence over all others," Ashling said.

"Aye, what you say is true and so it will be. Still and all, I don't have to like it," Eamon said with a sad smile.

Chapter Seventeen

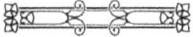

Everyone working at Grainne's large Northern California headquarters was doing their best to stay out of her way. On her best days, she could be amusing and even charming with her staff and followers. Considering her reputation as an evil warlord, it often surprised them when they saw her more pleasant nature.

Since she returned from visiting Cassiday in outer darkness, Grainne's good side was nowhere to be found. She'd been woefully impatient, surly, and short-tempered with everyone around her. While her bad moods had come and gone before, everyone thought she'd be thrilled to have finally pinpointed the location of Rundimahair.

Grainne did seem to be excited about finding her greatest enemies' location after centuries of searching in vain. But there was something about her incursion into the realm of outer darkness which had left her depressed and very short-tempered.

While she did realize that her behavior was unproductive, and might even be counterproductive, Grainne was struggling to shake off the fear that clung to her like a bad smell. Even though it had been a week since she'd visited Cassiday in outer darkness, the thought that she might end up there would not leave her mind. In truth, she'd prefer to cease to exist, in mind, body and spirit, rather than spend a single day in outer darkness.

"Carla," she snapped impatiently. "Have you located Rundimahair yet?"

"Not yet," Carla replied. "I've located the coordinates, based on what you gave me. The problem is, there doesn't seem to be anything there for miles around. It all appears to be farmland and rolling hills."

Carla was her top tracker and her talents were unsurpassed. Grainne had outlined everything she'd learned from probing Cassiday's mind tracks. She'd been confident that Carla would be able to locate her enemies quickly.

"I assure you it's there, Carla," Grainne said in a sugary sweet voice. "It's obviously hidden by their formidable magic, but that magic must be wearing thin after all these years."

"You're right about powerful magic at work in the area. It's so powerful that I couldn't see through it. I can feel the magic, although it's a variation I haven't come across before."

"That shouldn't come as too much of a surprise since they are protecting their lives and families with that magic," Grainne said sarcastically.

"I'm not really surprised," Carla said calmly. "I expected something powerful would be at work to hide them from us. The problem is, I can't work past it. I was about to suggest that you and I go onsite together and see if we can find a solution."

Carla's calm professionalism helped Grainne to get a grip on herself. She took a deep breath and exhaled slowly. "I like the concept," she said thoughtfully. "My only concern is that they'll feel our presence and be forewarned of our imminent attack."

"That's my worry as well," Carla said. "The problem is, we don't have any other option. You're the only one who has the powers to not only see through their defenses but also how to get past them."

After a few moments of consideration, Grainne said, "I think you're right. Go get some rest because we're leaving at midnight."

Carla nodded, while quickly grabbing her cellphone as she left the room. Once she was gone, Grainne muttered softly, "You'd better be right about this, for both our sakes."

"We're on," Ashling said suddenly.

"We're on what?" Sean asked.

"Grainne took the bait," Ashling said, smiling.

"How do we know that?" Sean asked.

"Could it be because I am a woman of unsurpassed magical ability?"

"I'd buy that," Sean said, smiling.

"It could be," Ashling said, returning his smile. "But in this case, we have someone on the inside."

"You mean we've got a spy in their midst?"

"We used to have several," Ashling said, as she stood and stretched. "But Carla is the only one left. Fortunately for us, she is also the closest to Grainne. I was reasonably sure Carla would be involved because she is the best tracker they have. She wouldn't leave the search for our hidden city to anyone else."

"So, if we have someone inside her organization, doesn't it stand to reason Grainne may have a mole among us?" Sean asked.

"It's very rare, but we've found a few over the years," Ashling said. "We usually discovered them when they try to get information to the outside world. It's impossible to get a message out while inside of Rundimahair. Anyone who leaves, for any reason, is tracked closely. Fortunately, we intercepted them before they could betray our location."

"What happens to them when they're caught?"

"What do you think, Sean? We're talking about the survival of our people. A traitor deserves and gets a quick and sudden death."

"When was the last time that happened," he asked thoughtfully.

"I executed the last one over a hundred years ago," she said.

"That must have been difficult for you."

"Indeed it was, but I have no regrets. They were trying to sell out their own families and loved ones. They left us no choice," Ashling said.

"I suppose the same would be true for this Carla if Grainne discovers she's a traitor," Sean said.

"Only her death would be slow and painful over the course of several days. It would also be done in front of everyone, so they understand what happens to a traitor."

"Then let's hope she isn't discovered," Sean said uneasily.

"I've put a protective mind block and false memories in Carla's mind that even Grainne shouldn't be able to penetrate. So far it's kept her safe."

"She must be highly motivated to live with such a risk day after day," Sean said.

"Her motivation is her husband and two children, who live two blocks down from our house."

"I can't think about that anymore or it'll drive me crazy," Sean said with a furrowed brow.

"Join the club, my dear," Ashling said as she leaned in and embraced Sean. "I pray every day that the Creator will watch over her and bring her home safely to her family."

"The same thing I do for you each time you leave," Sean said as he embraced Ashling.

"And I you, my love," she whispered in his ear. "Right now we'd better get some rest since we're going to be at our fake headquarters before midnight."

"You mean she's coming all the way from Ireland tonight?"

Ashling smiled and said, "She has a small compound in Northern California where they're staying now."

"Maybe we should just attack her there. They'd never expect that," Sean said.

"Too risky and the chance of success is small. She always has an escape plan in place wherever she goes. If we attacked, she'd be the first to leave and let her people die alone. If we can destroy her main compound in Ireland, we'll also destroy many of her followers. That would give us something even if we happen to miss her."

"I suppose you're right," he said thoughtfully. "But I really want to make sure we get her. You know what they say, if you want to make sure the snake is dead, cut off its head."

⊷◁ ▷⊶

"I hope she didn't bring half her army," Sean said, as they approached the counterfeit Rundimahair site.

"She won't bring many of her forces until she's sure this is the right place. I'm guessing they'll be no more than a half dozen of her best warriors," Ashling said.

"If they're anything like what we've fought before, maybe we should have brought Eamon," Sean said.

"First of all, we aren't planning on fighting them. We're only leaving a trail to make them believe this is Rundimahair. Aside from that, Da and I can't be in the same battle unless it's absolutely necessary," Ashling said.

"Don't want to lose both of you in a single fight?"

"Exactly so."

"So, I'm expendable, is that it?"

"Stop being a baby. We're not fighting tonight. We're just setting a false trail that will feel recent to them. If all goes well, we should be long gone before they arrive."

"Famous last words," Sean grumbled.

***

"This is it," Ashling said softly, when they arrived at the false site in Idaho.

Sean looked down and could see clearly in the dark night, since he was in his red-dragon self. Ashley was flying alongside him but suddenly swooped downward.

"It does kind of look similar to the land around Rundimahair," Sean said softly, when he glided in beside her.

"That was the plan," Ashling said. "Except this is in Northern Idaho, instead of on the Oregon coast."

"I can feel the magic from the protective shield," he said. "It's strong, but not as strong as the shield at Rundimahair."

"We don't want to give away all of our secrets," Ashling said. "This is a very powerful shield, which should be convincing. It's the same shield we had over Rundimahair until a hundred years ago."

"It might make her feel overconfident if she realizes your magic hasn't grown much in the past century," Sean said.

"Exactly the point. We want to convince her and keep her overconfident. That will be to our advantage if she ever does find the real Rundimahair," Ashling said.

"Wait! I can see homes and other buildings down there," Sean said.

Ashling gave him a surprised look and said, "Your powers really are growing. I didn't think you could see through this shield."

"Piece of cake," he said, although he'd had to really push his powers to penetrate the shield at all.

"We've built an illusion of a town similar to Rundimahair. We even have farms, rivers and streams built into it."

"Totally awesome," Sean said. "I wish I could do that kind of magic."

"We all have our own talents, Sean. Illusionary spells just aren't your strong point."

"Not yet," he said. "Just give me a little time to learn that stuff."

"Okay Mr. humble. Let's do a series of routes above the town. I want it to look like a lot of dragon traffic has been coming and going. I'll make some of the traces old and faint and others like they just happened earlier tonight."

"Man, it's so great to have you for my honey babe," Sean said.

Ashling was about to complain about his new nickname for her, but on second thought she decided that she kind of liked it.

Instead, she just said, "Let's crisscross each other's patterns, and then I'll do the work disguising them."

They spent the next hour flying routes across the valley above the phony Rundimahair site. On some of the runs they broke through the barrier. This would make it appear as though the Dragons were going in for a landing inside the protected city.

When they developed the false site, they'd added entrances from the air and from the road. They'd taken the time to move trucks full of equipment in and out of the area. This movement would be detectable to someone with Grainne's powers, although it would push her limits.

The idea of the subterfuge was to give Grainne the impression that it was an active site. She would be able to catch a vague impression that this was a hidden city protected by very powerful magic.

They wanted her to have to work hard and use all of her great powers to detect it. If it pushed her magical limits, she wouldn't suspect it was a trap. It was a fine line between making sure she found it, while she also believed only someone with her great powers could detect the hidden city.

"That should do, Sean," Ashling said, after they finished flying their routes.

"You think we've done enough?" Sean said.

"I can barely detect the site, and I know it's there," Ashling said.

"If I were here by myself, and didn't know it was there, I'd never find it," Sean said.

"That's good to know since your magical abilities are growing so quickly. It's getting to the point that only a rare few still exceed your powers," Ashling said.

"And Grainne would be one of those rare few?" Sean asked as they began to fly away.

"Let's hope so. Otherwise all of this hard work will go to waste," Ashling said.

"You're sure this is the area?" Grainne asked doubtfully.

"It's got to be close," Carla said.

"We've been at this for hours with no hint of anything," Grainne said. "If this keeps up, we'll be flying around in broad daylight."

"Wait! I can feel something," Carla said. "It's that feeling I had before of rare and powerful magic at work."

Grainne was about to say something sarcastic, but took a deep breath and let go of her frustration and doubts. She realized she'd been flying around with the attitude that Carla was wrong and Cassiday had given them bad information.

She slowly spiraled downward over the open fields surrounded by rolling hills. All outside thoughts and doubts were banished from her mind. Her entire focus was on seeking any touch of magic in the air.

Suddenly, Grainne arched quickly to her right and weaved back and forth. After crisscrossing the sky several times, she pulled up and soared back to where Carla waited.

"Anything?" Carla asked.

"You know for a slow moving gray dragon, you do all right, Carla."

Carla smiled and said, "You found it!"

"Dragon trails," Grainne said, smiling. "They're faint but unmistakable. I've locked onto the magic concealing them. You were right, it's some serious stuff. Even with all my powers of detection, it's taken hours to just get a whiff of it."

"If it's that strong, will we be able to break through it?" Carla asked.

"It's going to be a serious challenge, but there is no doubt I can break it down."

"What now?" Carla asked.

"I've got everything I need to prepare for the final assault," Grainne said, showing a wicked smile which bared her viciously sharp and deadly dragon teeth. "Let's head back."

Grainne was a magnificent, black dragon, which was even more rare than a red dragon. As far as she knew, she was the only black dragon still alive.

"Wait up," Carla grumbled as Grainne streaked across the sky.

In response, Grainne's voice echoed in her mind, saying, *"I'll meet you back at the base. I've got too many things to do to wait for a slow gray dragon."*

Carla felt insulted, but she was glad Grainne had surged ahead. It would give her a chance to check in with Ashling.

Sean and Ashling were already back home when she felt Carla's mind touch hers. *"She bought it!"*

Ashling did a return touch on Carla's mind for just a second. It was enough to let her know she'd received the message. They didn't dare leave any traces of Ashling in Carla's mind. Grainne could and did access her mind from time to time.

Carla's message also confirmed that Grainne would lead the assault on the false Rundimahair site. The good news there was they were now certain that Grainne was locked in on the false site. The bad news was that they wouldn't be eliminating her when they attacked her main compound in Ireland.

When Ashling confirmed this to Sean, he asked, "Why don't we attack her when she's occupied at the Idaho site?"

"I've contemplated the same question. I'm not sure why, but I know we're supposed to hit the Ireland compound instead," Ashling said.

Sean sighed and said, "Yeah, I got the same feeling when I had the prophetic dream about her stronghold over there."

"Those types of promptings have never led us down the wrong path," Ashling said. "Since you and I were both told to attack Ireland, we're going to trust the Creator has his reasons."

"I know you're right and all," Sean said with a downcast expression. "I would just like to take her out sooner rather than later."

"It's a frustrating situation to be in, but I believe there's a good reason why we're supposed to attack the Ireland site. We'll get her eventually, Sean. If we ignore the guidance we're given, we could be going into a disaster that we know nothing about. For now we stick to the plan and attack the Ireland compound," Ashling said.

"I'm with you all the way," Sean said. He embraced Ashling, kissing her passionately. When he finally came up for air, he asked, "Are we married yet?"

Ashling let out a deep sigh as she rested her head on his chest. "Not yet. Let's both get through this attack in one piece. Once we're back home safe, it will be time to remedy that situation."

"Just so I'm sure that I understand all the rules," Sean said with a quiet smile. "When we angels of light get married, we get to sleep in the same bed, right?"

Ashling looked up into Sean's fierce blue eyes and said, "Heaven help anyone who tries to stop us."

"Amen to that!" Sean said.

Chapter Eighteen

These things I warmly wish for you-
Someone to love
Some work to do
A bit o' sun
A bit o' cheer
And a guardian angel always near.

~ Old Irish Saying ~

"How many dragons did you say they have?" Sean asked nervously?

"Well now let me see," Eamon said. "If we assume Grainne will bring all but a few of them with her; I'd estimate they'll be no more than a dozen for us to deal with."

"A dozen?" Sean asked nervously. "I know we're fighting on the side of the angels and all, but we've only got eight dragons altogether."

"True enough. But their dragons are all grays except for Grainne–who is the only known black dragon in existence. You've fought the grays before, Sean. They're no match for a red, green, brown or blue dragon."

"I understand that, Eamon," Sean said. "The thing is, they could double or even triple team us with their browns and grays. On top of that, most of our eight dragons are young and inexperienced. They are still learning how to deal with their dragon-selves."

"What you say is all true, Sean," Ashling interjected. "That's why we're only bringing two of them with us."

"Says who?" Eamon asked with a furrowed brow.

"I already told you this, Da. Even the two we're bringing don't have any battle experience," Ashling said. "Those who have just released their dragon selves would get slaughtered against their experienced grays. I mean, it's not like we are all red dragons."

"True, but a brown dragon will whip a gray dragon anytime and anyplace," Eamon said.

"Experienced browns would. These new dragons are not ready to fight."

"Nor was I when I went into battle for the first time," Eamon said stubbornly. "If I say so myself, I did pretty well on that dark day."

"Come on, Da," Ashling said wearily. "You had a full year's training before your first battle. On top of that, you were surrounded by experienced dragons who kept an eye on you."

"And how do you know all about my first battle since you weren't even born yet?"

"From Mom and from you! You both told me the story often enough." Ashling said with growing irritation. "You know as well as I do that it's not fair to compare your first experience in battle what these children can offer."

Sean decided it was time to intervene between father and daughter, even though he really didn't want to get between them when they were arguing. At this point, he had no choice.

"I've got to side with Ashling on this point, Eamon. Other than David and Susan, the others who've recently accepted their dragon selves are not close to being ready. Even with those two, I wish we had more time before they're thrust into battle."

"Didn't you say that Susan is a golden dragon?" Eamon asked.

"That she is, and her powers are already exceeding our brown dragons," Sean said. "While she has awesome potential, there's no way she should be going into battle without more training."

"We have no choice but to bring David and Susan with us," Ashling said. "Bringing the other six young dragons into battle before they're ready would be like killing them ourselves. It's nothing short of a miracle that we're seeing new dragons after centuries without even one. We can't sacrifice this gift from the Creator to their own inexperience."

Eamon was silent for a few minutes, while he stood on the training grounds watching the newest dragons trying to complete very basic fighting drills. As much as he wanted to argue the point, he could see that Sean and Ashling were right. They wouldn't last for five minutes against Grainne's more experienced and ruthless dragons.

"Aye, I see the truth of what you're saying, Sean and Ashling. Even David and Susan will struggle in a real fight," Eamon said, dejectedly.

"Tis true," Ashling said. "So, Sean will fly with David and I will fly with Susan. We'll fight as teams to help offset their inexperience."

Eamon sighed and said, "Ashling, I should be going with you since no one has more battle experience than your old Da'."

Ashling stepped in and hugged her Da close as she said, "Truer words were never spoken, but we can't take the chance. If we were both lost in battle, it would be the beginning of the end for our people."

Eamon stepped back and looked at Ashling, his eyes filled with sadness. Finally, he nodded his head slowly and said, "You're right as rain, my dear, but I don't have to like it and that be the truth of it. You and Sean come home safe along with the young ones," he added with his voice choked with emotion.

⚜

"So, we're sure this thing is safe?" Sean asked nervously.

"You've traveled by portal with me before, Sean," Ashling said patiently.

"That's true, but this time we're traveling across the ocean. We're also taking five hundred of our people with us," Sean said.

"Faith and begorra, Sean. Do you trust me or not?" Ashling said impatiently.

Sean was silent for a moment before saying, "When you put it that way, I'd have to say open the portal and let's get this done."

Truthfully, Ashling hadn't opened a portal of this size for a hundred of years. The principle was the same regardless of the portal size. The difference was that it required massive amounts of power.

In the past, she'd relied on Eamon to strengthen her own great powers. This time it would be Sean lending a hand. It was their best chance since his own magical powers appeared almost unlimited.

"All right then. Let's get on with it," she shouted to her troops. "Sean, it's just like we practiced it. You stand behind me and wrap your arms around my waist."

278

"I like this part," Sean said as he took his place behind her with his arms around her waist.

"Typical man," Ashling said, smiling. "Once I get the portal open, you join your powers to mine." She turned and looked at Eamon and said, "Da, when we open the portal please keep everyone moving through it as quickly as possible."

"Will do, my darlin' girl, and may the Creator be with you all," Eamon said solemnly.

Ashling nodded in return, as she glanced back at the five hundred warriors lined up in columns behind Eamon. It was a comforting sight, but she also felt a pang of worry. All of their fates were in her hands.

As if he could read her thoughts, Sean said, "We've prepared them well, Ashling. They'll do their best and so will we."

"True and true," she said, as she put her hands over his. "It's time."

Ashling raised her hands high above her head and began reciting the incantation that would open the portal. Almost immediately Sean saw the air in front of them begin to swirl in a circular motion.

Within minutes, the center of the circle opened, and they could see green hills in the distance. Initially, it looked like the hills were shrouded in a gray fog, but as she pushed her powers deep into the opening vortex, the distant green hills of Ireland became clearer.

Ashling felt the terrible strain on her powers as the portal opened to a four-foot circumference. "Now Sean," she said in a strained voice.

Quickly, the painful pull on her powers began to ease. Sean's powers still amazed her whenever she felt the incredible depth of his magical strength.

Working together, Sean and Ashling pushed the portal opening until it was a swirling ten-foot circle. When Eamon was satisfied with the size and strength of the portal opening, he gave the order for their warriors to advance.

No matter how many times he'd witnessed it, Eamon was still in awe of his daughter's powers to open a portal. It allowed them to travel thousands of miles in a few short minutes. He was grateful that Sean was helping her since his formidable powers took much of the strain off Ashling.

Eamon watched with great pride as the columns of their best warriors hurried through the portal. When Eamon saw Sean and Ashling about to pass through the portal, he turned and spoke with one of the trusted council members. Although the council member couldn't hide his surprise, he smiled and nodded in agreement with his old friend.

In the night skies over Idaho, another portal was opening. Instead of a soft white vortex, this portal was as black as a dark, stormy night. Within moments, hundreds of huge, powerful, misshapen beasts passed through the portal. Once through the portal, they marched onto the hilltop a few feet below. Right behind the columns of warriors, ten fearsome dragons rushed through the portal and began circling the hilltop in the cloudy afternoon sky. Leading the swirling dragons was a massive, powerfully built, black dragon. Despite its size, the black beast moved with the grace and speed of a hawk.

The impressive and terrifying black dragon elegantly swirled downward and landed softly on top of the hill. A streak of light, similar to a lightning strike, flashed for a few seconds. When the light disappeared, Grainne was standing where the dragon had been moments before. She didn't really need the lightning strike to complete the transformation, but she couldn't resist the dramatic touch.

It was an isolated valley with only one old road providing access in and out. Even so, Ashling had placed a concealment spell over the valley, to hide their presence from any foolish humans who might try to interfere. She didn't want any bystanders watching when Grainne unleashed her vicious attack.

"You all know why we're here," Grainne said. "The last of our sworn enemies are hiding in the valley below. When I breakdown their defenses be ready to attack quickly and without mercy."

The horde of monstrous warriors pounded the staffs of their spears onto the rocky surface in unison, acknowledging their understanding and approval. It would have been a terrifying sight if their enemy had been present to see the terrible blood lust in their dull, gray eyes.

Without another word, Grainne returned to her dragon form. Ten dragons quickly appeared at her side and they flew off together. The dragons and the monstrous troops were united in their desire to destroy their old enemy.

⁂

Ashling's portal opened in the forest on the west side of the remains of an ancient castle. They wanted the concealment of the thick forest as a staging area for their attack.

281

She tried to place the ruins she was looking at, but they didn't seem to fit any of her memories of the ancient ruins of Ireland. While they looked genuinely ancient. something about the ruins seemed unnatural to her.

"I've not heard of or seen theses ruins before," Ashling said quietly.

"Are you telling me you know every ruin in all of Ireland?" Sean asked.

"That I do, Sean. The history of Ireland has long fascinated me. I've had a long time to study them closely."

"Okay, I'll take your word for it, since you are much, much older than me," Sean said.

"You left out the important part of that statement," Ashling said.

Sean smiled and said, "I didn't leave it out. You interrupted me before I could say that although you are as old as the hills, you actually look younger than me."

"Thank you. Although I could have lived without the 'old as the hills' part," she said, smiling.

"Good to know," Sean said. "So, if it's not a real castle, why would Grainne have put it here?"

"It's good cover, I suppose," Ashling said. "If anyone ever did happen upon her home base, they would only see another old pile of castle ruins. They wouldn't be likely to look any further."

"It makes sense, although it seems like it would just draw tourist to this area," Sean said.

"Did you not see the no trespassing signs?"

"Nope, where are they?" Sean asked.

"I see three of them from here. I'm guessing there are more on the other side and out front," Ashling said. "I've no doubt that she owns all the land within fifty miles in any direction."

"I guess that makes sense. Even if they did trespass, all they would see is old ruins. What's inside seems to be protected by some seriously powerful magic."

"I can feel waves of dark magic circling the valley and we're still nearly a half mile away," Ashling said. "That means we're going to have to watch and listen for magical traps. We don't want to set off any alarms if we can help it."

"You go first," Sean said, smiling.

"Trust me, I was planning to all along. You're sensitive to magic for a newbie. But I will sense things that would go right past you."

"Humble and beautiful," Sean said, smiling. "A rare and appealing combination."

Ashling smiled. She appreciated Sean using humor to ease the extreme tension they were under. She touched the minds of each group leader and ordered them to spread out and prepare to attack.

When they reached the edge of the woods, Ashling ordered everyone to stop. She searched the ruins carefully by letting her powers slowly roll over the ancient ruins like an invisible fog. After a few minutes, she shook her head in frustration.

"What's wrong?" Sean asked quietly.

"I'm not sure," Ashling replied. "I can sense Grainne's dark magic cloaked over the ruins, but I'm having a hard time finding the opening to her hidden compound."

Sean touched her mind with his and let their powers blend together. "It's right there," he said, pointing to an archway off to their right.

Ashling couldn't hide her surprise when she realized he was correct. "How can you see it if I can't?"

"Because I have been inside once before. It was in my vision—remember?"

She nodded her understanding. Ashling continued to focus on the archway Sean had pointed out. Suddenly, she saw a dark blue, magical gate shimmering in the archway. "Okay, I see it now. It looks like the gate is protected by at least three dark spells, blended together."

"So, it's probably not going to want to open even if we ask nicely," Sean said.

"We're not going to ask nicely, but I promise you that it's going to open," Ashling said.

Mind to mind, she ordered their warriors to stand ready and wait for her signal to attack. When she was sure everyone understood her order, Ashling and Sean quickly covered the ground between the edge of the trees and the gate.

Ashling began pushing spells at the magically locked gate. After going through a dozen spells, she frowned and said, "Grainne's put something diabolical into this protective spell."

Sean could see her growing frustration. Suddenly, he felt a strong urge to reach out and touch a large stone in the support column for the entry gate. It took a moment for him to recall this stone from his vision. Without hesitating, he reached out and placed his right hand on the stone. Immediately, it began to glow a soft, white light.

"What in blue blazes do you think you're..." Ashling's panicked rebuke stopped when she saw the stone quickly release a blinding white light over them. Immediately, the blue, shimmering light on the gate began to blink rapidly and then go out altogether.

He pushed hard on the gate and it opened easily. Sean looked back at Ashling and said, "Beginner's luck."

Ashling watched in amazement while Sean pushed the heavy old gate all the way to the side. "Ladies first," he said, smiling.

She couldn't help but smile back as she walked past him and said, "Did I mention how happy I am that you are here with me?"

"We're a great team," he replied as they hurried forward.

Once they passed through the dark magical barrier at the gate, the illusion of old castle ruins began to dissipate. In its place stood a stunningly beautiful, modern-day castle of immense proportions.

When Sean saw Ashling's reaction to the beautiful home, he said, "Pretty amazing, isn't it?"

"It's incredible. Can we take it home with us?" she asked.

"Wait until you see the rest of the place. It stretches out for miles. Down there are the industrial, military complexes. Over there," he said, pointing to the apartments and barracks area, "is where they house much of her army."

"I would have loved to see all of this in the daytime," Ashling said. "Grainne has built an amazing home for her followers. I actually hate the thought of destroying it."

"Let's focus on the industrial and military areas first. Maybe we can leave the housing complexes and the castle alone," Sean said.

Ashling stared at the castle for a long moment, before shaking her head. "I'm not sure why, but the castle has got to go. There's something very dark and ugly in the fortified basement."

Sean shivered as he thought of some of the ugly, terrifying creatures he'd already had to fight. He also recalled his scary visit to the basement in his spirit vision. If the basement area had anything to do with creating and housing the deadly savages, then it had to go. "I'm with you on that," he said grimly.

Ashling nodded thoughtfully as she touched minds with her captains of one hundred. Each captain was responsible for the hundred warriors under their command.

Sean heard her mind-to-mind communication as she said, *"Remember why we're here and what has to be done. Stay connected to my mind tracks so I can contact you instantly if necessary. Susan and David, it's time for you to join Sean and I."*

While Susan and David were hurrying to join them, Ashling continued to pass orders along to each captain. One of them was ordered to search the massive castle-like structure and to take no prisoners. She also ordered them to leave the basement area to her and Sean.

When Susan and David arrived, they all quickly transformed into their dragon selves. "Susan, you're with me and David is with Sean. Remember your training and stick to our plan. If anything changes, Sean or I will let you know."

Just as she was about to give the order to commence the attack, shrill sirens began going off all around them. They could see large spotlights coming on up and down the complex.

"Grainne must have a trigger warning in place if any strange dragons are sensed. Our transformation must have set off the alarm. Go, go, go!," Ashling shouted, mind to mind.

* * *

The dragons in Grainne's army attacked what they thought was Rundimahair. She took the lead, using her fiercely dark and powerful magic to break down the city's protective shield. She cast one spell after another and unleashed them at the invisible barrier.

Almost immediately, counter spells began crashing against her and the other dragons. One of the gray dragons was too slow to evade the spells and was blasted into oblivion in seconds.

"Spread out and watch yourselves!" Grainne shouted angrily. The attack had just begun, and she was already down one dragon.

Through the invisible barrier, there appeared to be thousands of people running around in confused panic. The others couldn't see through the barrier yet, but Grainne could. It filled her heart with a lust to destroy her longtime enemy. They'd fought against her, as their rightful ruler, for so many centuries. Now they were running amok, knowing that their doomsday had arrived. There would be no mercy given, and no prisoners taken. Only their entire annihilation would satisfy her terrible rage.

Grainne closed her eyes and focused on the devastation spell that she'd been revising and strengthening for over a hundred years. It took a tremendous amount of power and strength to cast such a gargantuan spell.

She swirled, dodged, and dove in unpredictable turns to avoid the protective spells being hurled at them from below. When she was finally centered over Rundimahair, Grainne nosedived toward the barrier with blinding speed. Just before she was about to crash into it, she unleashed the devastation spell on the barrier.

There was a tremendous explosion, as Grainne completed a reverse spin. The dark spell crashed into the barrier and spread across its surface like a gray cloud. Grainne didn't bother to watch it spread. She was desperately soaring into the dark night sky. If she didn't get clear of the spell's unleashed power, she might die along with everyone inside of Rundimahair.

⁂

Within minutes ten gray dragons were in the air above Grainne's Ireland compound. Eight of them closed quickly on Sean, Ashling, David and Susan, who were each in their dragon forms. The remaining two grays began searching for enemy warriors on the ground.

Ashling had ordered a captain of one hundred to take his warriors and attack the beautiful castle-like building. Everyone else had been ordered to stay under the cover of the trees until they could gain control of the skies above the compound.

Sean saw that Ashling was busy fighting two grays, while he and David were fighting three gray dragons. Two other grays seemed to be gliding close to the ground, searching for enemy ground troops.

The remaining three grays were closing in on Susan in her beautiful, golden dragon self. Sean had an urge to go help Susan, but he couldn't leave David alone against the three grays.

Two grays attacked Sean, from above and below, hoping to confuse him long enough for one of them to set him on fire. It was an attack strategy that he'd practiced countering over and over.

Sean arched upward suddenly, catching both attacking grays by surprise. The gray above him was forced to pull out of the dive he'd begun, which is exactly what Sean wanted. With his blinding speed, Sean was able to reach the dragon above him while the gray was trying to regain his balance. Having to pull out of his own nosedive had left him slightly out of control.

Slightly off balance was all Sean needed. As he streaked passed the struggling gray, Sean released a searing blast of fire into the belly of the enemy dragon. It was a perfect strike against the soft underbelly of the beast. Within seconds, his entire dragon body burst into flames as he spiraled out of control. He crashed hard into one of the barracks buildings below. Within seconds, it too burst into flames, leaving a fiery inferno no one in the building would survive.

Sean turned in time to see David closing on the other dragon that had been attacking Sean. A quick glance around showed Sean that David had already taken out the dragon he'd been fighting.

Trusting David to handle the remaining gray he was closing in on, Sean rushed to help Susan. She was desperately trying to keep three grays at bay, with her superior speed.

Sean could see she'd been singed along her back, as he approached the dragon belching flames at her from above. It struck Sean as a cowardly way to fight. He soared past the gray dragon, ripping a large hunk of back muscle off the creature with a vicious tearing motion.

The gray roared in pain as he turned to see what had attacked him. To his surprise, the powerful red dragon had already reversed direction, with a graceful arching movement. Before it could regain its balance, Sean blasted him with a red-hot ball of fire. The ball of fire struck the gray in the face, virtually melting its head, as it dropped from the sky.

Sean immediately arched away to his left; in case another dragon was on his tail. When he turned back to the sky battle, there were no grays coming toward him.

Susan had just broken one of the gray dragon's neck with a fierce twisting motion of her powerful jaws. When he turned to fly to David's defense, he saw the powerful brown dragon had just toasted the final gray they'd been fighting. He felt a surge of pride for how well the young dragons were faring in their first battle.

He felt a dragon approaching him from behind, but when he turned he realized it was Ashling coming to check on him. He knew grays shouldn't be able to keep up with her, but he was happy to see she was safe.

The four dragons gathered together high above the compound. Ashling took one look at Susan's scalded back and said, "I'm taking her into the woods to heal this. You two handle those last two dragons, who are still looking for our warriors."

Ashling nudged Susan toward the woods. Susan was in terrible pain, but she was reluctant to leave the battle. "Go!" Ashling growled loudly. Susan knew better than to argue and meekly flew toward the cover of the woods.

Sean and David came at the unsuspecting dragons, hovering over the castle, and blasted them from both sides. The grays didn't even have time to fight back before they were spiraling toward the ground, like twin balls of fire.

"You'd think they might look up once in a while," David said.

"I'd rather fight a dumb dragon any day," Sean said. "Let's head for the woods and get ready to cover our warriors when they start the ground attack."

※━━※

Grainne felt a rush of scalding heat rush past her, as she continued her desperate climb into the sky. It was very hot, and the heat seemed to steal the air from her lungs.

290

The explosive strength of her spell was even more powerful than she'd anticipated. It buffeted her with burning hurricane-force winds. If she survived this explosion, there was no doubt in her mind that Rundimahair would be fatally wounded by such immense power.

She managed to soar high enough into the sky that she finally outran the reach of the incredibly powerful blast. Despite her great power, Grainne felt a bit weak and unsteady, as she leveled off and looked down at the valley below.

"It worked even better than I thought it would!" she cried out, as she looked at the cracked and burning magical shield. Everywhere she looked there were signs of the splintering and cracking of Ashling's powerful shield.

Grainne circled away from the center of the blast and dove for the edges of the shield. It was apparent that it would soon be falling apart under the strain of the explosion. She forced herself to be calm and patient. This moment had been centuries in the making. She wanted to enjoy the success of her powerful shield busting spell.

She touched the minds of her squadron leaders and told them to advance on the shielded valley. As soon as the shield fell apart, Grainne wanted her troops attacking from all sides.

She instructed them to stay on the perimeter for now and not let anyone escape. She would lead the dragons on a sweep of the center of the city and force survivors out into the clutches of her ground forces.

When she reached the center of the shield, she could see large, jagged cracks, which were quickly spreading in all directions. She unleashed a series of powerful spells against the weakest points of the magical shield, anxious to see if finally collapse.

With her mind-to-mind communication, she warned her squadron leaders to be ready to fight. There would be desperate survivors trying to flee the city. Grainne didn't want any resident of Rundimahair to escape.

With the unrelenting attack on the critically damaged shield, it finally broke open and collapsed from the center outward. Even from her height, Grainne could now hear the shouts and screams of her sworn blood enemies down below. It was like music to her evil, twisted soul.

⁂

Ashling had treated Susan's severe burns with her best healing spells. She'd been surprised by the damage done to the young dragon's back. A passing blast of fire from a gray dragon shouldn't have done so much damage.

When she began exploring the wound more carefully, she felt a chill of dread touch her heart. There was more to the wound than just burns. This had the markings of a flesh-eating spell. Somehow, Grainne had embedded this spell into her dragon's fire.

She'd quickly warned Sean and the other dragons to watch out for this if any other dragons appeared. They couldn't allow their fire to touch them.

The other dragons and warriors were making quick work of destroying the rest of the complex. Now that the enemy dragon defenders were slain, it was only a matter of time.

After healing the damage from the flesh-eating spell, Ashling left their medics in charge of Susan, and the other wounded. She took to the skies as her dragon self. The scene below her was at once satisfying and heartbreaking.

The once beautiful and secure complex of housing, commercial and military structures, was going up in flames. She could also see desperate hand-to- hand combat going on below.

Ashling felt satisfaction in destroying the headquarters of an enemy bent on the destruction of her people. She also couldn't help but feel great sorrow for the needless loss of life and property.

Even though the enemy was committed to destroying Ashling's people, at one time they'd all been part of the same angelic Sidhe. The terrible waste broke her heart.

She and the other dragons searched for enemy troops that were not engaged in close up fighting with her warriors. Wherever there was sufficient space, they would sweep down from the sky and blast the bitter enemy with fiery destruction.

It was turning into a rout as their enemy began to flee. The dragons could have destroyed them to the last person, but Ashling couldn't bring herself to kill unarmed, fleeing soldiers.

"Enough!" she called out forcefully, mind-to-mind, to her squadron leaders. *"Gather our warriors to our planned point of departure."*

When Sean landed at the wooded departure point, he quickly joined with her in opening the portal that would take them home. Despite the weariness they both felt, the portal opened smoothly and began to grow. They would soon be on their way home.

Something was not right about what was emerging from the smoky destruction below her. She could hear the screams of her enemy and see shadowy forms running in all directions in apparent panic. What was wrong was that she couldn't feel their fear.

Grainne had reached out to touch the minds of the long-hated enemy. While there was a general feeling of panic and despair, she couldn't pin down individual fear or terror. It just felt wrong to her. A growing fear and anger began to build in her black heart as she finally shouted, "No!"

Without waiting for the smoky haze to clear below her, she streaked down through the broken shield and stayed low to the ground.

It only took her a few minutes to realize her worst fears were true. This wasn't Rundimahair, and none of her hated enemies were dying and fleeing for their lives. She had been well and truly duped by Ashling.

She quickly pulled up and out of the broken shell of a shield and into the clear air above. With barely contained rage burning in her heart, she reached out to touch Carla's mind. Grainne wanted someone to blame for this disaster, and Carla was going to be her scapegoat. After all, she was the one who'd brought Grainne here and convinced her this was Rundimahair.

After several unsuccessful attempts to contact Carla in Ireland, she reached out to contact her military leaders. A growing sense of dread touched her dark heart when she continued to get no response.

Grainne forced herself to stay calm as she continued to reach out to her generals. Finally, she felt a weak connection to one of her squadron leaders. She boosted her power with a fierce blow of magic and could finally hear his response from her Ireland headquarters.

"Under attack…everything on fire…dragons in the sky…soldiers everywhere…"

Her connection to his mind was suddenly cut off and she could no longer sense his life force. Was that why she couldn't reach her other military leaders? Were they all dead?

The magnitude of the great deception engulfed her, and she realized what Ashling had done. She ripped open a portal, pushing herself too hard because of the fierce anger and fear that controlled her thoughts.

The other dragons and soldiers quickly responded to her angry call to the portal. As they arrived, she pushed them hard to pass through the portal. Finally, she and the other dragons passed through and the hastily constructed portal quickly closed behind them.

❋◁ ▷❋

Ashling was just pushing the last of their warriors through the portal, when a black hole opened in the sky above the ruined compound.

A rush of gray dragons flew out of the unsteady portal, followed by a surge of ground troops close behind. The problem with bringing ground troops through the portal was quickly evident when they realized the portal had opened two hundred feet above the ground.

Dozens of Grainne's troops fell to their death, but she was beyond caring. She ordered her dragons to follow her into the woods. She sensed that Ashling was still in the forest, and that was all that mattered to her now.

The remaining troops had managed to stop from falling out of the front of the portal, but it only delayed the inevitable ending.

The poorly constructed portal began to close because Grainne was no longer there to support it.

Within minutes it collapsed and the remainder of her troops were crushed to cosmic dust. The only saving grace was that none of them had time to suffer.

All of this was lost on Grainne as she and ten dragons bore down on the location of Ashling's portal. If she could just catch and destroy Ashling, it would pull a great victory from the jaws of humiliating defeat.

⁂

Because Grainne was livid with rage, she hadn't properly masked her arrival. Ashling and Sean both sensed her at nearly the same moment.

"Something went wrong," Ashling said urgently, "Grainne is back."

"Not just her," Sean said. "I sense a pile of dragons with her."

Ashling was quiet for a moment before nodding her agreement. "I sense ten dragons plus Grainne's big black monster."

"Sounds right," Sean agreed.

"It's me that she's focused in on," Ashling said. "You stay here and finish getting everyone through the portal, Sean. I'll lead them away from here to give you time."

"Not a chance in hell that is going to happen," Sean said forcefully. "Susan and General Mahoney will stay here and make sure everyone gets out safely. You and I and David will keep the dragons busy."

"I'm in charge here, Sean. You'll do as I say," Ashling said, a tone of desperation in her words.

By way of response, Sean turned to David and asked, "You coming with me, big brownie?"

"I will if you promise to never call me that again," David said, with a grim smile.

"You've got a deal," Sean said as he morphed into his dragon self and streaked into the dark sky.

"Sean!" Ashling cried out in a mixture of anger and fear.

"You're wasting time, Commander," General Mahoney said.

"They need you up there. We've got this covered," Susan said.

Ashling hesitated a moment longer before realizing they were right. "Thank you both and get everyone home safe!" She shouted as she morphed into her dragon self and exploded into the sky.

She noticed immediately that there were only seven enemy dragons still in the sky above her. Sean and David must have surprised the enemy dragons with their sudden appearance. Taking a quick glance below her, Ashling saw one of the grays, falling to the ground, as a streaking ball of fire.

Ashling decided to take the same approach, as she rushed by several of the dragons trying to corner David, while Sean engaged in battle with Grainne. It would have to be a hit-and-run strategy, where she would engage the other dragons momentarily and then strike at Grainne. She had to keep the black dragon off balance, or she would take Sean down. He simply didn't have the experience to fight the dark angel alone.

With a power born of desperation and anger, Ashling ripped through two of the grays trying to attack David from behind and above. It was their enemy's typical style of cowardly fighting, but it was also effective.

She reached out with her long, sharp claws and ripped deep into the back of both grays without slowing much at all. There was a satisfying sense of flesh being torn asunder, as she continued forward and unleashed a fierce ball of fire into the face of the surprised dragon facing David.

In seconds, she'd managed to disable or kill all three dragons, while continuing to streak toward Grainne.

David only had a moment to admire her incredible fighting skill, while he finished off the two badly injured grays. Before he could take time to admire his own fighting ability, two more grays attacked him. The remaining two dragons pursued Ashling. They all knew she was the one Grainne wanted dead.

Sean was desperately trying to stay calm in the face of the black dragon's assault. He knew he couldn't fight her one-on-one for very long. He understood that he was outmatched. If he didn't fully comprehend it before, he certainly did after fighting with her for a few minutes.

He could sense the immense fury in her attack strategy. There was nothing subtle about it. She was trying to overpower him and crush him to dust. If she couldn't do that, she would settle for turning him into burnt toast. Sean sensed that her almost out-of-control wrath was keeping her from using some of her more subtle fighting skills.

So far, he'd only survived by sticking and moving. He used his own incredible speed to avoid a fiery finish to his life. Eventually, she'd figure out his strategy, but he hoped help would arrive before then.

Ashling tried to flash by Grainne and rake her back with her claws, as she'd done to the two grays. Despite her being preoccupied with battling Sean, the mighty black dragon arched into an impossibly tight loop and unleashed a fearsome stream of fire at Ashling as she rushed by.

It was only Ashling's stunning speed that saved her from taking a mortal wound from the belch of red hot fire. She saw Sean crash into Grainne from the side to keep the black dragon from following up on her attack on Ashling. When Sean arched away, he felt claws rip into the side of his left leg, leaving behind an incredible burning pain.

Grainne tried to follow up her success by blasting him with a ball of fire. Ashling managed to slash a cut in Grainne's side with the razor-sharp tip of her heavy tail. It was enough to turn the great black dragon's attention fully on her.

Sean turned to do another fly by attack on Grainne while her attention was on Ashling, but he was suddenly hit from the side by one of the gray's that had been fighting David. A burst of fear touched Sean's mind for David's safety, but he had no chance to even look that direction.

Claws dug into his left leg and pain exploded in this mind. Following his survival instinct, he dropped suddenly, which pulled the gray's claw from his leg. The pain was almost mind-numbing, but at least he was free.

Sean turned and unleashed a streak of fire at the gray, but this dragon had learned to be cautious, after seeing so many of his fellow grays fall from the sky. He'd managed to pull up suddenly when Sean had dropped away from him. The belch of fire from Sean had blown into empty air where the gray had been.

The final gray who'd pulled away from fighting Sean was now closing in on Ashling. Helping Grainne defeat Ashling seemed to be his new priority.

When Sean saw that Ashling was in serious trouble he forgot about the burning pain in his leg and exploded upward with a surprising burst of speed. The gray he'd been fighting thought Sean was seriously injured and therefore less of a threat.

Even so, the gray dragon managed to avoid Sean's sudden burst of fire, as he shot by the surprised dragon. The gray went into defense mode and kept some distance between Sean and himself. He knew the longer Sean fought with his badly wounded leg the weaker he'd become.

Ashling too had taken an injury when the final gray dragon flashed by her. With Grainne relentlessly pressing her attack, Ashling hadn't had time to look around her.

The gray had managed to singe part of her back and side with a deep burn. The pain was a shock that nearly caused her to lose her focus on the deadly black. She'd only barely been able to circle up and away from Grainne's furious rush at her. Ashling had been saved by the black dragon's lack of strategy. It seemed that Grainne could only attack with burning anger and try to overpower her opponent.

With her injury causing her terrible pain, Ashling knew that her enemy's strategy would eventually bear fruit. With the loss of blood and mind-numbing pain from her burns, Ashling would eventually slow down enough to allow Grainne to finish her off.

Ashling dodged another bull rush by the black dragon but realized too late it had been a distraction. Grainne waited until Ashling arched away and cut back to catch her back with her vicious fore claws. The cut was deep and Grainne ripped even deeper, as Ashling pulled herself free.

Sean heard Ashling's roar of agony and looked to see her pull away, tearing the black dragon's massive claws out of her back. When the gray saw Sean lose focus, he released a massive ball of fire at Sean's head.

Without a conscious thought, Sean suddenly disappeared from sight. The confused gray pulled out of his follow up attack and hovered in midair for a moment. It was an understandable but fatal hesitation as Sean suddenly crashed into the gray with all his power.

The gray fought desperately to pull himself free, but Sean already had all four of his claws ripping through the terrified gray. Fueled by the knowledge that Ashling was in trouble, Sean tore the gray apart with his claws and finished him with as blast of fiery death, as he pulled himself free. The gray dropped out of the sky. He was dead before he hit the ground.

Sean tried to disappear again, but still had no control of it. It seemed to come and go at will. Due to the blood loss from his many wounds, he feared he might pass out and fall from the sky at any moment. With the last of his strength, he streaked toward the gray, who was causing so much damage to Ashling.

The gray must have sensed Sean's approach, but he turned a moment too late to fend off the mighty red dragon's attack.

Sean locked onto the gray and began ripping and tearing into him with all his strength. The gray responded with a desperate defense to save his life. The two battered dragons began a slow spiral toward the ground, locked in mortal combat.

Ashling wasn't aware of Sean's desperate struggle because she couldn't take her eyes off of Grainne for a moment. The other gray dragons taking cheap shots at her back, while she'd been forced to fight off the mighty black, had left her weak from pain and blood loss.

Grainne seemed to sense her weakening condition and pressed her attack with new ferocity. She didn't care if she'd needed the help of her grays to wear Ashling down, as long as she was the one to take her life force. By adding Ashling's life force to her own, Grainne knew that she would be the undisputed leader of all of the Sidhe.

Ashling managed to break free from the black dragon's grip one last time. She flew straight up just to put distance between them, while she tried to think of any way to defeat the monster.

When she circled in the air to look down at Grainne, Ashling knew it was hopeless. She was struggling to even stay conscious. Her heart ached with the thought of how her people would survive without her.

As Grainne began to circle up toward Ashling, she appeared supremely confident that she'd won the battle. Ashling knew it was true, but she was going to do as much damage to the evil black dragon as she could before she died.

With Ashling and Grainne locking eyes on each other, neither of them saw the blur of blue streaking across the sky until it smashed into Grainne with incredible force. The great black's single focus on Ashling had left her wide open to attack.

Momentary confusion and surprise suddenly cleared. The massive blue dragon was her father. Never in her long life was she more grateful for Eamon's stubbornness. He must have slipped through the portal at the last moment and used his own great powers to keep it open long enough to pass through.

Ashling began to circle down toward Eamon and Grainne, who were locked in a deadly struggle. She lost consciousness for a moment and drifted sideways. The fearsome roar of the black dragon brought her back to the moment, but she'd drifted farther from the battle.

With her last remaining strength, Ashling surged toward the black devil dragon. Grainne had done nothing but cause pain, misery, and fear to her people for centuries. It had to stop now.

While the great black dragon was desperately trying to get her foreclaws onto Eamon's back, Ashling struck her from the side, ripping deep, massive cuts into her left wing and side.

When Grainne arched up and away from her battle with Eamon, Ashling anticipated the move and hit her hard with a burst of flame. She'd aimed it at her head, but the badly wounded black dragon managed to twist away. The searing fire struck her neck and right shoulder instead.

Ashling knew that the combination of wounds should be deadly, but she never counted Grainne out of any fight. Her caution saved her life.

Grainne managed to twist up and away from Eamon's deadly rush at her. She soared past Ashling and managed to singe her wing with a smaller but still effective fireball.

With the amount of magical energy she'd expended, Grainne was struggling to evade Eamon and finish off Ashling before she fled the battle. She knew if she didn't escape very quickly, she would be finished. Her injuries were quickly stealing her strength and powers from her.

While she lined up for one last rush at Ashling, a burst of red-hot flame struck the mighty black dragon's already injured wing. She knew immediately it was the red dragon.

She let herself fall from the sky, hoping they would think she was about to crash into her ruined compound below.

Eamon followed her down to be sure it was the end of their feared and hated enemy. Sean was about to join him when he saw Ashling transform into her human self and begin falling from the sky.

Sean rushed to a position just under Ashling and allowed her to land on his back. "Hang on!" he shouted and was encouraged to feel her clutch onto his neck.

Eamon looked up to see Sean catch Ashling, as she was falling toward the fiery ruins below. He quickly glanced down to see Grainne disappear into the blazing ruins of her military compound.

Without another thought, he surged upward to fly beside Sean. Together, they landed near the forest where the medics were waiting.

Several medics quickly converged on Ashling and began assessing her many wounds. After a few minutes, the lead medic covered her with a blanket and said, "We've got to get her back to Rundimahair quickly. These are life-threatening injuries."

Eamon nodded gravely and turned to Sean. Without a word, Sean joined Eamon and began pushing open a portal that would take them home.

When the portal was fully opened, Eamon said, "Sean, you take Ashling and I'll make sure the portal stays open until everyone is safely through.

Sean wanted to stay and help get everyone home safely but his aching desire to help Ashling took precedence. He carefully lifted her into his arms and rushed into the still growing portal. While he streaked through the portal, the sounds of fires raging, massive explosions, and the screams of the injured and dying began to fade away.

Sean prayed for the safety of their warriors and leaders. Most of all he prayed that Ashling would still be alive when he got her back to Rundimahair. They may have won the battle but there would be little joy or elation if it came at the cost of losing the love of his life.

Epilogue

May the road rise to meet you,
May the wind be always at your back,
May the sun shine warm upon your face,
The rains fall soft upon your fields,
And until we meet again,
May God hold you in the palm of His hand

~ Old Irish Saying ~

When Ashling finally opened her eyes, the sun was shining brightly through the window in her bedroom. A sense of peace and comfort drifted back and forth through her thoughts.

After a few minutes of enjoying the sunshine, she decided to get up and start her day. When she attempted to roll out of bed in her usual manner, pain arched through her back and side.

She couldn't keep from crying out, which brought a rumble of footsteps rushing down the hall outside her room. Moments later, Sean pushed the door open and hurried to her bedside. "You're awake!" he almost shouted.

While his volume hurt her ears, his warm smile and the relief in his stark, blue eyes helped her relax a little. "What… what happened?" she finally managed to ask.

"Oh, nothing much," Sean said, grinning. "You just defeated the evil Grainne in battle and pretty much trashed her great military base over in Ireland."

With his words, the memories flooded into her mind. The recollection returned of the great and terrible battle with Grainne and her dark forces. There had been losses on their side too, but nothing like the destruction heaped upon their long-time enemy.

"We won," she managed to say in a dry, squeaky voice.

"Indeed, we did, although we lost our share of good warriors too," Sean said.

"Why am I in bed?" she asked.

"Actually, you've been in bed for weeks," Sean said. "We came much too close to losing you."

Ashling felt his pain and fear in those words. When she looked into his eyes, she knew he'd feared the worst.

After a moment he smiled and said, "But you're out of danger now and gaining back your strength and powers quickly."

"David and Susan?" she asked fearfully.

"They're both fine and pretty much inseparable these days. This isn't just some puppy love going on here. They are totally gaga over each other."

"I'm assuming that being gaga is a good thing," Ashling said, softly.

"Oh, it is indeed. In fact, I am totally gaga over you and taking it to a whole other level."

"Good to know," she said, smiling. She felt the same way about Sean, but he'd never hear her describe her feelings as gaga.

"There's my girl!" Eamon said, stepping into her room. "It does me old heart much good to see your smiling face, dear Ashling."

He bent over the bed and gave her a gentle hug, as he softly said, "You had me worried, my dear."

"Sorry Da, and I'm grateful that you came along when you did that night. Without your help, Sean and I might both be gone from this life."

"Thank the Creator of us all that he chose to leave you here to finish your great work," Eamon said in a trembling voice. He turned away to wipe at a stray tear.

Ashling knew how difficult it was for Eamon to show emotions in this way. The fact that he was showing them openly meant he'd feared greatly for her life. It sobered her to realize how close she'd come to the end of her days on earth.

"We're just grateful that you're still here and psycho Grainne is cleaning up black dragon pooh in outer darkness," Sean said, trying to lighten the mood.

Ashling smiled softly but didn't answer right away. When Eamon saw the concern on his daughter's face, he asked. "You think she survived?"

After another long pause she finally said, "I don't know for sure, Da'. But I have a feeling we haven't seen the last of Grainne."

"Saints preserve us," Eamon said, with a furrowed brow. "I know those feelings of yours and that tone of voice only too well." Sighing, he continued, "Well, if she's not dead and gone then I hope the great Creator keeps her away from us for a good many years to come."

Ashling nodded thoughtfully and finally said, "Amen to that, Da.'"

It was too dark here–darker than any moonless winter night. Her initial fear was that she'd died and been banished to outer darkness. In outer darkness, most of her powers would be useless. Grainne knew she had many enemies that she'd sent to outer darkness over the centuries.

While the darkness surrounding her was devoid of any light, she began to sense that it wasn't the same as the atmosphere in outer darkness. That soul draining feeling that all hope is lost was unique to outer darkness.

On her few visits there she'd sensed terrible, lonely sorrow. The other pervading feeling in outer darkness was that you only had yourself to blame for spending eternity here. No amount of rationalizing or lying to yourself could change the truth.

Fear crept into her belly, giving rise to panic that she'd rarely experienced. Grainne knew that she had to get out of this place wherever it was. She didn't think she could stand another moment in this black hole.

When she tried to move, the fear spiked into terror. Grainne couldn't move at all. She was paralyzed from head to toe. She tried to scream, but she couldn't open her mouth or get her vocal chords to react. Other than her thoughts, she felt like she was made of stone.

"It is not yet time, mighty warrior," a soft, gravelly voice spoke from out of the darkness.

Her heartbeat escalated to a panicky, rapid pounding in her ears. The voice sounded like it came from close by. Perhaps only inches from her ear.

"Fear not, Grainne. It was my honor to rescue you from eternal confinement in the outer darkness you fear above all else. I have long admired you as you shaped this world to meet your own demands."

His voice soothed her fears and left her feeling comforted. If only she could speak. She desperately wanted to ask him who he was.

"All in good time," he said, as though he'd read her thoughts. "For now, you must rest. It will be months before you will once again regain use of your body. It will perhaps be years before you can access all of your once great powers."

The words washed over her like acid rain. All that she feared seemed to be echoed in his gentle voice. Would she be a vegetable, lying helpless in bed for years to come?

Again, he spoke as though he'd heard her thoughts. "I'm not sure why, but I can hear your thoughts and I know your fears. I sense that your recovery will not be so long. I have learned much of the healing arts in my centuries of life. I will do all that I can to restore you to health sooner–rather than later."

If she hadn't been paralyzed, Grainne would have flinched back when she felt his large hand on her forehead. His palm was rough and callused, like a man who'd worked hard all his life. While he continued to stroke her forehead, she began to feel more comfort wash through her.

"I will strive to make you better than you ever were before, Dark Queen," he said, as he continued to stroke her forehead. "When you have fully recovered and we work together, the revenge over your enemies will be assured. We will cause them to rue the day they dared challenge your right to rule your people."

Grainne again felt a surge of peace and comfort run through her heart and mind, as he continued to speak in his soft, gravelly voice. Even though it wasn't loud, she felt compelled to listen. She felt a great desire to hear what he would say next.

"Together we will accomplish what you could not do alone. You cannot imagine how long I hoped for the day we would meet and join together. With my help, I believe you can win your ancient war."

Grainne felt drowsiness creeping back while she listened to the stranger's voice in the darkness. She desperately hoped that she'd stay awake long enough to hear all his words, which filled her heart with hope. There was a subtle power in this gentle, well-spoken man. He may indeed be a great ally if his words actually came to fruition.

His hand slowly moved to caress her cheek as he said, "Sleep now, Grainne. When you awaken, we will begin the long journey that we've both waited for centuries to commence. It will be a journey that could end with the destruction of your enemies and perhaps much more."

The stranger was silent for a long time, and Grainne thought he was through speaking. His calloused hand continued to gently stroke her cheek, and she was nearly asleep when she heard him speak very softly.

"I have watched you struggle to defeat your enemies for centuries. I once fought to rule this planet. I have lost thousands of my friends and fellow warriors in battle against countless enemies."

Grainne felt empathy from the calloused stranger. She knew that he spoke the truth about his great losses and suffering. It was the same suffering she was going through.

"In the end, I alone survived to live on in a world that I was a stranger to. The only thing that kept me going was watching you and your relentless drive to claim your right to rule your people. In the end, we have both failed to accomplish our greatest desire. Together, we will finally achieve the victory that has eluded us for far too long. If we continue down our separate, solitary paths, we will both continue to fail. Only together will we achieve the final victory which has been denied us for far too long."

Even through the terrible physical, mental, and emotional pain she was suffering through, Grainne felt a very slight sense of hope. The fact that she wasn't alone, and the stranger believed in her, kept her going. She wouldn't give up, despite the odds against her ever becoming the great warrior she'd been.

The tremendous fury and hate she felt toward Ashling, Eamon, and the young, red dragon, would keep her going. It was going to be a long, painful journey, but she would be back. *"Hear my thoughts, Ashling. I will return!"*

LARRY FORKNER

has been writing novels for more than twenty years. He's published fifteen fiction and two non-fiction books. He also wrote and produced the musical: Erin's Promise. Larry founded Highest Star Productions to provide authors the freedom to be creative and to offer the support necessary to be successful in today's fast-changing world of writing and publishing. Visit his website at: www.larrylorkner.com.